SEEKER OF SECRETS

COVEN OF SHADOWS AND SECRETS

CROWNS OF MAGIC UNIVERSE

ASHLEY MCLEO

MERAKI PRESS

GLOSSARY

* the Beinecke - a library at Yale
* the Covenant - the supernatural ruling body of the human world. It's made up of three individuals from each supernatural order (example: three vampires, three witches, three phoenixes and so on).
* the Darkborn - people in the human world who follow the Princes of Hell. Some are Hellblooded, but not all.
* Hellblooded - individuals with demon blood. They are usually born in the human world and are forced to register by the Covenant.
* Hellborn - individuals who were born in Hell. Nearly all of these creatures are demons.
* Isila - another realm where magical beings live. It's comprised of nine kingdoms (four fae kingdoms, mage, dragon shifter, elf, vampire, and wolf shifter). Many characters in the Coven of Shadows and Secrets have direct ties to Isila's courts.
* *Lapis caelesti* - the sacred stones made by angels thousands of

years ago and given to seven witches to protect. They are great sources of power that can defeat the darkest evil.

* Ordo Aeternum - Also known as the OA, Ordo, or the Order. An elitist group of supernaturals who believe those of magical blood should rule the world (many believe they should enslave humans too).

* Ouroboros - The symbol of the Coven of Shadows and Secrets. It is a snake, formed in a circle, eating its own tail.

* Wolvea - royal wolves of Isila

CHAPTER ONE

MEREDITH

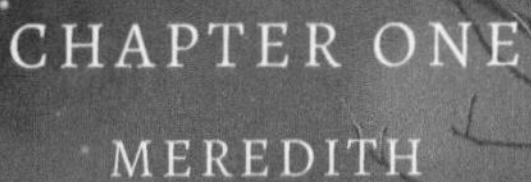

I GRIPPED THE ROPE AS MY PARTNER INCHED ME DOWN THE DUSTY stone shaft, my breath tight in my chest, my heart racing harder with each passing second. I wasn't scared of heights, the dark, or tight spaces.

And yet, I *hated* this situation. Irrationally, I both wanted Denz to lower me faster and pull me back up.

Alas, this was my only option to complete the job our boss had assigned. A ladder would be too wide to fit down such an ancient passage; plus, hauling it around would be a dead give-away and too clunky to slip past on-site guards.

Suddenly, gravity took me into a free fall. I let out a yelp and squeezed the rope tighter, as if that would save my ass from plummeting to my death. The rope snapped taut a second later, and my gaze seared upward.

"Sorry," Denz's baritone boomed as he peered down at me. "Thought I heard someone walking by. It was nothing, though."

I scowled at him. "Pay better attention, or next time, I'll make *you* stuff yourself down here!"

The threat was an empty one. Denzel, was too broad-shoul-dered to fit through the opening leading into the Egyptian tomb. His budding beer gut wouldn't help either.

Though he knew I was talking nonsense, he smartly didn't reply, just kept lowering me into the abyss at a measured rate.

A few minutes later, my feet touched down on sand. I exhaled my first long breath since I'd entered the shaft and released the rope. My legs wobbled from the combination of the adrenaline rush and the shifting ground.

"You there, Stone?" he asked.

"Yeah," I called back. "How deep?"

A brief pause told me he was checking the measurements marked on the rope. We were thorough criminals. It was why we were the best in the biz.

"Sixty feet. Really deep."

That *was* deep.

"Write it down," I said. We might need the data later, if this site proved fruitful. "I'm going to search." I fished around in my sack for my flashlight.

From our earlier reconnaissance, which had involved getting the site's archeology team so plastered they'd talk about their dig, we'd learned there was more in the tomb than just the treasure we were after. Something strange was hidden down here.

On the streets, Egyptians and visiting scholars alike gossiped about an item lost since the time of the pharaohs: a magical amulet last worn around the neck of the man occu-pying this very tomb. The wearer had the power to make others go mad.

The necklace had not been uncovered yet, but I had hope that I'd be the one to find it. That sort of artifact was an item our clients would pay a fortune for. As soon as my boss heard about it, the necklace became our primary target.

Thankfully, because the lead archeologist's right-hand man proved especially charmed while under the influence, he told me all about the dig. What they hoped to find. The eerie chill of the tomb. He even showed me—or the doe-eyed wannabe grad student he thought I was—a detailed map of the dig after we made out. The moment he'd fallen asleep, I swiped the map and ran to find Denz.

The young archeology professor was going to be pissed at himself for indulging in that last beer. Hopefully by the time he realized the map was missing, I'd be in Moscow or Paris, where my best buyers lived. I kinda felt bad about deceiving him . . . he'd been a good guy. But I didn't feel bad enough to pass up a gigantic payday.

Of course, first I had to find the damn thing.

I twisted my oversized toolbelt so the bag portion lay against my rear-end, turned on my flashlight, and dropped to my knees. My search revealed only one tunnel extended out of the shaft. I lay prone on my belly and army-crawled through it, doing my best not to sneeze as dust teased my nostrils, flooding them with the stale scent of earth that hadn't seen the light of day since the time of the pharaohs. As I moved, I prayed there weren't any creepy-crawlies down here.

Eventually, I climbed out of the tunnel and stood up in a larger room. Goosebumps pebbled my skin. The air was still and thick and all wrong. It lacked energy, flow, *life*, reminding me that I was breaking into the home of the dead.

"Cozy thought, Stone." I shuddered and turned to scan the area.

A door was set into each wall, but I knew which to take. Though, after I reached the end of the next hallway, I would have to rely less on first-hand accounts. The research team hadn't spent much time down this way.

That way okay. My intuition had not failed me yet, and after hearing most of the archeology team had sensed an odd, chilling presence down here, I didn't think it would fail me now, either.

It couldn't. There was too much at stake, and my boss did *not* tolerate losing.

I took the door on the right and prowled down a low-ceilinged hallway. Carefully, I reached up and brushed the stone above me with my fingers. Dry. Hopefully not also brittle and prone to collapse. I puffed up my cheeks and exhaled a long breath. This tunnel was tiny, but vast compared to the previous tunnel, and that hadn't fallen in. I had to have faith this one wouldn't either.

"Okay, let's see." I closed my eyes and allowed my senses to take over.

The best way I could describe my intuition was it felt like I was a ghost, walking ahead of my body. A trusted force guiding me, pulling me forward. I trailed my hand along the wall, collecting even more information. When it warmed some twenty feet ahead of me, I knew my intuition had worked like a charm.

"What have we here?"

I eased forward, careful of the uneven ground. I was not about to trip and knock out a tooth. Or stumble across a nasty snake or scorpion. Those suckers could live anywhere!

Still, I walked a tightrope of caution and speed. Night guards patrolled the dig area, so the longer we stayed here, the greater our chance of being caught. All they'd have to do was apprehend Denz and wait for me to reemerge at the surface.

I followed my instincts, and continued until I reached the

warmer portion of the blank wall. The moment I stopped in front of it, heat blasted from the stone, making my skin tingle. My intuition was telling me I'd discover a secret door somewhere along this stretch.

"Where are you?" I whispered, flashing my light along the wall.

I found something of interest high above my head. Hieroglyphics. I squinted, but I was unable to make them out because it was so dim, so I reached into my toolbelt to pull out a headlamp.

Once the band ringed my head, I turned it on and smirked. Thanks to the additional illumination, my vision improved tenfold.

I could read hieroglyphics, kinda. My boss, an enigmatic masked man who called himself the Ringmaster, had suggested I learn a few different ancient writings because, well, my job took me to weird places. I'd been studying for years, and while I wasn't a scholar, I could get by in a tomb.

It was amazing the sort of things people taught on the Internet these days. I could probably find instructions to perform surgery.

I stood on my tiptoes and squinted harder, as if it would enhance my hieroglyphic-reading abilities. When I reached a specific grouping of images, I paused.

"Is that for Isis?" I muttered, checking the arrangement against those I'd learned before concluding yes, it had to be the depiction of Isis.

If I was translating correctly, the tomb housed one of her possessions.

A thrill ran through me. Somewhere in this tomb an object —or objects—waited to be plundered. Something having to do with the queen of the underworld, a goddess of magic.

Of course, it was a bit much to believe I'd find an item actually owned by a goddess, but whoever was buried down here had surely made such a claim to elevate his own status. Braggarts existed in every age of history.

Taking a chance, I pressed my hand to the wall, searching for a crack. I'd barely moved an inch when a portion of the wall shifted. I pressed harder, and it swung inward to reveal that the whole slab was, in fact, a door.

"Hells to the yes," I whispered, gliding into the new tunnel —only to be stopped by a viper dropping from the ceiling.

I jumped back and screamed bloody murder as the snake hissed and retreated into the darkness.

"You've got to be kidding me," I whisper-yelled. "Why'd you do me that way?!"

It took a few seconds for my heart rate to slow, and when it did, I thought of something that made me cringe: my scream had been *loud*. Hopefully Denz hadn't heard it. Or the guards.

"I need to get in and out fast," I muttered, not wanting my partner to do anything stupid, like call our boss.

Not that the Ringmaster would come help—he had peons like us for that. Still, I didn't want him to know I'd screamed. I had a rep to protect.

"Stay around the corner, snake. I have a knife." I patted the blade against my hip. "And I'm not afraid to use it."

Headlamp shining on the ground, I inched forward. Soon enough, I'd made it so deep into the hallway, the door I'd entered through was but a dream. All along the wall, more hieroglyphics leapt out at me, the paint on them more vibrant than those in the first corridor. Many of them featured Isis too.

"Girl power," I whispered, trying to ignore the growing hunch that this might not just be a dead, rich guy's tomb, but some type of shrine.

Had the archeologists gotten it wrong?

The hallway led deeper into the earth, and I walked with even more care as the downward tilt grew steeper. I couldn't be sure how long I'd been going when I found myself in a large, open, square room.

Both headlamp and flashlight blazing, I scanned the area. A door graced each wall, and as I was trying to decide which to go through a distinct urge to turn around rushed over me.

Yeah, not gonna happen.

I needed to find what I'd been sent here to find. If I couldn't do that, I had to surface with something else of great value.

That was how this gig worked. If I came back empty-handed, the Ringmaster would be angry. And when the Ringmaster was angry, people tended to get hurt. The long scars along my spine tingled, a reminder of when I'd screwed up before. In the days after my caning, they'd hurt like hell, now the ugly lines were just a reminder. And to be honest, I counted myself as lucky that was all I got. Some people who disappointed the Ringmaster just disappeared off the face of the planet.

Sure, if I was dead, I wouldn't be a lackey to a psychopath anymore, but I'd rather live under the Ringmaster's thumb just a year or two longer and save up from my payouts to buy my freedom the right way. The only way that wouldn't result with him hunting me down.

Something—I'd bet a creepy, crawly snake—moved in the darkness, shifting rocks as it slithered ever closer. I scooted to my right, goosebumps erupting on my arms as the serpent loosed a long *hiss*.

"Pick a damn door, Mer." I double-checked that the snake was far away before I closed my eyes. All around, heat flared, but my intuition pulled me in one clear direction.

Straight.

So I crossed the room—or I tried to. I made it only halfway before a tile clicked beneath my feet and a side panel to my right groaned open.

My heart leapt into my throat, and I spun in time to see a flurry of daggers zooming toward me.

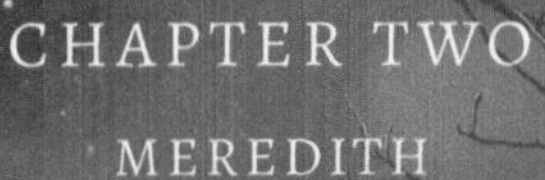

CHAPTER TWO

MEREDITH

My knees buckled. Rolling with it, I let my body go slack. When I hit the cool dirt, the flashlight flew out of my hand and spun across the room. A split second later, the air shifted, and the projectiles zoomed overhead, narrowly missing me to rebound against the far wall and clatter to the floor.

I exhaled and pressed my forehead to the ground. "Too close."

Sssssssss! Sssssssss!

Oh, hells no.

Slowly, I lifted my head to find another freaking snake only inches away. I pushed off the ground and rolled to the side, abandoning all thought of retrieving my flashlight as the snake sprang at me, fangs exposed.

"I hate snakes!" I yelled, allowing the momentum of the roll to take me.

When I was out of the little monster's reach, I stopped myself and scrambled to stand, not sparing a glance backward as I sprinted for the door.

When I burst into the adjoining room, my heart, which had been pounding a mile a minute, halted.

Sssss. Sssss. Sssss.

"Whyyyy?" I wailed. "Next time, Denz is doing this shit."

Snakes straight up infested this room, there were *hundreds* of them. I shuddered as they hissed and slithered over the dusty stone floor. Normally, it would be enough to make me run, but something else kept me there.

On the other side of the chamber, illuminated by my headlamp, stood a dais. A box sat atop it.

"Jackpot."

I yearned to rush forward, but experience stopped me. The snakes mostly kept to the sides of the room, so for now, they weren't too dangerous. But daggers had appeared from the walls, so I fully suspected there were booby traps in this chamber, too. I had to be careful.

Briefly, I considered going back to get my dropped flashlight, but dismissed the idea almost as quickly as it came to me. I might trigger more traps, and that meant staying down here longer than necessary. Or death. I cringed.

Put that way, I was tempted to leave the tool but that too would be foolish. Short-sighted. The flashlight had my fingerprints on it, and I had a record back in the States that would make me easy to identify. I had to get the light on my way out, and risk setting off another trap, but for now, the headlamp would have to do.

The box on top of the dais looked nothing like what some movies would have people think. It wasn't illuminated treasure, or pure gold. From my vantage, it just looked plain and black.

And yet, I was sure it held something valuable.

Eager to find out what was inside, I scanned the room one

last time before easing across the serpent-riddled space. Unlike in the antechamber, I didn't stumble across a rigged tile—a minor win. Although, the damned snakes still had me on edge.

They hissed from the sides of the room, their chorus sending shivers down my spine. One lingered alone near the center of the floor, watching me with dark, dangerous eyes, warning me to stay away.

Don't worry, buddy, I plan to.

I gave the serpent a wide berth.

How did they live down here, anyway? Ick!

I reached the platform and loomed over the box. For a moment, I considered grabbing the whole thing and running, but if there was nothing in it, I would have wasted all this time. Denz would be pissed.

My intuition screamed I was on the right track, but I had to be sure this was worth taking. So slowly, I lifted the lid. My headlamp shone down on the contents, and I sucked in a sharp breath.

A gold necklace lay inside. Nestled on a bed of black fabric, it featured a pendant of Isis. Her wingspan was approximately the length of my hand, making the necklace a chunker. On her head, she wore a crown made of many gleaming jewels. The one in the center was circular and shone dark as night with hints of blue and purple. It was beautiful and luminous as a pearl.

"Come here, pretty."

My fingers trembled as I reached for the necklace, and suddenly, the air in the room began to circulate. The snakes hissed louder, making my heart race faster.

I glanced up, expecting to find more daggers zinging toward me, but there was nothing. Still, goosebumps rose along my arms.

I was a practical woman, concerned with real matters in the world, but I'd also seen some crazy stuff in my twenty-one years. Unexplainable things. Was this tomb filled with ancient Egyptian magic or something? And down here, I was getting the sense I wasn't alone. Were ghosts floating around me?

I shuddered. Ghosts and hauntings were terrifying. I did *not* screw around with those—even if I couldn't prove they existed.

"If this tomb is haunted, let me know," I said warily. "I'd rather find out now before I piss you off. I don't want to be haunted for the rest of my life if I take this."

The shifting of the air ceased, and I exhaled.

"Okay, I'm gonna take that as permission granted."

I picked up the necklace. It was surprisingly clean for being hidden away for thousands of years. But my skin tingled and burned slightly where I touched the artifact.

"So beautiful," I whispered. My headlamp illuminated the glittering necklace. "It—"

I stopped. Save for my voice, the room had fallen silent.

What happened to the hissing?

My head snapped up, and a strangled yell flew up my throat. A glittering, silver mist inched inward from the sides of the room, engulfing the snakes and leaving them lifeless in its wake. And it was twisting, heading straight for me. Suddenly, the scars running the length of my back tightened and itched.

"I should have asked about curses too!"

I shoved the necklace into my toolbelt and took off at a dead sprint. The silver mist rolled closer to me, but I was fast. A girl who once lived on the streets had to be—it was the only way to survive.

Light-footed, I rushed out of the chamber into the antechamber. As I darted across the first room, I sent up a prayer. There might be more moving tiles, but I didn't have time to test for them. The sensation of the mist pressed at my back, tingling my skin, like when I'd touched the necklace.

The single snake that had tried to bite me before hissed again. I leapt over him in time to once more avoid being bitten. Dude was out for blood!

"Bastard!"

I continued to bust ass down the hall. I'd made it halfway to where I found the hidden door before I remembered I still had to grab the flashlight.

I worried at my bottom lip before chancing a glance back.

Oh my God. The mist hadn't just seeped out of the chamber . . . it was following me. Actually, it wasn't following, it was *chasing*! The silver cloud had expanded and taken on the form of a monstrous, three-headed dog—one that was alive and snarling and dead set on hunting me.

I put on another burst of speed. Sweat beaded down my face, and my heart rate spiked, but I would be damned if I gave up and let mist—even if it was in the shape of a three-headed dog—take me down.

I was Meredith Stone, and I never gave up without a fight, dammit.

The tunnel ended, and I took a sharp turn into the main hallway where the archeologists had been working, not bothering to close the door behind me. Between the flashlight and my newly found portal, after tonight, the crew would know someone slipped down here without permission.

But with the deadly mist chasing me, I found it pretty hard to care.

My heart hammering in my throat, I shot another look over my shoulder.

The mist is gaining! It—oh crap!

I stumbled over loose rock and slammed into the side wall, bracing myself with my hands to keep from falling to the ground. Suddenly, my skin burned, and the necklace sizzled inside my bag, as if someone had tossed it straight into a firepit.

What's up with this necklace?

I pushed off the wall and picked up steam again.

I didn't dare look around or behind me, in case I tripped a second time. The mist didn't need another advantage, it was already too close for comfort.

Still, from the corners of my eyes, I caught some of the hieroglyphics on the walls lighting up. Terror blazed through me. The tomb had lied. It was totally haunted!

Are Denz and I in over our heads?

Even as I considered the idea, I realized it was way too late to say I was sorry to whatever force controlled the mist. I was on the run, and I would either make it out of here with the necklace, or I wouldn't make it out at all.

I maintained my lead on the mist, and dove into the tunnel that snaked its way toward the shaft. I army-crawled faster than I had on the way in, screaming for my partner with each inch gained.

"Denz! Be ready! Do you hear me? Be ready to pull me up!"

I had a feeling that once I got out of here, the smoke would stop following me. Or I hoped it would.

Up ahead, my partner's deep baritone responded to my cries. "Stone? You hurt?"

"I'm coming! Almost there!"

I repeated those phrases over and over, so when I burst out of the tunnel and grabbed the rope, there was barely any hesitation.

"Stone?"

"Pull me up!"

"I—"

A garbled sound came from topside, and the rope went slack.

"Denz!"

The first tendrils of smoke seeped into the shaft, slower than before, but only inches from my feet.

"*Denz! I—*"

I shot up the shaft, gasping and clenching the rope tight, my gaze locked on the ground.

The smoke curled out of the tunnel, filling the space where I'd just stood. Glittering, silver tendrils drifted upward, but they seemed to be losing momentum.

Hope flickered. Maybe I'd been right and the mist couldn't leave its home.

With superhuman strength, Denzel yanked me up so fast, it was hard to breathe. When I reached the top, lights blazed into my retinas.

I whipped my hand up to cover my eyes. "Owwww! Can you turn those off?!"

No answer.

"Denz?" I blinked to dispel the light. "Turn that off. And check the shaft. Is there smoke coming up? If so, we need to run."

Still no answer.

As my vision returned, I learned why. My partner was sprawled on the ground in front of me, and his sunglasses, which were always perched on his head, lay across the room, as if someone had hit them off.

I looked closer and gasped. Blood pooled from his head.

What had happened? Had he fallen backward while

pulling me up? Dude would have had to seriously put his back into it for that to happen.

I moved to check on him. "Denz . . . are you—"

"I'll be taking that," a male voice said. "Thanks for extracting the Pearl of Hell for me."

Something hit me in the back of my head. I yelped and fell to the floor, narrowly missing a collision with a rock. Once I was down, a knife slashed the strap of my toolbelt and the weight of the bag lifted from my hip.

No! We need that!

"Hey! Come back here!" I pushed myself off the ground and spun, only to find no one there. "Come back here!"

Of course, the thief didn't make a peep.

On the ground, Denz groaned. I was about to go to him when another sound rang in my ears: footsteps, fast and purposeful.

A male voice shouted something in Arabic, and another answered.

Oh shit.

I sighed as guards rushed around the corner and pointed their guns straight at us.

CHAPTER THREE

MEREDITH

THE CLANGING OF A METAL DOOR WOKE ME.

"What time is it?" I groaned, uncomfortable on the stiff bench they called a bed.

No one answered.

Freaking typical.

I peered outside the bars, hoping to catch the guard's eye. I wasn't going anywhere, so I supposed it didn't matter, but it was the principle of the thing. Was it night? Day? Too early for any sane person to be awake? I had no freaking idea. My body was so screwed up from the jet lag, and now I hadn't seen the sun for what I suspected was three days.

It was inhumane, but the Egyptian authorities didn't seem to care.

And though I felt like I was in the twilight zone, I was sharp enough to deduce patterns. A guard was making the rounds, so it had to be the top of an hour. What hour was yet to be decided.

I slid my hand outside of the bars and waved. The uniformed man down the way saw me and scowled.

What a friendly guy. We would soon become besties for life. I was sure of it.

"What's the time?" I asked.

The guard snorted, but came closer. "Morning."

"I need to make a call."

"No."

Most of the guards spoke a little English. Not that I expected them to speak any English, when I was in Egypt. If anything, *I* should learn more Arabic. All that aside, I was sure I had the right to talk to someone.

"I'm pretty sure I deserve a phone call. In my country, it's the law."

"You stole from us," the guard barked back.

Yes, I was a tomb-raider, which meant I stole his culture and sold it to the highest bidder. I understood I was in the wrong. But I was between a rock and a hard place. If I didn't do as my boss said, I'd likely end up dead. If I had to rob a few graves to stay alive, then so be it.

"I demand my phone privileges."

"What are you going to do if we don't give it to you?" He smirked.

What an asshole.

My jaw tightened. "Eventually, I will get out of here, and I'll go public. I'll do my damndest to make it go *viral*. Hell, if I have to show some tit to do it, I will. You'll be famous for all the wrong reasons."

"That's assuming she ever gets out of here, isn't it, officer?" A new voice, one with a rumbly, panty-melting English accent with just a hint of posh, rang from the depths of the station.

I peered around the guard.

A man approached. He wore a suit, all black and perfectly tailored and crisp, though not buttoned up. He was tall and pale with longish gleaming raven hair that would cover his ears if it weren't styled, and the most vibrant green eyes I had ever seen in my life.

Total smokeshow.

"Who are you?" the guard asked.

"I am here on behalf of Miss Stone."

What?

I didn't hire this guy. Had the Ringmaster hired him to be my lawyer?

"Who let you back here?" The guard dropped a hand to his hip, ready to grab his weapon.

"Your compatriot," the man replied smoothly. He didn't look at all worried that the guard would pull a weapon on him. In fact, he walked unlike any man I'd ever seen, his motions smooth and graceful, but with a distinct undercurrent of danger.

My brow furrowed. The new guy reminded me of a predator, closing in on prey.

"You're not allowed back here. Leave," the guard demanded.

Instead, the newcomer continued approaching, his swagger and assurance astounding. When he reached the guard, he placed a hand on the man's shoulder. Green eyes seared into dark brown ones, and the new man gave the guard a small smile.

"I insist that you release Miss Stone right away." The rumble in his voice developed more grit. "I have spoken with those in your office, and they agree."

"She's charged with stealing antiquities," the guard said. His voice remained level, though very different from before. Dreamy, almost.

"Yes," Suit Guy said. "She has been a terrible person. But I think she'll soon be working to rectify her past." For the briefest second, his eyes met mine.

I took a wary step back. I swore they had been green before, but now they looked black as night.

The events in the tomb came rushing back. I'd spent a few days considering what I'd seen; after much rumination, I could think of only one explanation.

Whatever had been in the tomb had to have been magical. A *true* curse. The mist had killed the snakes, and if it had touched me, I would have gone the same way.

Why did this guy remind me of the mist?

"Release Miss Stone."

What tightness remained in the guard's shoulders went slack, and he turned toward me.

Again, confusion washed through me. Not only were the dapper gentleman's eyes odd, but the guard seemed dazed.

What was going on?

The guard approached me. A moment later, the door swung open. He stepped aside, waiting.

I arched an eyebrow. "You sure about this?"

The guard waved me on, his expression still dazed.

"Most people don't ask to be locked up again," the man mused. "You *are* different." His gaze latched onto me, and his eyes resembled emeralds once again, even brighter and more hypnotic than before.

I shuddered. Suit Guy was different, possibly dangerous, and he knew more about me than I liked others to know.

But how? And why come to collect me?

"Come with me," Suit Guy demanded.

I stepped out of the cell, arms crossed over my chest. "Thanks for getting me out. But I don't have to go anywhere with you."

"In that case, I'll tell the officers in front we're not actually working together." He nodded to the guard still standing there like a puppet. "As you can see, I can be very persuasive."

Dammit. I did want out of the cell. Out of the country. Once I left, I wouldn't be coming back, either—not without a convincing false passport.

I believed this guy when he said he would toss me under the bus, so I needed to go along with this charade. At least until we were far away from the building and I could lose him.

"Fine. I'll go with you."

"Good choice."

I followed the man out of the jailhouse. Although the authorities saw me leave, no one tried to stop me. All of their eyes were dazed, like the other guard's.

What did Suit Guy do to them?

When I stepped outside, warm Egyptian sunshine washed over my face. I sighed and instantly wished I had sunglasses. I'd even take the ugly Terminator-style ones Denz favored.

Oh my God! Denz!

"Did you get my partner out too?"

"He's not my concern," Suit Guy replied. "I was told to retrieve *you*. He'll have to make his own way. Come on. We need to get well clear of the jail before my influence wears off."

Influence . . .

So that's what he was calling what he did to the guards. I was pretty damn sure it was magic, but I would go with 'influence' for now. And I, too, wanted to get further away from the police station. Then I'd make a run for it.

Once I was free of Suit Guy, I'd figure out how to get Denz out of jail.

I followed the man down the street and around the block.

He was eerily silent, and seemingly fine with it, but I needed to fill the quiet.

"What's your name?" I asked. "You already know mine, so it only seems right to reciprocate."

"Tobias."

"Nice to meet you. You told the guard someone sent you to get me out. Was it my boss?"

I didn't use the Ringmaster's moniker. If Tobias worked for him, he'd know why.

I'd met my boss only once, the day he pulled me off the street, and I'd never seen his face. He always wore a mask, black with a silver sheen. The mask was all elegant planes, as if pounded from metal by a master metal-worker. No one who worked for him had seen the visage beneath. Not even those who claimed to have taken in-person meetings with him, which was practically nobody.

"Not your boss," Tobias said. "Come in here." He opened a door.

I peered past it, into a dark, dank, narrow hallway. My gaze flashed up at Tobias. His suit, his accent, his entire demeanor, didn't scream serial killer, but what if he was trying to traffic me or something?

"No way. Do you think I'm an idi—Hey! Let me go!"

He'd snatched me up and darted into the hallway. I kicked, and a scream tipped my tongue, when he set me on the floor and took three steps back.

"What the hell?!" I looked around, in case someone else lurked in the shadows, waiting to jump me.

"We need to be out of sight," Tobias said, his tone so smooth it calmed me. "I have something to give you."

"What?"

"This." He reached into his pocket and pulled out an envelope.

The sender had sealed it with wax, like a king would have done in the old days. In the wax, an image of a snake eating its own tail stared back at me.

I took the letter. As I did so, our skin touched, and a waterfall of cold washed down my backside.

No way.

Tobias was attractive, but this was *so* not the time.

"What is it?" I asked, brushing off the spark I'd just felt. "And why the snake?"

"It's an ouroboros. Open the letter."

"What else would I do with it?" I replied, pretending to know what the hell an ouroboros was as I pried off the wax, and pulled the message from the envelope.

It was thicker than normal paper, creamy too. Expensive stuff.

I unfolded the note and read the spiky, EKG-like scrawl. When I finished reading, my gaze lifted. "There's a safehouse waiting for me?" I asked Tobias. "In New Haven, Connecticut? But why?"

The Ringmaster clearly had nothing to do with this. As a minor he provided me housing, which was part of the reason I was in debt to him. Now, that privilege was gone. My boss paid me to get my jobs done, and nothing more.

"We need to make sure you're safe."

"From what? And who is *we*?"

Tobias leaned in close. The heady scent of him, fresh but with a hint of leather and spice, filled my nostrils, making me dizzy. Why did he have to smell so damn good? "Did you memorize the address like they asked? And where they hid the key?"

I nodded.

"Good."

Tobias pulled a lighter from his pocket and plucked the letter from my hand. In a flash, he set the page aflame and dropped it to the ground. The spiky scrawl disappeared, eaten up by an orange glow.

He reached into his suit pocket and pulled out something else. "Do not return to the rooms you were renting. Go to the airport. This is your new identity until we say otherwise."

I took the item: a passport. Upon opening it, I saw that this was an excellent fake, one with money tucked in the center—both U.S. dollars and Egyptian currency.

Tobias might look proper, like an upstanding citizen, but he wasn't legit. Then again, neither was I.

"You'll find a ticket has already been purchased in your name at the Air Egypt counter," he continued. "Get on the plane, go to the house, and wait quietly. Do not leave. Do not make a ruckus."

"What if I don't want to get on the plane?" I challenged.

I hated when people told me what to do. It was the Taurus in me.

"The choice is yours." His shined leather shoe stomped on the letter, now blackened beyond recognition. The flames snuffed out, and he kicked the ashes around. "But if you don't, you're going to wish you had."

He turned toward the door and opened it. "The person who took the Pearl will hunt you, and you're not prepared to fend them off. If I were you, I'd take the deal."

Then he left me standing in the dank hallway, alone and utterly confused.

CHAPTER FOUR

MEREDITH

I stared at the door of the house, my prison for the last three days, toes tapping on the hardwood floor in staccato bursts.

Okay perhaps *prison* was too strong a word. I had arrived here of my own free will. I'd locked the door behind me with my own fingers. And honestly, the place was nice, though minimal. Keys lay in a ceramic bowl, white on the outside, gray inside. The furniture was modern, with bright pillows for flare. A gas fireplace provided ambiance at night.

Best of all, the home had a ton of books, and a well-stocked fridge that always had exactly what I wanted. I swore a block of my favorite smoked cheddar hadn't been in there yesterday, but it had appeared like magic when I'd gone rummaging this morning.

All of my stuff from Egypt was present too. Well, almost all of it. My phone appeared to be missing, but that didn't surprise me. There was no phone in this house. No computer, either. Zero means of connection to the outside world. Tobias had said to wait quietly, which apparently meant no phone calls.

The only part that didn't quite fit the rest of the home was the garage. It was stocked with car parts and the scent of oil hung heavily in the air, hinting that whoever owned the place worked on vehicles. Posters of motorcycles and luxury cars were pinned on the walls too.

So yeah, 'prison' wasn't quite right . . . but the trapped sensation was all too real. Stifling. Almost like death was closing in on me. I hadn't seen or heard from Tobias since I'd learned someone was hunting me, and I was dying for information.

I turned away from the front door, and a sigh gusted out of me. "What the hell am I doing here?"

It was one of the many questions I kept asking myself. Along with: what had happened to Denz? How was I going to get my most recent arrest off my record so it didn't haunt me for the rest of my life? And why would the person who took the Pearl be hunting me?

Probably the most terrifying question though, was what my boss thought of me just up and leaving without contacting him.

The Ringmaster had claimed that if someone working for him ever left his employ without paying him what they owed, which was a lot of money, he'd find them. He'd end them.

No one left this game without the Ringmaster's blessing.

So did that mean I had two people hunting me? An unknown person and my boss? Had coming here, even to avoid an unknown threat, been a huge mistake?

The scars tracking the sides of my spine tightened. Most of the time I could go weeks pretending that they weren't there, but not since I'd arrived in this place. My anxiety over my boss made that impossible.

I shuffled to the kitchen and opened the fridge. The block of smoked cheddar stared back at me. I shook my head and snatched it up. Once I had sliced off a mountain of cheese, I relocated to the living room and sat on the couch, perching the plate of cheese on my lap.

Last night, I pulled a few books from the shelf. All of them were occult in nature, except for a piece of fiction about a supernatural spy school. It looked fun, but I didn't have the brain space for fiction right now.

I was living one hell of a story myself.

I flipped open one of the larger tomes. It was leather-bound and stank. I'd never understood people who said they like the smell of books; the old ones were musty and gross.

Inside this one, there were symbols, and explanations as to what they meant. Some spells, too, though I couldn't decipher them.

The Ringmaster made us study the occult, because a lot of people we stole from believed in magic or the old gods. But I'd never read a book quite like this one.

I was in the middle of the volume, flipping nonchalantly, when the air in the room shifted. I stiffened, a piece of cheese hanging halfway out of my mouth. Then, inexplicably, I twisted toward the front door.

Neon blue and pink symbols flashed above it.

My mouth fell open, and the cheese tipped out onto the floor. "Are those *runes*?"

As if in response, someone knocked.

I shot out of my seat, flinging the plate of cheese all over the ground. If this wasn't someone coming to kill me, I'd have a hell of a mess to clean up later.

I was being ridiculous. "A killer wouldn't knock, Mer."

And there I went, talking to myself again. I really needed to get out of here.

I stared at the door. Would they knock again? Had it been a mistake, like UPS had gone to the wrong door?

My gaze flashed up. The runes had dimmed, but another knock came, and the runes flashed bright blue and pink again.

"Meredith Stone?" a male voice called out. "I am . . . *friends*," the word didn't sound right on the man's lips, almost as if he hated to admit it, "with Tobias Aston. He sent me to fill you in on what's happening."

He was a colleague of Tobias, last name Aston. Suit Guy.

So, not a killer.

Or would the killer say that?

I mulled it over for about two seconds before deciding I'd chance it. I was desperate for answers.

I rushed to the door and flung it open.

A blond man with bright blue eyes and a scar along his jawline stared back at me. He wore dark jeans and a patterned button-up. A hint of tattoos peeked out of his sleeve.

I'd spent a lot of time staring out the window, watching students pass on their way to summer courses or their job or whatever they were doing. I'd imagined a hundred different scenarios. And this dude looked like a Yale girl's dream—clean enough to be within limits, but with a hint of bad boy.

His eyes dipped to take me in, judging me. Easy to do, considering I was in sleep shorts and a tank top stained with yesterday's food.

Jesus, why hadn't I put on real clothes?

Oh, maybe because I've been in this house by myself for three days?

"Who are you?" I demanded.

His lips twitched. "Hans Novak. This is my home."

He removed my hand from where it rested on the doorframe and waltzed right in.

I blinked. *His home*?

No photos or personal effects lined the walls or shelves. Although, now that he mentioned it, the place had a masculine edge. More metal and leather than I would expect from a woman's home. Less color. Still, I'd thought it was a rental.

"Surprised?" Hans smirked, and in that single word I caught a hint of an accent. Eastern European of some type.

"You're not who I pictured owning this place." As the words left my mouth, I recalled the garage. With his tats and scarred jaw, that was the only part of the home that seemed to fit him.

"I hired a professional to decorate," Hans shrugged. "Didn't have time for it."

I got the distinct sense he also didn't really care what his home looked like on the inside. Odd.

"Right," I replied, trying to make sense of the man before me. "So why have I been in your house for three days?"

"It was a safe place to keep you until we decided how to proceed. Also, I sleep at headquarters a lot because things always crop up that need my attention. I see you made yourself comfortable." Hans gestured to the cheese all over the floor.

"Your knock startled me."

"Right." He smirked.

"I should change," I said, feeling stupid, way too underdressed, and like I needed a moment to think.

"Brilliant idea."

I rushed back to the bedroom—his bedroom, probably—and fished my favorite ripped-up jeans and tank top out of my bag. All the while, trying to make sense of what was happening and the man in the living room. I pulled them on quickly and glanced in the mirror.

I looked like hell, but I didn't want to take too long getting ready. I wanted answers. Clearly some sort of organization had put me here. Why? And who?

Quickly, I ran a comb through my hair and brushed my teeth. After, I applied mascara and cleaned up the flecks that always dotted my lower lash line, then I called it good.

I waltzed back down the hallway like I didn't have a care in the world, even though my heart was thundering.

When Hans's eyes landed on me again, his eyebrows lifted. "You're 'Cute but Psycho', huh?"

How dare he look at my beloved tank in such a way? I'd gotten it at a concert, tickled by the message, but clearly Hans was not into it.

Well, screw him.

"Yeah," I said defensively. "About sums me up."

"Why do you say that?"

"Eh. I've always been a bit off. Different."

I robbed graves and tombs. I broke into high-security buildings to steal. I ganked treasures from rich people so other rich people could buy it. And I did it without getting caught. My intuition was strong and nearly always right. Heck, even my appearance was unique. Not many people had different colored eyes, in my case one blue and one green. So yeah, I was different, though not crazy. The shirt was just cute.

"Anyway," I deflected. "I'm in your house, and now you're here. Why have I been here for days? Who put me here? And most importantly, who's going to kill me?"

Hans nodded. "Direct. I like it."

"Most people say the same, but they don't mean it."

He chuckled. "You're hanging out with the wrong people."

My lips parted in shock. I had thought the same many times. My honesty always charmed people at first, but eventually, whether it be days, weeks, or months later, I always said the wrong thing. Then they no longer considered my direct nature cute. Annoying, more like.

He motioned to the living room. "Take a seat. I'll cover as much as I can."

Only then did I notice that he'd picked up my mess of cheese while I'd gotten ready. That surprised me, but I didn't let it show on my face as I dropped into the chair across from the couch, accommodations for one. I didn't need Hans sitting next to me, no matter how hot or clean he was. Anything that insinuated we were buddies was *not* happening.

"Tobias told you that your life was in danger," Hans said. "He's right. I suspect after what happened, you have many questions."

"What do you know about what happened in the tomb?"

There were no surveillance cameras down there, just a million snakes and dust—and mist. Deadly mist. None of which I'd mentioned to the police.

"We don't know a lot," he admitted. "Only that you and your partner were there, and someone knocked him out before the authorities came."

"What happened to him?" I asked.

"Your partner? Or Tobias?"

"I don't care about what happened to Tobias."

Hans smiled.

Yeah, he and Suit Guy had some sort of beef.

"They have released your partner, though not with any pressure from us," he assured me.

"Who is *us*?"

"You're not familiar with Yale, are you?"

"Why do you say that? My shirt?" I didn't like his tone. I could be rocker-chic *and* smart.

"More like your past history, which we've been studying," he retorted, not at all apologetic.

I crossed my arms over my chest, but didn't interject.

"There are many secret societies at the university," he continued. "Shadows and Secrets—which is 'us'—is one of the oldest landed societies. Also, one of the most discreet."

"Like Skull and Bones?"

I'd heard the name on a TV series. Or maybe in a book.

"Skull and Bones is one of the other landed societies. They're popular and produce lots of presidents. However, we are far more selective."

"This is starting to sound a lot like a 'who has the biggest shaft' competition."

He snorted. "Well, to be in our group, you have to be special. And, as it turns out, Meredith, you fit the requirements to a T."

He leaned forward, placing his elbows on his knees in a relaxed position, though his eyes remained serious. "To be part of Shadows and Secrets, you need magic. And you have it, Meredith. You have a *lot* of it."

My mouth fell open, and I leaned back into the chair as shock washed over me like a tsunami.

I'm magical?

I'd had crazy experiences throughout the years that led me to believe things existed that couldn't be explained. Like mist that transformed into an animal form and chased me through a tomb.

Goosebumps dotted my skin. As if he could feel them too, Hans's gaze darted to my arms. Still, he said nothing, waiting.

I cleared my throat. "Do you mean magic like hocus-pocus? Spells and potions? Or ghosts and stuff?"

His full lips twitched, bemused. "Hocus-pocus is part of it. Ghosts exist too. You want me to dive deeper for you?"

"Yes," I said, not sure if it was the truth.

"There are witches and wizards and mages, although mages are pretty rare. Most live in Isila, though a handful are here for whatever reason. Some people belonging to those orders turn dark and prefer the term 'sorcerers'. They're assholes." He pursed his lips before continuing.

"There are also shifters, vampires, demons, those of demon blood in this world, which we call Hellblooded, necromancers, and many other creatures. I assume you've heard of most of those, though?"

My eyes practically bugged out of my head. "They're all real?"

"They are."

"So, necromancers . . . Why aren't there armies of the dead?".

"It would take a necromancer of incredible power and skill to command such an army. Though they can raise a few of the dead, and perform other valuable feats of magic, I can't say there's ever been one quite so powerful to control an entire army."

"Thank goodness."

"That *would* be terrifying," Hans agreed, his gaze softening, as if he were entertained by me.

For once, I didn't even care if someone thought I was silly. I was just relieved no one could raise a troop of zombies. I'd seen the movies. I knew how that ended.

Not good, Houston.

"Modern stories get a lot of the finer points about magic wrong, but the creatures are all real."

He lifted his hands and snapped his fingers. A flame erupted in his palm, and danced up and down his arm.

My heart rate jumped as I pushed back into my seat. He wasn't burned at all, not even red where the flame licked his skin. "What are you?"

"Wizard. And we suspect you are of my kind—a witch."

"The terms are gendered?" I wrinkled my nose. How old-fashioned.

"They are," Hans said. "But as a group we're called witches. Long live the matriarchy and all that." He winked and earned a few more points in my book. "Anyway, because we're similar, I was sent to explain about our group."

I waited, so he continued.

"Shadows and Secrets is not just a secret society on campus, we're also a coven of sorts. The 'landed society' part is so we blend in better around Yale."

"A coven of witches." I shook my head. This was freaking wild.

"Not quite. That's why I said *of sorts*. We're a coven of all types of creatures. Take Tobias, he is a—"

"Vampire," I breathed.

I'd watched the popular shows. I'd seen how vampires could use compulsion to sway what others thought. That had to be what Tobias had done to the guard in the jail.

Am I living a YA trope? But I'm twenty-one!

"Bingo." He looked impressed. "You're quick to catch on."

In my line of work, it was either catch on quick or die.

But, oh my God, vampires?!

"Wait. They can walk in the sun?"

I'd seen it happen, but who could blame me for questioning it? Perhaps Tobias had a daywalker ring, or whatever.

"They can walk in the sun," Hans confirmed. "Humans just made up some lore to make themselves feel safer. All supernaturals can walk among people at any hour. Most of the time, they never learn of our existence."

I closed my eyes briefly. "I cannot believe this is happening to me."

"Really?" He arched an eyebrow at me. "You said you've always been different. Did you feel things?"

I gulped. *The mist. The runes.*

My intuition?

"I-I've always had good intuition, especially when finding old artifacts. And I've seen some weird shit." My gaze veered to the door. Nothing was there. "Even here, I swear I saw runes flashing above your door before you came in."

"You did. They alert those inside to someone approaching, and more importantly, they keep out the rabble." He shrugged. "Or townies selling junk. You wouldn't believe how many kids sell candy door-to-door. Poison, I tell you."

"Do the runes hurt people?" I asked, ignoring his babbling over sugar and trying to make out the marks he'd confirmed were present. I couldn't find a single trace of them.

"No. Mostly just alert and deter people. I can teach you how to do that for your own place, eventually."

My own place? I hadn't had a permanent address in years. I traveled the world, stealing artifacts and ancient treasures and reselling them. With that kind of life, who had time for a home?

"Maybe." I pulled my gaze from the door, back to him. "Obviously, you guys knew I was in jail, but how did you find me?"

"The necklace you removed from the tomb created a ripple around the globe. It's dangerous. Deadly."

"The person who took it after *I* did called it the Pearl of Hell."

Hans rolled his eyes. "Vampires have a flair for the dramatic—Tobias aside, of course. He's as dry as sawdust."

So they thought that person was a vampire. Might explain how he moved so fast.

"What does the Pearl of Hell do?"

"Should we discuss this at headquarters?" he asked instead. "Are you comfortable leaving to see Shadows and Secrets Hall?"

I stood. "Let's go."

The moment I stepped outside, I breathed in fresh air for the first time in three days.

I threw my arms wide and tipped my chin to the clear blue sky. "Aaaaaaah!"

Hans gave me an amused expression. "Feeling cramped in there?"

"It's a nice place, but yeah. I'm usually more active."

I wasn't about to admit my activity was usually a result of casing new places to swipe ancient goods or valuable art from. This coven knew enough about me, while I knew nothing about them.

Except that they were made up of supernatural creatures and called themselves 'Shadows and Secrets'.

Goosebumps crawled up my arm. I had known some shady characters in my life. Were these people shady?

"The hall isn't far," he said conversationally. "S&S is one of the oldest societies, so she's kept her tomb on campus, even though we've become less active in the Yale community over the years."

"Wait? Tomb?" I eyed him sidelong. That sounded sketch.

"Oh, yeah. Just another word for the hall." Hans shrugged. "Headquarters. It's kinda archaic, but other societies use the term for their halls, so we do too."

I nodded and looked away. Head spinning, I fell into silence. Hans didn't say anything either. He must have sensed that I needed a moment.

We walked past a bunch of kids on the way to classes even though it was late summer. They were around my age, but looked so naïve. I was sure a lot of them had traveled the world on Daddy's credit card and stuck to the tourist trails. A few might have volunteered to build huts for the less fortunate or something.

They lived charmed lives. Not necessarily innocent, but not truly dangerous either. I doubted any of them had seen the seedy underbelly of the world. The part that would rip you out of your comfort zone and throw you into a pit, just to watch you claw your way out.

That was the world I had been raised in. It was nothing like this ivy-league fairytale.

One guy winked at me, his J.Crew attire far too clean for my taste. I looked away, uncomfortable.

"Hey, that's a great sign," Hans said. "We need members who can pass as students here when the Fall term begins. Gives us more credibility."

"You don't have actual students applying to S&S?"

"No. Too dangerous. Instead, we have members get into the school who can pose as students. They have to take and pass classes, though, otherwise the society would be in trouble. Term starts in a couple of weeks, so Luca will have to set that up quickly."

I couldn't believe what I was hearing. This was *Yale,* and I'd only gotten my GED. As a young teen, the Ringmaster had plucked me out of my shitty personal situation, promised me protection. After living on the streets and fending off men who sought to take advantage, I'd immediately agreed. I wanted safety, love.

I got the former, and only when I did what my boss asked.

I'd been working to pay off debts owed to the person who'd gotten me off the streets ever since. I was almost there too, just a year or two more of thieving and I'd be able to repay the Ringmaster and go my own way.

"Is that something you'd like?" Hans asked when I didn't leap at the offer.

I mulled it over as we walked, studying the campus.

I enjoyed learning, but Yale? I wasn't sure I had what it took to even pretend to belong here.

I glanced down at my tank top and ripped jeans. Man, I really did stand out.

"We'll talk about it." Hans filled in the silence I'd left. "The coven leader will meet with you and go over your role in more detail—if you're accepted into S&S, of course."

I pressed my lips together, not liking being yanked around. Either they wanted me, or they didn't. And seeing as they'd hid me in Hans's house for three days and were protecting me, I suspected they did.

But why? Did they know I worked for the Ringmaster? Or even who he was?

"We'll see." I tried to match his nonchalance.

We fell quiet as we walked across a long campus green. All around, people darted into buildings. Though the semester hadn't even started yet, there were so many students. As the days passed, I expected more bright, rich, young things would trample this area with their designer boots and sneakers.

What a strange place.

I was still busy checking everything out when Hans took a sharp turn down a very narrow street. I followed, and a wave of cold washed over me. Rubbing my hands on my arms, I looked around, though I found no source for it.

"A ward," Hans offered. "We can't have students traipsing up to our front door. We like being in the heart of the university, we've been here for centuries, but the location comes with liability."

"And no students notice the ward?" I asked as we walked down the lane.

If I had magic and didn't know, other people had to be in the same boat.

"They might, but our warder makes sure they don't feel inclined to explore this area," he said and stopped before a door.

"But . . . I can't imagine there aren't any kids at Yale who have magic. Wouldn't they sense something?"

"They know better than to come snooping."

I arched an eyebrow, examining the entrance to the so-called secret society. "I don't know. It looks like a door to a plain back-alley pub to me."

"Exactly the point." He smirked. "Ready to have your mind blown?"

"It's already shattered to pieces."

"Miss Cute but Psycho, you ain't seen nothing yet."

He placed his hand on an ouroboros, a symbol that—given my experience in the tomb—made my mouth go dry. The serpent lit up bright gold, and he pressed the door inward.

CHAPTER FIVE

TOBIAS

"You can't be serious." I paced in front of the expansive mahogany desk. My hands were clasped behind my back, my face placid as I tried to conceal how much the coven master's choice irritated me. "The girl doesn't know a thing about our world, Luca. When I spoke with her in Egypt, she looked like a doe staring down a crossbow."

My claim wasn't entirely accurate. Meredith Stone had handled herself relatively well. Impressively, even—for someone blind to the hidden world. But did that mean she belonged in Shadows and Secrets?

Absolutely not.

Luca's eyes twinkled as he glanced up from the paperwork strewn over his desk. "You know, Tobias, a gun would be a more common reference nowadays. Please say you're not using antiquated turns of phrase on missions?"

I gave him a withering look, which had absolutely no effect on the mage. "One, people have been hunting with guns since I've been alive. And two, I excel at playing my roles."

I'd been acting one part or another for 150 years, a wolf in sheep's clothing.

Although, I had to admit, recently I'd been pining for my human days. A time when I'd lived openly. I didn't know why, just that there was something missing in my life.

Or maybe it was the opposite? Perhaps it was time to end my long life?

My heart—the one that had rarely beat since the day my maker turned me in a dingy London street reeking of mud and piss and debauchery, some of which I was to blame for—gave a hard thump in protest.

I cocked my head slightly, bewildered.

"You know as well as I, the girl found the Pearl of Hell," Luca pressed. "She could be useful. At the very least, we need to learn *how* she found it."

"I doubt she knows."

Luca leaned back in his leather chair and arched a single gray-dappled eyebrow.

He was younger than me, but not by much. However, looking at us, no one would guess I was the elder. Luca appeared to be around fifty, though he claimed to be more than triple that age, whereas I'd become a vampire at twenty-five.

Mages, vampires, fae, dragons, the wolvea, all creatures in Isila lived very long lives and retained their youth for most of their years. Or, in the case of vampires, they remained the age they were when they were turned. Usually, that was fairly young.

I'd only met three vampires who'd been turned when they were over forty years of age.

"She must have some inkling as to how she did it," Luca

mused. "And if we can teach her how to use her power, she can find other items."

"You're forgetting one key thing."

He sighed. "And I suspect you'll enlighten me?"

"If you're lucky."

The coven master snorted. "As if you could refrain. Go on, then."

"She found the Pearl of Hell, and she *lost* it." I leaned back against his bookshelf, the top half of which contained leather-bound tomes from across the ages. Drawers lined the bottom half, filled with weapons and other items the coven master wanted close.

"Of course she lost it," Luca replied, unbothered. "It's no secret the Ordo Aeternum are after it. I would not be surprised if they were the ones to possess it now. What chance did she stand against them?"

I had to agree that the Ordo was our prime suspect—even if we had no proof. And if Meredith was pitted against the supernatural group that wished to rule both the magical and human communities, she wouldn't stand a chance in Hell.

And yet, even if it would keep her safe, even if she did have a raw talent we could utilize, I couldn't stand the idea of that girl joining our coven. Protecting her was one thing. It was what S&S did. But did Luca really have to welcome the thief with open arms?

I was about to plow forth, to convince Luca that allowing someone so naïve and with such flimsy morals into S&S would be a dreadful idea, when a knock came at the door.

"Yes?" Luca called.

Shay appeared, her long, brown hair falling like a curtain as she poked her head in the door. Ever-present excitement rippled across her fine features. "She's here. Should we show her to your office?"

The coven master stood and shook his head. "Not right away. I'd like to see how she reacts to our hall."

Interesting. For all of his talk, he might not trust the girl either.

"I should get going." I pushed off of the bookshelf. "I'll return to the Beinecke and see if I can't dig up more clues."

I knew as well as anyone who had been privy to the disturbances shaping our world that I wouldn't find a damn thing on any of the seven *lapis caelesti* in the Beinecke Library.

Only one book held the location of the mystical stones—the very gems the angels had created and used to give rise to magical creatures in the world. The stones that unknown creatures from the past had separated from each other and hidden because they were too powerful to keep together.

The gemstones which, in the hands of one person, had the power to ruin the world.

"The missing tome isn't going to just appear in the library, Tobias," Luca chided. "That's why we need her. If I'm right about what she is, this girl is the key to heading off the devastation before it comes to pass."

"Fine. Then I'll jus—"

"You'll come with us and give the girl a proper reception."

Behind Luca, Shay smirked.

"Tobias is on the welcome committee? Talk about a shocker. Try not to scare her off, Stiff. Maybe even smile a little?" She beamed, showing off perfectly straight teeth.

I bristled at the nickname, but hid my annoyance. Shay loved getting a rise out of me, and I hated giving her what she wanted.

"Same to you," I retorted. "Keep your wings hidden. They're a bit much. Too showy."

Shay stuck out her tongue, which gave me a little satisfaction.

Luca shook his head and laughed as the three of us filed out.

The corridors buzzed with excitement as we made our way to the heart of the coven's hall. For days, people had been asking me about the young woman I'd lifted from an Egyptian jail—as if I'd taken the time to get to know her when there were more important matters on the line.

Why weren't they more concerned that the Ordo Aeternum likely possessed the Pearl of Hell? What little history we had to go on told us the Pearl could rip away a man's sanity. If combined with any of the other *lapis caelesti*, it was said they could do much worse.

And if they're all together . . .

I shuddered; a gesture Shay didn't miss judging by the arch of her eyebrow.

Not that she missed much. There was a lot about the perky young woman that annoyed me, but her powers of observation, I respected.

"What's she like?" asked the wisp of a woman at my side.

"Why aren't we discussing the Pearl?" I growled, ignoring her and focusing on the mage.

"It has been hidden for thousands of years, Tobias," Luca answered. "Whoever took it from Meredith will ensure the Pearl of Hell continues to be hidden until they're ready to use it. Have you heard of explosive signs of madness occurring around the globe yet?"

"No," I admitted grudgingly. "Still, we should be narrowing down our choices."

"We will. When she's ready," Luca replied, patiently, never one to be rushed. So Italian. "When the person in possession of the Pearl uses if for the first time, we'll know precisely where to search—and I for one hope that doesn't come any time soon. Until then, we focus on training the girl. She'll need to look past magical protections to find the Pearl, and we need to help her."

"And you didn't answer my question, Tobias." Shay placed a hand on her hip, annoyance brimming in her usually bubbly tone. "What's she like?"

I shrugged. "Naïve. Too young."

Intriguing. Mysterious . . . Argumentative.

My jaw tightened at the last.

"Compared to you, everyone is young," Shay scoffed.

Luca twisted, his eyebrows pinched together. "Old age will come for you too. If you're lucky."

Shay was a nephilim, which in the *Bible* referred to a group, a race of giants, but in magical society meant something else entirely. Nephilim were simply part angel and part human beings. They could live well over two hundred years, but rarely more than five hundred. At some point, the angel blood could no longer constrain the human blood in their veins.

We traversed the halls, and others fell in step behind us. They were trying to be smooth about it, but were not succeeding.

To think, these people were members of a coven that hunted dark artifacts and evil creatures. We were the shield protecting the human world from beings that wanted to destroy it. How were they not more covert?

"Aren't you worried about her being a thief?" I tried once more to get Luca to see sense.

The coven master gave me another mildly irritated,

amused look. "No more than when you told me you were a mudlarker. That's not too far from being a thief."

"People lost things in the mud off the Thames all the time. It was no crime to dig up those items and sell them—at least, not until after my larking days were already over. Even when it *was* a crime, larkers did not steal priceless treasures from heritage sites."

"True," Luca said. "But I suspect you weren't so innocent as a sailor, either."

My eyes narrowed, which made the mage chuckle. "I'm only teasing. I've heard you, Tobias. And I still believe she could be useful, and I would like to introduce her to the coven."

I exhaled—something I didn't need to do to live, but the habit stuck, particularly when frustration gripped me.

We had capable creatures. Why risk bringing in someone so easily trailed by the Ordo Aeternum? Or, in the off chance they hadn't been the ones to take the Pearl of Hell, trailed by anyone else? It was asking for trouble.

"There she is!" Shay pointed over the railing, into the atrium below.

We paused and leaned over the banister. Indeed, there was Meredith Stone, walking next to Hans with stars in her eyes.

I scoffed and shook my head.

If the girl was struck by the hall, how would she react in front of real treasure? Or real adversity? Those in S&S often put their lives on the line. It was our job. Would she crack?

She didn't in Egypt.

I frowned. No, she hadn't, but she hadn't been facing down real danger with me. I'd merely delivered a message.

Down below, Hans stopped to introduce Meredith to

people. A few bore the signs of their magical orders: wings, horns, scales and fangs.

Shockingly, Meredith held it together. Until she came across a compatriot of mine with blood-red eyes. Then she took a step back.

"See." I nudged Luca.

"Reggie didn't feed. He should have," the coven master replied. "Red eyes would frighten anyone."

"They don't frighten me."

"Because you see them in the mirror when you don't eat enough," Shay interjected. "Believe me, they're freaky as shit."

"Such foul language from the heavenly," I retorted, affronted.

I'd always been considered a handsome man, but being a vampire made one a touch more vain than normal.

She shrugged. "Blame it on my human half."

I was about to reply, when something caught my eye: a dark figure, moving far too fluidly, too snake-like.

It darted from the opening of the hallway, moving in on the interloper to the coven. Hans was too caught up in talking to a siren to notice, while Luca and Shay remained too focused on Meredith herself.

No one spied the shade as he put on a burst of speed. Nor did anyone notice as he pulled a glowing, red blade from his black cloak.

My heart gave another hard thump, and something inside urged me to move.

I didn't question it. I leapt into motion, hurtling over the railing. Gravity took me, and I plummeted.

People shrieked as I flew past them, three levels to the ground floor of the atrium. The shade glanced up, its glowing red eyes latching on to me. He sped up, trying to reach the girl before I did.

"Bloody hell," I muttered, still falling.

What was Hans doing?

Clearly not paying attention to his charge.

My feet hit the ground, and I sprinted toward the thief, a blur to all who saw me. When I reached her, I pressed Meredith into a wall and shielded her with my body.

"What's going on?!" the young woman gasped.

By the distortion of her words, I figured her face must be pressed against the wall—or perhaps my back. Though she might be uncomfortable, that was better than dead. I continued to protect her body with my own.

"Let me go!" Meredith yelled, louder this time.

Hans turned, his easy smile falling from his face when he caught sight of me. "What are you doing?"

"Your job, Novak!" I yelled as the creature of darkness closed in. "Shade! At your back!"

The dark spirit hurled itself at Hans, who whirled about just in time to block it. A flurry of activity followed, and for a moment, Meredith stopped struggling.

"What is that thing?" she asked, her tone smaller than before.

"A shade."

"A what?"

I rolled my eyes and pivoted when the shade slithered past Hans and got close enough to swipe its hell-cursed blade in our direction.

My skin took the brunt, slicing open. I hissed as it knitted back together, and prepared to retaliate, but Hans hauled the devil back. I stayed put, knowing I was best used as a shield for the woman who wouldn't survive a blade created in the pits of the underworld.

"A shade is an evil spirit from hell; right now it seems to be partially corporeal. They can only take human form temporarily, and even then, they usually flicker in and out. This one has been sent on a mission."

"A mission?! What kind?"

"Probably to kill you."

"What?!"

I smirked. "Welcome to the Coven of Shadows and Secrets, Meredith Stone."

CHAPTER SIX

MEREDITH

Tobias crushed into me, his body as solid as the wall at my back. The effect should have been suffocating, but the damn vampire smelled so scrumptious, it almost made up for the pompous line he'd spouted.

'*Welcome to the Coven of Shadows and Secrets, Meredith Stone.*'

His words ran through my mind in a high, nasally voice that was nothing like his rumbly English accent. Still, mocking Tobias, even just in my head, gave me great satisfaction.

Why did he have to be so smug? So I hadn't known what the creepy person-thing was.

Actually, I still wasn't totally sure about it, or what the shade could do. The fact remained I did not appreciate his tone.

The shade let out a hair-raising shriek, exposing fangs that made me shudder, as more people descended from the floors above. Some held balls of light—magic—in their hands. Others seemed to radiate power from their every pore. A brunette woman fluttered from above on pure white wings.

The shade launched itself at Tobias, one last-ditch effort to get to me before the gathering crowd drove it off. It tore wildly at the sleeve of the vampire's black suit, and again, Tobias took the brunt of the attack, as if he were made of steel. But the creature got close enough to snap its mouth within inches of my earlobe.

Rotting breath filled my nose, and I pressed my body flat against the wall as the creature's slitted nostrils flared danger-ously. Thankfully, the next second, Hans leapt forward, pulling the monster off Tobias and hurling the beast across the atrium.

I exhaled, trying to level out my jangled nerves.

Okay, maybe I needed *a little* help. But just until I got my feet under me.

"Move!" a male voice cut through the crowd.

People scattered to the side, and a man appeared, running our way. He was a silver fox if there ever was one.

Yes, it was a poor time to be checking someone out, but what could I say? I had hormones. And eyeballs.

At the sight of the newcomer, the shade loosed another horrible shriek, pivoted away from me, and soared away.

But the silver fox was already on him. Magic, like wisps of glittery smoke on the wind, bloomed from him in a myriad of colors and caught the monster in a net of light. The shade screamed, eyes bulging as it thrashed about.

"Stand back!" Silver Fox yelled.

Immediately, everyone darted backward, making room. Hans uttered a spell, and a dome—a shield?—wrapped around me, him, and Tobias.

The older man was in the middle of the fancy atrium, the shade levitating in front of him. I was wondering what would happen when he conjured a sword out of thin air, also glit-tering with magic, and with one swipe, cut the shade in half.

Thick tar and inky smoke exploded throughout the chamber, spraying as high as the third floor. It would have covered the others if they were still close by—or me, if Hans and Tobias hadn't protected me. As it was, it only covered Silver Fox, who dropped to his knees and fell to the ground unconscious. A moment later, the halves of the shade joined him on the floor with a *thunk*.

A rotten scent wafted through the air, the stench of the dead creature, and I swallowed, disgusted but also awed.

"Cleanse him!" Tobias growled.

Hans leapt into action. "Witches! Wizards! Help!"

Tobias didn't move, so neither did I, but a half-dozen people darted closer, dancing over the goopy tar to reach the older man.

Hans poured magic over him. It was obvious he was cleaning up the residue the shade had left behind, little by little. As more people joined, the process sped up, until the man looked as if he'd stepped out of the shower. A few magic workers then moved on to clearing the puddles from the ground so we could walk.

Suddenly, Tobias shifted, freeing me, and I fell forward.

He caught me, his bare skin tingling against mine, and his gaze dipped down to where his hand clutched my arm.

He felt that too, huh?

Before, I'd thought it was adrenaline, but now that I knew magic existed, I wasn't so sure.

Tobias snapped out of it first, lifting his eyes and scanning the crowd. "Luca needs to lie down. Even if the poison is gone, some will have seeped in through his skin. Or worse, his mouth. He'll be weak."

Poison.

So when a shade was killed, it spewed poison, possibly killing anyone nearby. Interesting. Now it made more sense why the others had fought it, but not as aggressively as the man who'd actually slain the monster. They had been scared.

"I think we took care of most of it pretty fast. Still we'll need a healing elixir." Hans pointed to a woman in her thirties with long blonde hair and a buxom figure. "Can you make it, Daph?"

"On it. You'll be in Luca's office?"

Tobias glanced at me, nose wrinkling.

Did I stink? I refrained from sniffing my pits because even if I was ripe, there was no way I smelled worse than the dead shade. This was twice in ten minutes he'd been kind of a dick.

I crossed my arms over my chest.

The vampire's green eyes caught the gesture, and he turned away again. "After he wakes, he'll want to proceed as planned."

Hans looked at me and nodded.

"Come, Meredith," Tobias instructed. "I'll take you to the coven master's study. Hans, you have Luca?"

"Right behind you," Hans said as the older man—Luca, apparently—levitated. "Watch out for missed poison puddles."

I sucked in a breath. This was all so crazy! Before the attack, I'd been staring at the place all wide-eyed and probably making a fool of myself. Now that the danger had passed, I couldn't keep from doing so again.

From the outside, it looked like a hole-in-the-wall dive bar, but on the inside, the hall was all gleaming wood and old-world charm. The symbol of one of my least favorite creatures, a snake, was everywhere. In the images the serpent ate its tail, just like the wax seal on the letter Tobias had delivered in Egypt.

Ornamental gold rings hung from the ceiling, spinning, one

inside the other. A few such decorations dangled at different levels and caught light coming in from skylights, reflecting it and spraying gold across the vast space. I wanted to ask what they were, but everyone was so focused on Luca that it felt wrong.

I stayed quiet and continued following Hans and Tobias as they, and the winged woman, marched down the hallway, up the staircase, and into an office.

They laid the man down on a navy velvet couch—mid-century modern style, if my memory served—while I scanned the area, eyebrows knitted.

The entire room was a strange mash-up of different eras. It was also rich, posh. This kind of wealth wasn't flashy or ostentatious but it was so enmeshed in the design that to erase any sign of it, someone would have to tear the whole place apart.

"You okay, Luca?" Tobias leaned over the man.

"Fine," he said, apparently having come to while we walked. "Weak, but fine. Is the girl okay?"

I stiffened. As a general rule I didn't like being called *'the girl,'* but this man had risked his life for me, so I'd let it slide.

This time.

"I'm fine," I said. "Was that normal? The shade attacking here?"

"I'm glad you made it," Luca replied, his voice breathy. "I'm Luca Moretti, Coven Master of Shadows and Secrets. No, shades don't normally pop in like that."

"Telling that it did though," Hans said. "Someone has been talking. Someone connected to one of the Hellblooded or a sorcerer."

Hellblooded . . . Sorcerer. Hans had just told me that they were bad—assholes, he'd so eloquently put it. If they could send, or worse, control, a shade that descriptor seemed pretty accurate.

"Yes," Luca grunted as he shifted his weight. "We'll speak of that later." Again he turned his gaze to me. "I wish your arrival had been less climactic, but while shade attacks are unusual, I will admit, things are rarely boring around here."

"Which brings us to the point," I said, unable to hold back any longer. "Why am I here?"

"You're here because the night you found the Pearl of Hell, a disturbance registered all around the globe. We traced it to the tomb you . . . ahem, *explored*. From there, we found you and your partner in jail. It took only a moment to tell you were the one who caused the disturbance, not the man you were with. And yes, you have magic, a very particular kind."

"Which is?"

"We'll have to test you to be sure, but I believe you're a witch. A seeker."

"What do they do?" Judging by the name, I had an idea, but wanted to be crystal clear.

Luca smiled wanly. "Seekers are known for finding magical artifacts, which is what my coven specializes in. Although, there hasn't been a seeker alive in many centuries, and it's probably not as easy as I make it sound. Some artifacts don't want to be found. As far as we know, some exist only in legends."

I *was* fantastic at finding ancient artifacts and relics. Had they been magical, and I never knew? The mist in the tomb had clearly been magic, but I'd taken hundreds of objects and never come across magic before my time in Egypt. And speaking of the tomb . . .

An image of the damned flashlight I'd dropped popped into my mind. If they wanted me for something, I'd ask them to take care of that. And my new criminal record in Egypt. But not yet. I didn't want to give them leverage, just yet.

"If I am a seeker, what am I here for? I presume you have a use for me."

Luca chuckled. "You're smart. Good. If you decide to join us, you'll be attending classes at Yale, and it's always easier to hide the whip-smart acolytes in the crowd of Ivies. I—"

He coughed, and Hans and Tobias shared a glance.

"Are you sure you're okay?" Tobias asked, then sniffed the air.

Could he sense something was off about Luca? Like when a dog sensed their human was ill?

"Fine." The coven master brushed off the concern, collecting himself and turning his attention back to me. "You see, Meredith, supernaturals are rare, and seekers even more so. Many would want your magic."

"Many, like you?"

"Precisely," Luca replied. "I won't deny that we have use for you in the coven's ranks, and you can be certain others will too—those who seek the same things as us, but for far darker means."

I blinked. Like the guy who had taken the necklace from me. I'd wondered how he'd known to be there. Had he sensed the 'disturbances' Luca spoke of?

"We don't want our adversaries to get ahold of certain objects," the coven master added. For a moment, he looked conflicted, as if unsure if he should continue.

"When that guy took the Pearl in Egypt, he probably didn't know what I am, right?"

"We believe he did not. If he'd known, and if he's from the group we believe has the Pearl, he would have taken you too. Used you to search for other powerful artifacts." Luca swallowed. "Your identity and magic is safe for now, though if you join the coven and the hunt for the Pearl, it likely won't be that way forever."

After I paid off my debt to the Ringmaster, my main plan had been to live in sublime anonymity. Maybe in a chill beach town in South America. Would this take me further from my plans?

Even if it did, I couldn't deny I was interested in learning more.

"So, this Pearl of Hell," I ventured. "What will it do?"

"If used for evil, the Pearl will bring about chaos in the world. It could, if paired with other sacred gems, create destruction unlike the Earth has ever seen before."

My stomach dropped. "Not good."

"No," Luca agreed. "It's not. But if you join us, we can make sure the Pearl, and the six other *lapis caelesti*, do not fall into malicious hands. We would also offer you protection, and a sort of family."

I drew a breath. A *family*.

I'd been working my ass off to pay back the Ringmaster and go off on my own. But if what Luca said about the Pearl of Hell was right, and the baddies already had it, we could all be in grave danger.

What if the world went crazy because of something I unearthed? Living with that knowledge would be impossible.

As much as I yearned to be a free agent, to lounge on the beach and sip from coconuts, I couldn't do so with this on my conscience. I had to learn more about this world, and right my wrongs. After all, the Pearl would still be buried under tons of sand if I hadn't found it.

And that was another thing: what if, as Luca feared, someone came after me because I could find other powerful items? After seeing the shade, knowing that dark entities that I didn't understand might control them, I wasn't about to turn down protection.

Once I got my magic up and running, I'd reconsider going it alone, but for now, I needed help.

"A trial run suits me. I'm not sure how long I'll stay, though, after we find the Pearl." I swallowed. "Before you broke me out of jail, I was actually considering a change of career."

What an understatement. I'd wanted to break away from the Ringmaster forever, but Luca didn't need to know about my troubled past. I held that close.

"This one might suit you," the mage said.

"True. Does it pay?"

Luca's lips curled up a touch. "Of course."

I mulled that over. Then eventually, I'd be able to pay my debts the right way.

"Perfect, then I have only one request."

"Which is?"

Some people would flat out ask for the debt to be taken care of, but I wasn't like that. I'd taken on the debt, I'd gotten myself into this situation, and I'd pay it. In no way did I want to feel as if my debts had just been transferred to the coven. My stubborn pride couldn't handle it. In fact, I didn't want anyone here to know about what I owed. But I *did* need help, and suspected that S&S had the means to deal with my issue.

"Erase my criminal records in Egypt and the United States. I dropped a flashlight in the last tomb I raided. That was probably found and used as evidence, so it will need to be confiscated too."

"Consider it done."

"Oh, ok," I said, surprised it would be that easy. "Then, I'm in. For now."

"Very well, Meredith Stone," he said. "Then we have no time to waste. We'll start tonight by testing your abilities with a sort of scavenger hunt. I'll need to arrange the event, so in the meantime, you can either stay here or return to the safe-house. After the test, we'll induct you into the coven—temporarily or not—and begin training. Whether you leave later is your choice. If you do, we'll perform a memory modification for your time here. Do you consider that fair?"

"I'd get to know what I am, still, right?"

"Correct. We'd only erase sensitive information you learned about Shadows and Secrets, and your memories pertaining to the coven. For our safety, of course."

I nodded. "I can live with that."

It would suck to forget parts of my life, but so much of it was a blank anyway. What were a few more weeks, when years were already gone?

"We have a deal." Luca's gaze switched to Tobias. "You will be one of two racing her for the treasure."

The vampire's lips twitched, and his shoulders loosened.

Something in the gestures made my spine straighten.

"What was that about?" I asked, frustration mounting at the dismissive look on his face.

"I beg your pardon?" The vampire's brows knitted together.

"Your lips twitched like you were trying not to smile."

Or laugh, but I wasn't saying that out loud.

"You did the douche thing," the winged woman, who reminded me a lot of Selena Gomez, piped up. "The thing where you think you're better than the rest of us."

"I do not."

"Then you think I have a chance of beating you?" I asked point-blank.

His lips twitched again.

"See!" The young woman pointed, blue eyes wide. "He doesn't even know he's doing it, and it's annoying as hell!"

I agreed. But instead of digging in, I waited for him to answer.

"Was that a serious question?" Tobias asked.

"I don't like to waste my breath."

"I'll admit I don't think you'll be able to find whatever item they hide before I do. I'm a hunter, by title and nature."

"And I'm good at finding things."

He paused. "Undoubtedly. However, my belief has not changed."

My fists clenched. "Well, I guess I'll have to show you what I can do. Then you'll be forced to admit how wrong you were."

The vampire's face hardened.

I twisted to Hans, who appeared to be enjoying the show. "Can you show me around? Or take me wherever I need to wait for the test? I'm done here."

Shifting my gaze back to Tobias, I finished, "I have a victory to plan."

CHAPTER SEVEN

MEREDITH

My hands wrapped around a mug of hot chocolate enhanced with hazelnut syrup as I scanned the café.

After I'd agreed to test my abilities, Hans had escorted me back to his home. For the rest of the day, I'd paced the house, wondering how I'd beat a vampire at my task, and ate my emotions while I waited for instructions on what to do next.

Thank you, magic refrigerator!

Finally, twenty minutes before, I'd received a text instructing me to meet in the café down the street from the house.

So here I was, waiting.

If there was one thing I disliked, it was tardiness. It was so rude for people to be late, like their time was more valuable than anyone else's.

I'd nearly decided to leave and go straight to the coven headquarters when two young women burst through the café door. One was the brunette with wings I'd seen before, but her wings were gone—which was good, 'cause I was sure they wouldn't go over well in the middle of Yale. Still, I couldn't help but wonder where she'd put them.

Do they retract into her back?

I watched the ladies scan the room. When the brunette's gaze latched on me, she rushed over.

Again, she reminded me of a blue-eyed Selena Gomez, sexy in a way that would always draw attention, but she could pull off the innocent look too.

"I'm so sorry we're late," she said breathlessly. "Harper had to make sure everything was perfect. Yell at her."

"Or don't," the other girl countered as she joined us. She had straight red hair and glittering emerald eyes.

They both looked like models, and though I was no slouch, I felt plain by comparison. I sat up straighter to compensate for the sudden pang of self-consciousness.

"Luca would hate if everything wasn't *just right*," the ginger added. "Let's get a coffee, then we can fill her in." She didn't bother apologizing, nor did she appear remorseful as she turned and strode to the counter.

Someone was confident.

"You want something else?" The Selena-lookalike gestured to my cup. "They make a mean latte here. Organic beans or something. I don't know. Maybe it's magic." She winked.

"Yeah, your names would be nice? I need to stop referring to you in my head by your hair color."

The girl facepalmed herself. "Duh! I'm Shay, and the ginger is Harper. But I gotta get a latte—I'm so dead! Be right back, 'kay?"

I nodded, and, apparently reassured I was not upset, Shay trailed Harper to the counter.

I observed them as they ordered. They interacted with the

familiarity of friends, even if one was clearly annoyed at the other.

Truthfully, I couldn't remember what close female companionship felt like. It had been so long since I'd had a bestie. Denz was the closest thing I had to a friend, and he was much more of a coworker than a pal. He didn't even know what I was up to, or anything about my past—not that I knew much about his either.

Moments later, Shay bounded back to the table. "Just got a text. They're not quite ready for you, which is perfect. We have a bit of time to chill and get acquainted."

I frowned. "They had all day to prepare."

"True." Harper joined us. "But we're hiding something from a vampire who is good at finding things, a wolf with one of the best noses on the East Coast, and someone who might be a true seeker. The coven is taking their time covering their tracks. No one wants this to be too easy on you."

"Of course not." I snorted. "Don't throw the clueless one a bone or anything."

Shay laughed. "You found the Pearl of Hell! You know how to use your power a little. We only need to see how well you manage it."

"I don't," I insisted. "I know nothing. You might as well call me Jon Snow."

They exchanged unsure glances.

So I'm the only nerd here. Awesome.

For a moment, I tried to guess what kind of magical beings they were, but gave up. I was only wasting time speculating. So I asked outright.

"What sort of supernaturals are you two?"

"Wolf," Harper said. "Shifter, that is."

I blinked, shocked. She had a sort of stiff-upper-lip vibe;

her appearance fit in at Yale, as did her designer jeans and crisp button-down. But wolves brought to mind someone much more rugged. Wild. Raw.

"She likes to be different," Shay explained, correctly interpreting my stare. "As for me, I'm a nephilim."

I tilted my head at the strange term. "A what?"

"Nephilim. We're half-human, half-angel. Though I'm not quite *half*-angel, but pretty close."

"And what do nephilim do?"

"Tons of things! We're strong. We can fly, although I rarely do because I have to hide my wings."

"Where?"

"They just disappear with our magic."

"What kind of magic?"

"We have powers of the heavenly sort," Shay continued after a beat, which didn't really answer my question, but I let it slide. "We're the basis of supernatural creatures, after all. My kind—"

"She means full *angels* are the basis of all supernatural creatures in this realm," Harper cut in. "They created magical beings, both light and dark—though of course they didn't mean to make the latter. Her kind, nephilim, are a byproduct of an angel tussling with a human."

I was about to ask what she meant by 'this realm,' when Shay stuck her tongue out at the shifter.

"Whatever, Miss Encyclopedia." The nephilim turned to me, her eyes twinkling with mischief. "Harper belongs at Yale, which is nice when I need help on assignments, but other times, she's Miss Know-It-All."

"You get used to it," the wolf replied with a sly smile.

She apparently took no offense at the jab. Actually, she seemed to relish it.

Shay rolled her eyes, but amusement still lined her face. "Kinda."

Her comment was followed by a muted buzzing. Shay pulled her phone out of her pocket, glanced at its screen, dropped it on the table, and clapped her hands. "They're ready! Let's go!"

With the wolf and the angel practically vibrating with excitement, and my stomach weathering an odd mixture of anxiety and determination, we rose from our table and left the café.

As soon as we stepped onto the sidewalk, I stopped and stared at them. "Now what?"

Shay still had her phone in her hand. She faced the screen toward me, and I looked at the image on it: a book with leather bindings and a cover engraved with a gold pentacle.

"Find that," Harper explained. "It's an ancient grimoire, a witch's book of spells and knowledge. It once belonged to Bridget Bishop and still resonates with her magic."

I had no idea who Bridget Bishop was. Or how to find this book.

"You're not going to give me any sort of clue?"

"Why would we? If you're a seeker, you should be able to find what you want to find."

"What are you here for, then? If I can find that with *no issue,* why do I need help?"

"Someone has already attacked you," Harper pointed out. "Our group has been keeping tabs on you all day."

"No they haven't," I said, skeeved out by the idea. "Hans dropped me at his home and left, and I was alone until I came here. I even walked to the café alone."

The redhead gestured upward, where ravens perched on the telephone lines. "Just because you walked by yourself doesn't mean you weren't being watched. We can't make it too obvious who you are because you've drawn enough attention already. But a necromancer in our coven can see through the eyes of ravens. Anytime you're outside, they'll be watching you."

Shay looped her arm through mine. "So, you know what the book looks like. Now you have to dig into yourself to find it. Hans and Luca hid it, and they will have covered their tracks—magically, of course."

I sighed. "And I'm up against a wolf and a vampire. Both with good senses?"

"Excellent senses," Harper confirmed. "As much as I hate to compliment him, because he'd never let me hear the end of it, Gunner is far superior to Tobias in that respect. Don't tell him I said that, though."

"Tobias probably hates how keen Gunner's nose is too." Shay laughed.

"Absolutely," Harper replied, a smirk playing on her lips.

"Which means you have to beat them!" Shay turned back to me, excitement in her blue eyes. "We need some lady power at the top of the hunter charts. Harper and I are on Team Meredith."

I promised nothing, but looked down at the phone again. If they expected me to find the book before a vampire and a wolf, I needed to make every second count.

"The guys have already been told the hunt has started?"

"You're not getting an advantage because you're new," Harper said bluntly. "They start at the same time and were given the same parameter: the item is hidden within a six-block radius of campus."

I didn't think the limit of a six-blocks in any direction was such a huge boon, but Harper clearly did, so I wasn't about to argue. That might make me look weak.

"We *really* need a seeker." Shay's tone was softer than the wolf's but no less serious. "Luca is hoping you work out, but we need to watch you in action first. Make sure the Pearl of Hell wasn't a fluke—which, it totally wasn't, but you know." She shrugged. "Then we can induct you into the coven and show you all our secrets."

"There are more?"

"We're not called Shadows and Secrets for nothing." Harper snorted.

Shay winked at me. "Girlfriend, you only saw the tip of the iceberg. Find the grimoire and you'll be invited into a whole new world."

"I should probably get moving, then." I closed my eyes.

Calling up the image of the book in my mind, I tried to access my intuition. To my great surprise, the picture was crystal clear, and a faint pull, originating from somewhere in my chest, thinned my breath.

Had this happened to me before?

"You okay?" Shay asked.

"Yeah." I opened my eyes. "I feel different."

"You've been around supernaturals now. Your magic might be responding." Harper examined me like I was a science project.

"It's possible," Shay said. "And if this helps you beat the dudes, all the better."

My lips tugged upward. She had an excellent point. Perhaps this was the advantage I needed.

"Only if you hurry, though," Harper said, bringing both Shay and me back down to Earth.

"This way." I turned right, not entirely sure why, but determined to go with it.

Heck, it had always worked before. Why not now?

We went down the street, the faint tugging in my chest guiding my way. Since I was concentrating, our trio was unusually quiet, which garnered a few strange looks from passing students.

I ducked my head, feeling exposed as a group of ten straight up stared. Apparently, three girls couldn't walk in silence.

"It's because we all have magic," Harper said softly.

"What?" I asked, still moving, still following the pull.

"Whenever supernaturals gather together, we get more attention than when we're apart. Humans can't help but feel the otherness coming off of us. Our trio—a witch, a nephilim, and a shifter—probably feels very odd."

"Oh. It's not 'cause we weren't talking?"

"It's both," Shay said. "Can you sense the book?"

"I think so," I murmured as we turned onto a quieter street.

My eyes narrowed as I took in our new surroundings. Large buildings lined both sides; though a touch cold, they also felt expensive. Important.

"Where am I?"

"Two landed societies have their tombs on this street." Harper grinned, unable to hold back her excitement. "I bet Luca called in a favor. You're probably on track."

Though I had no idea how I could tell, I was sure she was correct.

My gut was telling me to veer right, toward a large, unassuming building with immaculate landscaping. The moment I stood before it, I exhaled. "Here."

"Skull and Bones," Shay whispered. "Try it. If you're wrong, they won't let us in anyway."

I nodded and led the way to the door, which wasn't visible from the street for whatever reason.

Raising my fist, I let it fall to the wood in a knock, and the hollow sound rang out, echoing through what must be miles of hallways. Before I'd returned my hand to my side, the door opened a couple of inches.

"Your purpose?" a voice asked, though the person—male, I thought—didn't show his face.

"I, uh . . . I'm here to find a book. Sent by Luca."

The door opened the rest of the way, and suddenly, I was standing face to face with a man in a stark black robe and plague mask, his face visible only from the upper lip down. "Your hand."

"Why?" I asked, my fists clenching instinctually.

"A blood sacrifice is required to enter. Do you wish to walk among the bondsmen?"

Blood sacrifice?

I gulped. For a moment, I considered turning away, but the idea was gone before it even fully materialized.

I couldn't. I needed to know about the magic inside me. Know what I was, what I could do if trained up a bit and given a chance. I needed to right the wrongs of unleashing evil on the world.

So, trembling, I extended my hand.

Grinning, from the folds of his cloak, the man whipped out a blade.

CHAPTER EIGHT

TOBIAS

Twenty minutes earlier ...

Gunner's phone rang, the sound a howl . ... which was quite appropriate for the shifter. Before it could do so again, the wolf snapped it up off the scratched table and checked the screen.

His overly large mouth spread in a grin and he ran his hand through his shoulder-length hair. "We're up, my man!"

He placed his piss-water beer on the bar top and threw down a couple of bills, sending another grin to the young bartender with a ludicrous mustache. "Thanks, Dean. See ya later."

"Cheers." I mirrored the wolf's motions, paying for my scotch, only half gone because it was barely tolerable.

I preferred a nice, rich claret, but the pub had a piss-poor wine selection, so I'd settled. The smokey aroma of peat would remain lodged in my nose all evening.

Together, Gunner and I left the bar and turned toward the campus. Those who'd hidden the grimoire would have also notified Meredith that the hunt was afoot, so I sniffed the air, trying to locate the young woman with two-toned eyes.

Nostrils flaring, I caught many scents, most of them familiar and comforting. Coffee. Cheap ramen noodles, fresh from the microwave. Steak served at the nearby steakhouse, which professors and alumni frequented and most students could not afford. Gasoline spilled somewhere on the road. A too-strong perfume.

Soon, autumn would descend; I could smell that too. But try as I might, I couldn't smell the witch. Wherever Shay and Harper had requested to meet her must not be in the vicinity.

"You take right, and I'll hang a left?" Gunner asked, his southern drawl thick as the mud on his boots.

Seemingly fetching, too, as the girls passing by stared at him. One even batted her eyelashes, which caught the wolf's eye.

"May the best creature win." I lowered my voice.

The wolf grinned at the ladies, but managed to tear his gaze away, back to the task at hand. "Looking forward to seeing what this gal can do. Catch you later, Toby."

My lips tightened, but before I could remind him that I despised that nickname, he was already running off, lost to the hunt.

I huffed and strode to the side of the street. There, I closed my eyes to better listen and smell. My senses were the key to finding the grimoire.

It could be anywhere within six blocks of Yale's expansive grounds in New Haven—even my own home, though I doubted Hans and Luca would sneak in to hide the book. They had to have guessed I would lay traps for anyone stupid enough to breach my modern security system. Even magic could not discern all the snares I'd laid—which was how I wanted it. A vampire with my lineage and past could never be too careful.

Still, I could guess at some of their tactics. Hans and Luca would do their best to cover their scents, so Gunner and I were on the same level as Meredith.

But they couldn't completely erase their presence. Any hair freed from their scalps, any item they had touched, they would leave behind faint traces. Not all vampires could detect those traces, but I knew the men well and my senses were sharp, so I could.

I simply needed a starting location, which I hoped the loquacious students of Yale would provide.

As I listened to the sounds of human chatter, punctuated by the occasional creature passing by, I tried to keep the competition out of my mind. However, where one of my competitors was concerned, the feat turned out to be impossible.

Even if Meredith wasn't a seeker, but a less-gifted, hedge witch, she could use magic to find things—just not nearly as easily. And some things would always remain hidden from witches who did not carry a seeker's gift.

The question was, how would these differences manifest? And how strongly? If she was not a seeker, or someone worth bringing into this dangerous world of secret societies and lost dark artifacts?

Harper and Shay were tasked with watching Meredith as she worked. From their observations, we'd know if the girl's discovery of the Pearl of Hell was a fluke, or an innate talent that, with proper training, might be honed into something incredibly valuable for the coven.

We all had to bring something to the table.

Down the street, a dog barked, reminding me of my other opponent: a man I already knew was worthy of being in S&S.

Gunner, like me, came from a distinguished bloodline, which he'd use to his advantage. He would shift somewhere and call on other wolves. His strong alpha blood, his connection to the wolvea, the original wolf shifters in the immortal realm, and more specifically in Gunner's case, the *Royals* of Isila, meant others would have to respond, they'd seek him out. And if a wolf had noticed the coven master and the wizard—which they would if they were anywhere in the area because the duo was *powerful*—I would be screwed. The wolves would divulge their paths to Gunner, and he'd be on his merry way.

Gunner beating me would be irritating. But Meredith finding the grimoire before me would be downright unacceptable.

So set your head to rights, Tobias, I scolded myself and bore down my focus.

With my thoughts no longer scattered, it didn't take long to hear my first hints.

"I still can't get him out of my head. He looked like a Ken doll. A sexy, tatted one. How have I never seen him here before?"

"I liked the Italian better."

"I wonder what they were doing on campus. You don't think they're professors, do you? If so, sign me up for that class."

"Cheers, sis!"

The women devolved into giggles, but I turned away.

I had what I needed.

Hans, with his blond hair, chiseled jaw, and strong build, certainly fit the description of a Ken doll—although, once you spoke to him, that squeaky-clean image deteriorated some-what. He had a dark streak that a doll could never manage. One born in his blood and bones.

Good looks often deceived, seduced people's trust—vampires knew that better than most—but no one could hide their true self forever.

Luca had to be 'the Italian' in that conversation. Together, they'd caught the wandering eyes of coeds, as I'd hoped.

I made my way to where the young women were hanging out in front of a bar, sipping drinks, about half a block away. With their cloying perfumed scents in my nose, it was easy to follow where the girls had walked before.

Finally, two streets away, I caught another scent I recognized: car oil and sage. Hans loved tinkering with cars, and he also 'cleansed' himself often with the herb. The wizard had been in the area.

I searched for another sign of the duo, and found a second clue at the stoplight. Hans had pressed a button to cross the street.

I traversed the same road and continued to scour the campus and listen, catching additional clues here and there. Some markings from my covenmates proved older and worn away. Others were fresh, like the many times Hans had touched a lamppost or fingered a flower as he passed.

Bloke needs to keep his hands to himself.

But part of me was grateful; those markers led me to a notable landed society's sandstone tomb.

Skull and Bones—or as some of their new brothers liked to call it, the Brotherhood of Death—was likely who my coven master had sought out to hide the grimoire.

I scanned the street, searching for Gunner and Meredith. They were nowhere in sight.

Either I was off my game, or they were.

My lips curled up. As the top hunter in Shadows and Secrets, I liked my chances.

I prowled forward to search around the tomb, staying to the opposite side of High Street. With each step, sharp pangs of determination burned through me.

I had to show this Stone woman I was the best. That I would not be challenged by her, or anyone else. Luca might believe she was the key to finding the Pearl of Hell, but I still held significant reservations. Her thieving past being one; the strange effect she had on me being another.

Which was more concerning, I wasn't sure.

Focusing again on the task at hand, I listened, but found nothing of note across the street. So finally, sure of my findings, I crossed the road and walked straight up to the tomb's door.

My footsteps echoed in the recess that partially hid the door from the street. I listened for students or townies nearing, and when I was sure no one would walk in front of the threshold, I bent at the waist and sniffed the metal door handles.

Air tore down my throat, and a scent forced my spine to stiffen until I stood ramrod straight. A coppery tang filled my nostrils, making my mouth water insatiably.

Someone had been bleeding here. Recently, too. Someone with the most *delectable*-smelling blood.

A moan crept up my throat, but I stopped its vocalization seconds before a group of students walked by, peering curiously into the recess, perhaps hoping to catch a peek of a bonesman entering their hall.

One young man's eyes lit up, a young one excited to get a glimpse of a bonesman, or so he thought. His pulse quickened, sending the vein in his throat throbbing. The blood rushing through him called me, *sang* to me.

I whirled away, and resolutely stared at the door, seconds from losing all restraint.

The students passed as a fresh wave of need—something akin to desire, but also a frightening need to control—came over me. My throat burned as though someone had poured lava down it, and I trembled from head to toe, as my fangs threatened to emerge.

Control. My fingers dug into the wall, as if trying to wring liquid from stone. *Keep it together, Tobias.*

Sucking in a breath, I pressed myself into the corner of the building, allowing the sandstone to support me as I composed myself.

As I hid from the outside world, more people passed, the area too heavily trafficked. Though I didn't dare turn, I could feel their curious gazes burning a hole in my back.

I couldn't blame them; the tomb was an attraction, a mystery to most. And though they didn't know it, the person huddled in the doorway's recess was an even more uncommon sight.

It was doubtful that any of them had ever seen a vampire on the verge of bloodlust.

CHAPTER NINE

MEREDITH

"YOU'VE GOT TO BE KIDDING ME," I HALF-WHINED, HALF-ACCUSED to the man who stood before me. "I suck at riddles."

Wasn't the blood enough? The masked Skull and Bones member waiting inside the door had already made me give a 'blood offering' to enter their hallowed halls. All he'd done was slice open my finger, but he'd made it seem like a much bigger deal. A bit dramatic, if you asked me—though Harper explained the exchange was for the sake of symbolism, as well as to show trust. In the rare situation when an enemy—basically anyone not a part of their society—entered their halls, they'd be weaker.

The prick on my finger was still oozing, and not wanting to get blood on my clothes, I brought it to my lips and sucked. The metallic tang of blood filled my mouth, somehow sharpening the moment, making it more real.

The man who stood before me now wore a robe and mask like the one who met me at the door. His face remained largely hidden, but his mouth was on display. "No one ventures deeper into the bonesmen's tomb unless they prove themselves cunning."

My gaze swept down the long hall that had brought us from the door to this T in the corridors, trying to get a sense of this place and what kind of people joined the society. The bonesmen I'd seen so far wore plague masks. Images, gothic and dark in nature, lined the hallway, decorated in dark colors and lit only by the buttery glow of candles.

I was getting the sense that death reigned here. It gave me the willies, but it also intrigued me a little. This was a challenge, as well as an honor. They did not show many outsiders the tomb of Skull and Bones.

"Tobias will be good at this," Harper murmured behind me.

The girls had been pretty quiet as I'd followed my instinct, my magic, through the streets of New Haven. Actually, the coffee shop had not been far from the windowless stone society hall I'd stopped in front of. Not far at all.

I was sure that wasn't on purpose, because both girls seemed as surprised as me when the man at the door asked for our blood and let us in. The proximity was, however, a nice perk.

"He will be," Shay agreed. "He's brainy. And old, so he's had time to accumulate lots of random knowledge."

No way in hell was the vampire beating me. I had to hurry.

"Let's do the damn thing." I cracked my knuckles like a boxer heading into a fight.

"Very well, then. Here's your riddle. You only have one chance to answer." The man could not contain his excitement as he spoke. "There are two sisters: one gives birth to the other and she, in turn, gives birth to the first. Who are the two sisters?"

I blinked. No way did I get so lucky. Did Luca tell this society I'd studied other cultures? Classics too? Although admittedly, the classics weren't my fave, they were good to know for parties, a great cover for fitting in with people who cared about that sort of thing.

But how would he know that? Other than the fact he knew I robbed a tomb, which indicated some knowledge of Egyptian culture. But no one wanted to advertise an initiate to their society as a grave robber.

I bet this dude would not suspect a girl wearing a shirt with 'Cute but Psycho' written across it to be very cultured. I so wanted to prove this mainstream-asshole wrong.

"Can you repeat that?" I asked, wanting to make sure it wasn't too good to be true. Riddles were such tricky assholes.

He did so, his smile growing. This bonesman probably got off on the idea that he had me cornered.

I mulled the riddle over and couldn't discern a trick. It was one of the lesser-known sphinx's riddles from *Oedipus Rex*. "Day and Night are the sisters."

The robed man's face fell. "Correct."

"Yaaaas!" Shay howled, and then slapped her hands over her mouth. "Shit, I hope Tobias or Gunner didn't hear that!"

"Well, what are you waiting for?" Harper directed her question to the robed figure. "Let us through!"

Anxiety laced her voice. I twisted to see her nose twitching. Did she smell one of my competitors?

My insides turned cold. I wasn't even sure I wanted to be a fully-fledged member of S&S, but I *did* want to beat Tobias and wipe that aggravating smirk off his face.

The man stepped aside. "At the end of the corridor, take the final door on the right. There you will find one more trial.

It has been set up by the Grand Master of Shadows and Secrets himself."

They didn't call Luca a coven master. Was that because they didn't know S&S was a coven? Or did they want to keep Shadows and Secrets in line with their own traditions?

"So close, Mer!" Shay whispered as we walked down the hall.

I was about to tell her not to call me Mer. Only people I loved—all of whom were long gone—called me that, but she looked too elated for me to chastise her. She was here for me, excited for me. I hadn't had a cheerleader in a long-ass time, so 'Mer' would work for now.

"Let's hope she can finish strong," Harper said, her tone more scrutinizing than Shay's.

We reached the end of the hall and turned right. All the air whooshed out of me as a library complete with thousands of books, antlers over a hearth, and a huge globe in the corner, spread out before us.

"Of course," I muttered, half in awe, half annoyed. "Why *wouldn't* they hide a book in a room full of other books?"

"The bonesmen dabble in the mystical, so some of these books might be magical," Shay said. "You'll have to use your gift to narrow it down."

I turned. "How would Gunner or Tobias find it faster?"

Harper tapped the tip of her nose.

"Some of these might be so modern, they'll be able to sniff out the old one." My gaze raked over the room.

"Use your power," Shay prompted.

To get here, I'd followed my intuition down the streets. There was always a faint pull, drawing me forward. I could only hope it would be the same here, so I closed my eyes, allowing my intuition to guide me.

One step forward. Then two. I imagined the grimoire in my head as I walked, begging it to call to me.

Silence rang in my ears, almost deafening. But one tone was higher, clearer. It resonated through me, familiar but also strange. It reminded me of the mists chasing me.

Magic.

It pulled at me, and I turned right, eyes still closed. Behind me, I could sense Shay and Harper standing still. I would bet my favorite shirt that Shay was holding her breath, and Harper's eyes were narrowed.

I followed the pull until I could no longer move forward, and only then did I open my eyes. A wall of books stared me down, climbing from floor-to-ceiling. My eyebrows knitted together.

Usually, when I hunted relics to sell on the black market, something would jump out at me. But right now, I seemed to be looking at a regular library.

Steps alerted me to the others' presence.

"They all look too new," I murmured. "Is there such a thing as a spell that hides stuff? Like makes it look different?"

"For sure." Shay's voice bubbled with excitement. "Fae have glamours. They can apply them to people and things other than themselves. Other supernaturals can cloak objects or disguise them. Luca and Hans can."

"So what I'm seeing might not be real." I chewed on the inside of my cheek.

Nothing on the wall called to me, but I still felt the pull coming from the shelf.

Or maybe from *beyond* the wall.

Following a hunch, I cast my gaze to each side of the bookcase. Mostly, it contained books, but one object struck me as odd: four paces to my right, an old-fashioned candelabra was mounted on the wall. It certainly fit the decor of the old-world library, but its placement was off.

I crossed to it and placed a hand on one of its arms. The moment I touched it, a zing of energy—magic—zipped through me.

Bingo.

I pressed up but found very little give.

Wrong way.

Reversing the direction, I pulled down.

The library wall clicked open, revealing a secret passage.

"Wicked," Shay whispered. "I keep telling Luca we need one of these."

"I'm shocked S&S doesn't have a secret room."

"We do, but not in the library." Her shoulders rose and fell. "It's always cooler inside a library."

"If you say so."

I pushed the door open and found myself in a stone chamber full of robed people wearing plague masks. Hans and Luca stood among them.

The coven master stepped forward. His olive coloring looked wan, which I suspected had to do with fighting the shade, but when he smiled, it lit up his face.

"One more test. Which is the real grimoire?" He pointed to a table on which two identical books lay.

I allowed my intuition . . . er, my *magic*—it would take some time to get used to thinking about it that way—to guide me, but when I approached the table, I knew immediately.

I pointed to the one on the right.

Luca's eyes locked on me. "Are you sure? The stakes are high on our missions. Members of Shadows and Secrets must always be sure."

I hesitated, and at that moment, the room shifted. A breeze flew by me, and Tobias appeared.

He picked up the other book. "She's wrong. This is the correct grimoire."

CHAPTER TEN

MEREDITH

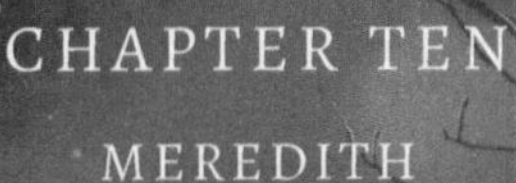

No one spoke. No one moved. The air vibrated with a heady mix of excitement and tension.

My eyes locked on the vampire who had stolen my thunder. I wanted to punch him, but refrained. Not out of the kindness of my heart, but out of a sliver of fear wiggling through me.

His chest heaved. He looked crazed, like a wild animal. One set to snap at any moment.

I took a half-step to the side.

Hans tensed to strike. Luca noticed the vampire's state, too, because his eyes were wider when he dragged his worried gaze back to me.

"Meredith? Answer me. Are you sure?"

I closed my eyes and it only took me a moment to verify my intuition was as strong as before. Tobias claimed I was wrong, but I didn't think so. I'd chosen correctly, I was positive.

"It's that one." I pointed to the book still on the table.

Luca studied me for what seemed like a never-ending

moment before his face split into a grin. "You're correct. Sorry, Tobias. A powerful fae glamour tricked you. Meredith won this one."

The vampire didn't speak. Didn't move. Then a muscle feathered in his jaw.

My eyebrows knitted together. *Are his nostrils flaring? Is he smelling me again? What the—*

Tobias slammed the imposter book down, making me jump as he spun on his heel and marched toward the door.

Hans watched him go, caution in his gaze, and hands at the ready, as if he, too, still worried that Tobias might attack.

"Whoa." Shay gaped as the vampire exited the hidden room. "Talk about a sore loser."

"I don't think it's just that." Harper frowned at where Tobias had disappeared. "Something's up with him."

"I guess," the nephilim hedged. "But what?"

I barely had time to process what had happened before a robed, masked man stepped out of the circle.

Why were they here? To intimidate me? To make me feel even more on display? If so, they'd partially succeeded. I hated all the eyes on me.

When I'd been myself, not playing a role for the Ringmaster, I'd rarely mingled in a room with this many people. And when I had, it was at a rock concert. They were a rare indulgence and one of the few places where I could lose myself and not mind the crowds.

"We want to hire her to find property stolen from our tomb," a bonesmen said.

Luca held up a hand. "While we'd love to help you, Grand Master, Meredith needs to be inducted into Shadows and Secrets first. She needs to take the vows of secrecy and train before I send her on a single mission."

"How long?"

"I suspect not very. A week or two at most. With the right partner, she might be able to go out earlier."

"She's naturally in tune with her magic," Hans added. "Training shouldn't be too hard."

Luca's eyes sought mine. "If she still wants to go through with it?"

My heart skipped a beat. To my surprise, I wanted to join much more than before. Normally, I wouldn't tie myself down, but this didn't feel like that.

As the person who'd found and unleashed the Pearl of Hell on the world, not only did I feel a moral obligation, but this was something I was good at, the people seemed decent—and the gig sounded like it would pay well.

I couldn't ignore that factor. If the Ringmaster came calling, I'd need the money to pay my debts and buy my freedom— even if I wouldn't be alone, like originally planned. Sure, the people in the coven were odd, but I liked them well enough.

Most of them, anyway. Tobias's scowl came to mind.

Plus, I liked how Luca had presented them as a family.

I hadn't had one of those in many years.

"I do want to join Shadows and Secrets," I answered finally.

Luca beamed, but his happiness quickly succumbed to a fit of coughing.

The Grand Master of Skull and Bones observed him. Through his mask, his eyes shone with concern.

"I'm fine," Luca rasped when his coughing fit petered out. "It's dry in here." The coven master straightened. "Once Meredith is inducted and trained, your job will be her first. Unless you'd rather hire someone else before then? Is it urgent?"

"This particular item has been missing for weeks, so it is not urgent, more of an annoyance." The Skull and Bones Grand Master paused. "I think I'd like to hire the other man, too. The girl is talented, but new. And she only beat the man by a few seconds."

Ugh, fabulous. I'll have to deal with Tobias on my first gig.

"As you wish," Luca agreed. "Hans, will you undo the enchantments we set?"

The wizard nodded.

"Very good." Luca gave a small incline of his head. "Gentlemen and gentlewomen, I thank you for accommodating us this evening and allowing us access to your tomb. If there's nothing else, Shadows and Secrets will bid you goodnight." He scooped up the real grimoire and nodded for Shay, Harper, and me to leave.

As we did, a tall, broad-chested man with longish hair and a frat-boy air about him entered. "I'm too late?"

"Afraid so," Luca said with a wry grin. "You're the third to arrive, Gunner. Better get your nose checked."

The man snorted. "I blame the beer. Shouldn't have had that second one." He looked at me. "Welcome to the club. We have a hell of a good time."

"Thanks."

He, unlike Tobias, was a gracious loser.

"We're leaving, Gunner," Luca said. "Don't want to overextend our welcome."

We exited the tomb of Skull and Bones and stepped out into the cool night air. I looked around. Tobias was nowhere to be seen.

"What's next? Do I get inducted tonight?"

"I need to prepare a few things first," Luca said. "Tomorrow."

"Oh, okay." Strangely, I felt let down.

Luca turned to Harper and Shay. "Ladies, will you escort Meredith back to where she's staying?"

"Of course!" Shay said, her tone animated.

We split from the guys, and all the way to Hans's home, Shay chatted on and on about how cool it was that I'd beaten Tobias.

"No one has done that. Ever!" she gushed as we strode up the walk.

"Thanks," I replied, exhausted from being in her vivacious presence.

Harper closed her eyes briefly. I sensed she might feel the same.

Introverts unite!

"Well, thanks, ladies. I guess I'll see you tomorrow?"

"You will," Harper answered before Shay could. "We wouldn't miss the induction for the—"

She paused, her nose wiggling. "Are you still bleeding?"

I looked down at my cut. "No. It stopped."

An ear-blistering stream of curse words left the wolf's lips. "Open the door."

My heart rate spiked at her tone, but I did as she said.

"Stay there," Harper instructed, as she eased into the house. Shay was right behind her, leaving me on the doorstep like a lost puppy.

Screw this. I followed. Harper didn't seem surprised when I caught up with them. Nor did she say anything. She was too busy searching the room.

"What is she looking for?" I whispered to Shay.

"Nothing good."

Harper bounced from the couch to the fridge and then

walked back toward the bedroom. We followed behind her, my shoulders knotting tighter with each step.

When we entered the bedroom, I exhaled. Everything was in order.

But then we checked out the attached bath, and what reassurance I had left shattered. A sentence was scrawled in blood on the mirror.

You owe me, Meredith.

I sucked in a breath. That could only be from one person. But how had he gotten past the protections Hans had around his home?

Harper whirled around. "Who do you owe and what do you owe them?"

"The Ringmaster. He was my boss. I owe him money, which is why I work for him. He supported me for years, protected me, and later used me for his own means. If I don't pay in full, he'll kill me."

"Shit! Shay, call Luca. Tell him she can't stay here."

"Right! Where instead, though?"

Harper paused. "Our place." She turned her gaze on me. "It's earlier than we expected, but it looks like we're your new roommates."

"Has that always been the plan?" I asked.

"It has," Harper replied, fishing in her bag as she turned away from me. "We'll tell you more later."

I wanted to ask why their place would be more secure than this one, but Shay was already on the line with Luca, and Harper was taking samples of the blood.

She keeps vials in her purse? Talk about weird.

The other two were a whirl of activity, pacing, analyzing. I didn't want to screw anything up, particularly since this threat was aimed at me, so I waited somewhat patiently for them to do their thing.

When Harper finished gathering blood, she turned to face me. Her brows squished together. "What are you just standing there for? Get your belongings!"

"Oh, right!" I was leaving this house for good.

As I gathered my stuff, I marveled at how Hans's house had actually started to feel like home. Surely, if the wizard had been here with me the whole time, that would not have been the case, but he hadn't been.

My teeth dug into the side of my cheek. I'd never had female roommates. Actually, I'd only shared a room with another female relic hunter once. We hadn't gotten along, and the Ringmaster had never put us together again.

Still, the worry of rooming with Harper and Shay vanished from my mind. How could I worry about something so trivial when someone had threatened me in *blood*?

The vampire's pissed off expression from earlier flickered in my mind. Was it Tobias?

No . . . that would be totally insane. Tobias had been acting off earlier, but something told me he wasn't crazy. My first inclination had to be right.

The Ringmaster had done this.

After my parents died, I'd found myself in a horrible situation, and he'd been the one to support me—though not just out of the goodness of his heart. He expected a lot in return. Had my boss done so because he'd known what I was? Or had he been honest when he told me he just saw something in me? Something, as it turned, he could use, and did. Often.

Did he see the magic?

It was impossible to know with him; he wasn't the most trustworthy guy. And writing a note in blood was both disgusting and creepy. It was more in-line with the supernatural world than the one I'd grown up in—violent and cut-throat as that had been.

"Ready?" Harper prompted. "Wow, you don't have much, do you? Thank the Old Ones your new room is furnished."

"So, I was always supposed to room with you eventually, rather than stay here? Why?"

Shay approached. "We have the space, and Hans doesn't want a girl in his home permanently. But we needed to be sure you were good enough to join the coven. And that you wanted to, of course."

"Right."

I threw the last few items of clothes into my duffel and closed it, in a hurry. If I left something, it wasn't a big deal. I owned little of value.

"Ready."

Shay had already called a rideshare, and as the car pulled up, I glanced up at the runes, flashing neon blue and pink. I took a cleansing breath, and followed my new roommates out of Hans's home.

We stayed silent during the drive, and it wasn't long before the car pulled up in front of an old-fashioned, Victorian-style house. It was gorgeous, with a tower at two corners.

"You *live* here?" I asked as we got out of the car.

"Yup. It was my mother's," Shay said. "She let me buy it when she moved."

I blinked. Shay had bought this place? But she had to be around my age, and this house looked super nice.

"Trust fund," she explained.

"And she calls *me* a snob." Harper strolled past us.

"Not like you're from the streets," Shay retorted.

Not like me.

I kept that bit to myself.

The girls teased each other a bit more, but their chatter ceased when Harper opened the door and showed me inside.

"Welcome to Chez Haray. Harper-Shay!" Shay flourished with her hands. "We'll have to figure out how to put a bit of your name in there too. Might take me a few days to come up with something catchy, though."

"I can't believe this place."

This was some real rich-people shit. Everything on the first level was picture-perfect. Like, straight out of a Pottery Barn catalog, but with the charm one would expect from an old home. Cute built-ins, ornate staircases, and even a stained-glass window above a fireplace. And . . . something I couldn't put my finger on. An off aura.

"Why does it feel weird in here?"

"Angel magic," Shay supplied. "And mage. Mom made a deal with Luca to have him ward the house, to supplement my magic. She can't stop me from being in S&S, so she wants to make me as safe as possible. The combo of angel and mage magic is harder to break than pretty much anything else. Most people don't know enough about either to do so."

"Oh."

I had so much to learn.

"Your room is up here." Shay bounded up the stairs.

I followed, but Harper hung back.

"I'll make tea," the wolf said.

"Biotch! You better pop that champagne!" Shay called.

"She was just threatened!"

"*And* she passed a wicked-hard test. Make tea and pop the bottle!"

"Whatever. Fine." Harper huffed and continued into what I assumed was the kitchen.

We crested the stairs, and Shay led me down a hallway. As we walked, I scoped out the photos—all of them depicting a dark-haired girl with overly large blue eyes and a mischievous grin. Shay. A woman with long, blonde hair often paired the girl, an amused smile on her face at Shay's antics.

"Here you are!" My new roommate pushed open the door at the end of the hall. "I hope you like it."

I entered the room, and all of my breath left me in one go.

They'd given me a tower room and, though it was minimal in furnishings and decor, it was *beautiful*. A homemade quilt covered the queen bed, and the gray-blue of the walls, made the space feel homey in a way that none of the hotel rooms I often stayed in had ever managed. Off to the side, I spied a bathroom. My very own. A luxury.

My chest tightened.

"Get comfy and come down for some champs, B!" Shay patted me on the shoulder. "It's time for us to get to know each other better."

"Be right there," I said, surprised to find I looked forward to it.

Could I find some normality here?

Maybe—and that was a *big-ass* maybe—but best not to get my hopes up.

CHAPTER ELEVEN

MEREDITH

I stared down at the image ringing the doorknob the snake in a perfect circle, eating its own tail, and willed the door to open faster.

"The ouroboros symbolizes wholeness or infinity," Harper watched me carefully, just as she had the entire walk to the tomb.

"Cool," I said, not really caring at all. This sort of distraction would usually work on me, but not today. After the threat last night, I was jumpy.

But so far everything this morning had been normal. The alleyway leading to the entrance of S&S's hall was quiet and still. And yet, my heart thundered so hard in my chest, I wondered if the others could hear the sound. Were they freaked out too? They weren't showing their cards.

I inhaled, trying to calm myself. *Stop freaking. Think of something else.*

I averted my attention to the nephilim still winding her hand around the doorknob in an intricate pattern. Gold magic trickled from her, and Shay closed her eyes, as if concentrating.

"I don't understand," I said, annoyed that the door had not opened already. "Hans simply touched the knob, and it glowed and let us inside."

"Security has increased since the shade attacked you, chickadee," Shay replied, her gaze trained on the ouroboros. "Good thing, too. Hans's home is well warded and someone *still* broke in. We need to be more alert."

"It'll stay this way until you can fight back," Harper added, making my heart sink lower. "Or until we're sure of who's out to get you and we can catch them. Whichever comes first."

"I already know the Ringmaster was the one to break into the house last night, and am not surprised," I admitted, feeling guilty for causing so much trouble. In addition to being worried about the threats on my life, I didn't like when others made a fuss over me, and this was a huge deal. "He has eyes everywhere."

"Does he control shades?" Shay asked.

My stomach dropped. If he did, that made him even more powerful than I'd ever known. "I'm not sure."

"You can bet the coven will find out," Harper said. "But I'd say it's not out of the question. If the Ringmaster broke past Hans's runes, he has supernatural ties." She arched an eyebrow. "You never suspected?"

"No." My fingers danced against the side of my leg as an image of ice-blue eyes behind a cold black mask sent shivers along my body. "I rarely saw my boss, and only over video chat. He has a lot of secrets."

I'd always wondered if magic was real, suspected it might be. So many strange things happened around me—though I usually tried to explain them somewhat rationally.

Harper shrugged, as if me being so oblivious was nothing. "Well, right now you should only worry about initiation and getting trained up. Other members are looking into the Ringmaster . . . who he is and how to deal with him. The shade too."

The question of paying off the Ringmaster climbed up my throat, but I closed my lips, stopping it before it could be born. If they paid him off for me, I would owe someone else money. It wasn't a true solution, just a transfer of my debts to someone kinder than the Ringmaster.

It embarrassed me to owe so much.

A *click* sounded, and the door opened.

"Freaking finally. Let's roll, babes!" Shay exclaimed.

I followed her inside, the wolf bringing up the rear. With each step, my eyes grew wider, more enamored. Although I'd been here, the building still stunned me with its occult, old-world beauty.

Yet, it wasn't enough to cut through the nerves jangling through me. The further we walked into the hall, the more my hands trembled. I wasn't sure what would happen during the induction. I expected there would be a vow and magic. Besides that, Luca might be planning to send me to Timbuktu—I had no idea.

We passed into the atrium where I'd been attacked, and Shay turned to the right to fling open a pair of double doors. Stepping inside, I gaped.

Fifty people filled the room, most of whom I'd never seen. Luca stood in the center. A bowl crafted of black stone rested on a dais, glowing slightly.

"Who are these people?" I murmured.

"Curious witnesses from the coven." Harper arched her eyebrows.

"Are there more? Isn't S&S small?"

"We only have about twenty more active members who

aren't present. Those who aren't retired or raising families." Harper lifted a shoulder and let it fall. As she did so, loose, red curls slithered over her shoulder.

That number didn't seem small to me, but then again, I usually only worked with one partner. Aside from Denz, I didn't even know many of the people the Ringmaster employed. I'd never wanted to, until now, when one might be hunting me.

"People are excited about having a seeker in the society." Shay beamed at me.

My natural talent for finding things *was* handy. To Shadows and Secrets, it was the key to changing the world. To me, learning how to use my power better was the way I'd right my wrongs.

If I didn't, a freaking apocalypse might happen.

A lot rested on my shoulders. It made me uncomfortable to be here, to be a part of something so big, and even to be getting to know people—and of course, I hated that someone was after me. But I had to stay here and figure out how to use my magic. To use it for good. Turning away after I'd released the Pearl of Hell was impossible.

Luca ambled up to us. Dark circles ringed his eyes, which were filled with concern. He looked paler than normal. Paler, and more worried about me. "Are you okay?"

How many people besides Luca, Shay, Harper, and Hans knew about the break-in? My eyes darted around the room, only to land on Tobias. His gaze latched on me too, almost predatory.

I shivered. That was one competitive mofo.

Determined to put the vampire out of my mind, I turned back to the coven master. "I'm fine. And Shay tells me her house is well-protected, so everything's good now."

"We can put this off for a day or two." Luca's voice was soft. Reassuring. "Give you time to settle in. You've been through a lot."

I'd rarely met a person as genuine as the man standing before me now. It was strange to think people like him even existed.

"Nah, I'm fine. Let's do this and get to training."

The sooner I could take care of myself, the better.

He nodded and gestured for me to follow.

We approached the dais, and when we reached it, my eyebrows drew together as I studied the bowl. It was about the size of a large popcorn bowl, but made of black marbled stone. The liquid seemed clear, but because the stone was dark it was hard to tell. "Is it water?"

I knew that was unlikely. None of this was run-of-the-mill.

"A potion. It will inform us if you harbor any duplicity in your decision to join. It's traditional for all coven initiates, not exclusive to you."

I swallowed. "What would happen if I were to be duplicitous?"

"When someone who is lying drinks the potion, it causes them immense pain. Their cries tell us they are not here for the right reason, and we don't induct them into our society."

The way he regarded the liquid told me I did not want to feel its full effect.

That was no matter. I wasn't trying to con them. In fact, I hoped that by joining the coven, my conning days would be over.

"I'm ready."

Luca gave me a long look, as if those brown eyes could see to the pits of my soul. He picked up a small cup, no larger than a thimble, and dipped it in the liquid.

"As Coven Master of Shadows and Secrets, I invite Meredith Stone into our fold. She will act in good faith, on behalf of all that is right and true. She will do everything in her power to bring dark artifacts to light and keep them contained. She will, when required, take on positions to fund the coven." He paused. "And she will keep our secrets and those of our clients. Understood, Meredith Stone?"

"I agree and understand."

"I give you this elixir, before everyone in the coven, to ensure you are true to your word. Drink. Once you come out the other side, we will complete the binding oath."

I took the tiny cup and shot the liquid down. It barely grazed my tongue, but a hint of mint tickled the back of my throat.

All around, coven members tensed and the air stilled.

How many people had failed this test?

I stood still, not sure how long the elixir would take to work its way through me. Or what to expect. My heart rate kicked up, but so far, nothing crazy was happening.

I swallowed thickly. Surely *something* should be happening, right?

My chest tightened.

Ten long seconds later, Luca beamed. "She is true. Take my hand, Meredith."

I exhaled the breath I'd been holding as my palm landed on his. The moment our skin touched, electricity shot up my arm.

I jerked, and Luca's eyes grew wide, concerned.

"Meredith, your magic is not right. It's blocked."

Blocked?

"I don't understand. You said I use it."

"You do, but I don't think you use the full scope of what you possess. Someone has bound you, and allowed only a trickle of your abilities to be released—perhaps to protect you from the adverse effect of bottling it up. You're more powerful than we realized."

A lump rose in my throat. I didn't know who'd bound me, but I had a guess: the people who used to know me best.

I could barely remember my parents, even though I should be able to. They'd died when I was thirteen, and yet, they lingered in the back of my mind, faceless.

When I thought about them, I saw a flash of red, a glimmer of green. Sometimes, I heard a feminine laugh, or a man singing softly. Other than that, I couldn't touch my past—couldn't get mad at a perceived childhood injustice, or reminisce happily.

I'd always thought it was because of the car accident that took my memories from me. Experts had claimed the wreck traumatized me, and I might never remember the events of my early life.

But now I'd discovered a whole new world, I realized there might be a more complex explanation. What if, before they'd died, they'd wanted to hide all traces of themselves? Or of me?

Had my parents been well-known in the supernatural world, and that was why the Ringmaster had approached me? Was that how he had found me on the streets, huddled in the cardboard box I'd made my home?

I'd never quite understood how he'd shown up right when I needed him.

My stomach hardened. I wished the days of my homelessness could stay buried as firmly as the memories of my parents.

"I can unlock your power before you take the oath. I would feel wrong not doing so," Luca whispered, startling me back to the present moment. "Would you like that?"

I hesitated, but only for a second. "Will it improve my training?" I asked, trying to be deliberate, though my heart immediately screamed *yes!*

"It will. It also might hurt."

"And will I remember the past?"

Shock flitted across his face. Apparently, he hadn't realized so much was a mystery to me. "I'm unsure on that front. If you want to, then I hope you can."

I pulled a steeling breath into my lungs. "Do it."

I wasn't sure how I'd found my way to the Coven of Shadows and Secrets, but now that I was here and things were unraveling, I wanted to understand what had led me here. I had a million questions, like . . . who was I? What was I meant to become?

Were these secrets tied up inside me, too?

Luca placed both hands on my forearms. "Close your eyes."

For reasons I couldn't fathom, my gaze flickered to Tobias, standing amongst the crowd. He was leaning forward, as if watching a riveting show, though his eyebrows were pulled together menacingly.

Weirdo, I thought right before my eyelids fell.

Darkness overtook me for a second, then something electrifying trickled through me.

Magic.

Luca tried to be gentle. His power seeped in through my skin, warming me before the stabbing pain started.

I gasped.

"Are you okay?" he whispered.

"Fine. Surprised." I drew myself up, not wanting him to stop.

Even someone like me, someone not used to magic, could

tell he was dealing with me tenderly, but he hadn't been joking when he said that unlocking my magic would hurt.

The more he pushed his power into me, the more pain I experienced. After barely a minute, I couldn't hide the agony any longer. My teeth ground together. My legs shook, and sweat dripped down my brow.

Luca asked again if I wanted him to pause. Again, I said no.

Deep inside, something was building, threatening to blow me up from the inside out. I held fast, but as the pain grew, a whimper escaped my lips.

"Hold on," Luca reassured me. "Almost there. I—"

I didn't hear the rest of what he said because the pain exploded through me like a firework.

Fire spiraled through me, piercing the scars running the length of my back, threatening to flay them open. The edges of my vision began to blur, to bruise gray, and suddenly, all my breath ripped out of me.

"No!"

I gasped as images, *memories*, horrible and dear, flooded my mind. A brunette woman. A soft hand caressing my cheek. The car losing control, and the fear in Dad's blue eyes as they locked on me in the rearview mirror.

They vanished as quickly as they had appeared, leaving nothing. A blank canvas, like the one I'd known all my life.

Frantic, I whirled, ready to chase my recollections. Maybe, if I ran fast enough, I might catch them by the tail and pull them back to me.

I made it exactly two steps before my knees buckled, and I collapsed to the ground.

CHAPTER TWELVE

TOBIAS

My spine grew ramrod straight as Meredith fell. Heat built in my veins, the impulse to shoot forward mounting ever higher.

Luca was at her side in an instant, fingers reaching for her pulse. He was calm and deft, and normally if someone was in peril, that would be a welcome sight.

But not now.

His touch on her skin forced a territorial rumble up my throat, but some small, conscious part of me stopped it before I could make a sound. But then my nostrils flared, and the fresh-floral scent of her filled my nose, and the growl worked its way out anyway.

At my side, Gunner twisted my way. I couldn't see his expression—that would mean breaking my stare from Meredith—but then a powerful, meaty hand wrapped around my wrist. Holding me in place.

I tensed and going against my instincts turned to face the alphablood.

"Dude, what's up?" Gunner asked when I said nothing.

"He's touching her."

Gunner arched his brow. "Yeeeaaaah. *You* need to chill, my man. Luca is helping her."

Rationally, I understood those words to be true. So why did I feel like this? Why did my body insist Meredith was in danger and I needed to be the one to save her?

"What's going on?" Gunner asked in his slow, southern drawl.

If he wasn't a wolf and hard as nails, he would already be running away from me. Few supernaturals were brave enough to take on a vampire, or try to control them, but wolves were among those who would challenge my kind. Particularly the strongest alphabloods, those most closely descended from the royal wolvea lines, like Gunner.

"Did the little witch get to you, Toby?" The wolf's tone softened, and he swaggered closer. A playful grin lined his face, though his hand still firmly encircled my wrist. He recognized that I was teetering on the edge of reason. "Did she work her way into that cold, undead heart?" He shook his head mockingly. "Say it isn't so."

The bloody arse was *teasing* me.

He courted his doom.

My fists tightened, my nails drawing blood from my palms. I tried to tell myself he was a friend, a colleague. Tried to be calm and collected.

It didn't work.

A snarl burst from my lips, and in response, the air pulsed with heat. Gunner was about to shift, about to try to take me down.

Not until I check on her.

I ripped my arm from his grip and darted through the crowd to Meredith's side. The instant I was close enough, I dropped to my knees and brought my ear closer to her body.

Luca didn't look up. His hand remained on her pulse, his attention on her face. That should have been reassuring, but it was not.

Her eyes—one blue, one green—remained closed. Her breath trilled in and out of her slowly in a whisper. Too faint. Listening harder, I realized her heart beat weakly too.

I scented the air. There was something different about her.

What had Luca done?

Behind me, people whispered—about me, about the young woman—but I wasn't paying attention to hear what they said. I couldn't. My focus was entirely on her.

Every time I looked at Meredith, I was overcome with either intense anger that she'd beaten me, or an undeniable need to shield her. None of it made any sense; I hadn't felt like this in Egypt. But with every passing encounter, my emotions toward the witch grew.

"What did you do to her?" I tried to level my tone, but it came out as a growl.

For the first time, Luca's gaze met mine. His eyes widened, recognizing the signs of a vampire on the brink. "Tobias, listen to me. Get back."

"Tell me what you did."

"Someone bound her magic, but she had no idea. I unleashed it."

"Of course, she didn't! She didn't even know what she was!"

Footsteps shuffled as everyone at my back scooted away, like I was touched in the head.

Was I?

"Tobias, I said *leave*." Unlike the others, Luca wouldn't back down. His warm brown eyes, a shade reminiscent of the espresso he favored, snapped up before returning to me. "Gunner, you ready?"

"Ready for anything."

The voice was closer than the wolf had been a moment ago. He'd snuck up on me—planned to restrain me.

Bloody hell.

Irritation raged through me. Together, the wolf and the mage would be strong enough to stop me if I grabbed Meredith and ran out of here.

I blinked. *Grab her and run? Why would I want to do that?*

The question had barely materialized when the girl groaned. Her eyelids fluttered open, and the next second, mismatched eyes latched on to me. The scent of jasmine became overwhelming.

She frowned, and though a part of me took offense, another part rejoiced. She was okay!

I shook myself. Why did I care so much? This woman was an annoyance, a thief. She meant nothing to me.

"You said that would hurt, Luca. Not that it would knock me into next week." Her tone rang accusatory, if weak.

"I apologize," the coven master said. "I didn't realize. Are you okay? Don't get up yet."

Meredith didn't reply right away. She looked down at her body, as if trying to find something new there. Finally, she nodded. "I am tingly and kinda weak, but yeah."

"Your magic, I expect. It was locked up tight. Having it flow freely through you will throw you off balance. Do you know who might have done that to you?"

For a moment, she looked like she would answer, but then she shrugged.

If she had information—and I suspected she had a hunch, at the very least—she wasn't ready to share yet.

Meredith was a better fit for the coven than I'd thought. She could keep a secret.

And kick my ass in a hunt.

Annoyance rose in me once more, forcing me to my feet.

Meredith's gaze flickered to me, those strange, magnetic eyes roving over my face, making me feel as if I were laid bare.

Suddenly, her attention jumped back to Luca. "So, I'm part of the coven now?"

"I still need to perform the binding oath, but close enough. Once you can stand, we'll do that, and you can begin training right away. That is, if you feel up to it?"

"Can I eat first? I feel so weak, I should do that even before I take the oath. But I would like to start training today."

"Harper and I can train her," Shay offered, coming around to where I could see her.

Judging by the closest scents, the only other people who had not inched away from me were Harper and Hans.

Shay caught my stare and arched an eyebrow. "After all, we're her roomies. It will be good for bonding."

Luca shook his head. "I'd rather one of her kind, a witch or wizard, start teaching her about her magic. And someone skilled in a different sort of fighting."

"I'll do the fighting!" Shay volunteered again.

"No. You use magic too. I mean physical fighting." Luca's gaze landed on me. "Tobias, you will be her sparring partner. Hans, you help her with her magic."

The skin on the back of my neck tightened. "But I—"

"You seemed concerned a moment ago, Tobias. I'm giving you the chance to be of some help."

My fists balled up. Though a part of me wanted to be close to the girl, this didn't feel right. Luca may be the coven master, but I had the right to refuse.

However, it was usually inadvisable to deny a mage. I'd done it a time or two, back when I was a young, dumb newblood, and regretted it each time.

Slowly, Meredith sat up, and another jumble of emotions rushed through me.

I blinked. I couldn't distinguish a single one among the mix. The chaos confused me, and I *hated* being unsure—almost as much as I despised being out of control. I needed to seek sense.

"Fine," I finally gritted out. "I'll help. Someone come find me when she is ready to work. I'll be in the library."

I marched out of the room with the sensation of many eyes on my back and a hundred questions bubbling in my mind. I exhaled, trying to calm down, but as I increased the distance between Meredith and me, the opposite happened.

My heart rarely beat, I rarely had reason to draw breath, but currently, both functions were happening. As I stormed down the empty corridors of the headquarters, my body trembled. It was as if my very cells were revolting against me.

What is going on?

In my centuries of life, I had never experienced something like this. Sure, there had been bouts of lust capable of scattering my thoughts. Bloodlust, too; particularly early on after my change. The latter was far more dangerous, but that hadn't happened for over a century.

Until the other night.

It all started when Meredith Stone came into my life, which meant she had to be part of the problem. But how? As far as I could tell, she was a witch—a seeker witch, but a witch all the same. I'd never met a witch who brought up this well of emotions inside me. Was she enchanting me?

Though the idea was, theoretically, possible, that couldn't be the case. She seemed as put-off by me as I was by her.

That frustrated me more.

I flung open the front door. The late-summer air smacked me in the face, steadying me somewhat, but I didn't halt in my escape from headquarters. I kept going, with only one place on my mind.

Luca believed Meredith was a seeker. I did too. After all, she'd found the Pearl of Hell when no one had in many millennia, and she'd done it without realizing what the stone was capable of.

But was she something more? Something that could unhinge a vampire? Or were seekers just like this?

It had been a long time since one had been born, and back then, I hadn't cared to know about that type of witch. Or any witch, really. The last known seeker had died when I was a new vampire, babysat by my maker, preoccupied only with blood.

But if Meredith had power over other supernaturals, she was more dangerous than any witch I'd ever met.

The question continued to burn in my mind as my feet carried me all the way to Yale's Beinecke Library. Soon, I would have to return to coven headquarters to help Meredith. By then, I wanted to know as much as I could about the strange girl and her kind. I needed to know why she affected me so strongly.

The rare books haven—more specifically, the supernatural section—was where I'd start. The enchanted section was as old as the library, though humans wouldn't know it. They couldn't see it. The wizard who'd created it had done a stellar job at hiding it in plain sight. Now, all supernaturals appreciated it as a repository of knowledge.

That special portion of the Beinecke was the only part of the university library that might help me. I could only hope it wouldn't fail me again, as it had in my search for information on the *lapis caelesti.*

No. It couldn't. This matter was quickly becoming as pressing as our concerns over the celestial stones. If I couldn't control myself . . .

I shuddered to think what would happen.

The last time I'd lost control had proved disastrous and deadly. Articles had even been published in the paper. Londoners didn't leave their homes for days; some, weeks.

Blood-filled memories flashed in my mind, and I forced them down, unable to deal with them when my mind was in so much turmoil.

There were things about my past I'd never be able to change. Or forget. Usually, I pushed away people, places, and things that elicited those savage, dark emotions.

And right now, Meredith Stone was conjuring up the most dangerous parts of me.

CHAPTER THIRTEEN

MEREDITH

After I ate, which made me feel a million times better, I took the oath. The words were fairly straightforward. A promise to be true to the coven. To use my magic for good. To not abuse any of the dark artifacts they sent me to retrieve.

Tobias was not present during my oath, and something about that bugged me, but the annoyance did not last for long. It couldn't, because shortly afterward, my training began.

"It's a beginner's conduit," Hans explained, igniting a ball of blue light until it pulsed in his palm and illuminated the sleeve of tattoos climbing up his arm. He was trying to show me how to call my magic into my hands, and I watched everything he did, listened to what he said, very carefully. "You try."

I nodded and held out my hands, palms up. My eyes narrowed as I called the power Hans had helped me isolate inside my body.

It had taken the larger part of an hour for me to get it, but now that I recognized what the thread of direct magic felt like,

I couldn't ignore it. The energy responded to me, like warm water flushing through me, pulsing in my veins.

I directed it toward my hands, and suddenly, the skin of my palms glowed.

"Wow," I breathed. It was nothing compared to the distinct ball of light Hans held, but to me, it was damn cool.

"Nice work!" His own ball of light vanished. "Try to push it out of your skin. When people are first training, they like to use their fingers and hands to point where they want stuff to happen. It helps with control, but once you've got that, you can grow out of it. Watch this."

He murmured a word I didn't understand but that sounded like Latin. Across the room, a chair lifted—then another, and another.

"All you need is the skill to control your magic and a strong intent. As long as you have those, you can do anything you want. Within the bounds of your powers, of course."

"What does that mean? The bounds?"

"Well, like I'm not a warder, so while I can do basic protections, especially if I use a tool like runes, no one would trust me to ward the coven hall. Warders can create shields for specific places and against specific people. It's quite a precise job."

"A warder," I tested the word out. "So what are you?"

Hans drew back, his eyes narrowed. "I told you that I'm a wizard."

I blinked. Did I strike a nerve?

No . . . he's probably just annoyed he had to say that twice. That means his student isn't listening. Or a dummy.

"Right, sorry," I said, not about to be thought stupid. "I meant is there a word for the type of wizard you are? Are there, I don't know, basic witches and wizards?"

A strange look of relief crossed his face, and he smiled at me.

"Good question. Sometimes, people don't have specialties," Hans replied. "But there are many different types of witches. I'm a caster, though I can still do what we consider fundamental magic—we call that hedge magic. People with only hedge magic dabble in many areas but are not considered particularly strong. They are usually very connected to nature too."

"But you said you're also a caster, so you are strong," I said as if I hadn't already known. "What can you do?"

"As long as I know the spell for the action I want—which I have acquired a prodigious lexicon of over the years—I can do many things. The magical words help direct my power."

"Could you break a dam?"

"Uh, why?"

"I saw a movie recently where some superhero did it. I'm trying to learn how powerful the spells are."

"Ah." Hans looked relieved. "Probably not. Maybe if I had a dozen other casters helping, but I'm not going to try it, so don't get any ideas."

"You're no fun."

"Or not crazy."

I chuckled lightly. "Could knowing spells help me?"

"Maybe. Casters can handle the widest range of spells, but even those with hedge magic can use simple spells."

"What is considered simple?"

"Lighting a candle. Ringing a bell. Getting rid of the dust in your house."

"That last one sounds pretty damn useful."

He grinned. "It is. How else do you think my place is so clea—"

The door to the room flung open, and Tobias stormed in.

Hans crossed his arms over his chest. "Good of you to show up. We've already been at this for almost an hour."

"I didn't need to be here for the basics of witchcraft."

Apparently unable to argue with the surly vampire, the wizard turned to me. "How do you feel about a change of tempo? Like Tobias says, he is not useful with magic, but you'll need to know more than magic. Luca wants to make sure you can defend yourself and fight."

My shoulders rose and fell, but the act of nonchalance resonated within me as forced and fake. The instant Tobias had entered the room, my every nerve had lit on fire.

"I've studied street fighting. It was necessary to have some skills when I worked for the Ringmaster."

"Great. But like I said, you'll need to learn how to defend yourself too."

"I've taken self-defense." I scowled.

This conversation was beginning to rankle. Did I look like a weakling?

I glanced at the vampire, who wore a smug smirk.

Then again, maybe it was just his presence irritating me.

"Not against supernaturals, you haven't," Hans clarified. "The SING method works mostly with humans. It *might* gain you a second or two of advantage against a vamp, but you really won't be able to fend them off by stomping on their instep."

No, I supposed not. Though I hated to compliment him, Tobias was made of stronger stuff than flesh and bone; his chest had felt like steel when I'd fallen into it before. It would take a lot to injure him—even more to break him.

Not that I wanted to *break* him. Although, right now, I

would settle for slapping him across his annoyingly handsome face.

"If you can protect yourself against my kind," Tobias interjected, "You'll be able to do the same against necromancers."

"Necromancers? What could they do to me that others can't?"

"If they manage to kill you, they can sell your magic to the highest bidder. It's the only way, besides genetics, in which magic can be transferred." Hans's face hardened. "It's foul, and only the worst necromancer would do such a thing, but it's not unheard of . . . And your magic is rare."

My blood turned to ice.

"Got it," I said, determined not to get offed so someone could steal my magic. "What do I need to do?"

Hans instructed us to stand in the center of the room, which was empty save for the tables and chairs that had been pushed to the side so we had a space to train.

I faced off with Tobias, and was wondering what exactly sparring meant, when Hans explained.

"The rules are simple. You're going to fight until one of you is on the ground, immobilized."

My heart rate stuttered. "Wait. Don't I get tips on how to fight a vampire?"

"You wouldn't win anyways," Tobias muttered.

"Like I didn't win last night?" I spat back.

"What I meant is," Tobias's jaw ground from side to side, "you should focus on defense. You wouldn't be able to incapacitate me with your level of magic. There are certain spells that can injure my kind, and make staking them or decapitating them easier, but I doubt you can wield such power yet." His gaze shifted to Hans, who shook his head.

"Too advanced. We've been working on calling magic,

recognizing the sensation of using it, and the pulse of it within."

He made my accomplishments sound so small, and that kind of hurt, because I'd been proud to pinpoint that flow of power and see the glowing light. But I didn't want to show weakness, so I drew myself up and put on a mask of confidence.

"As I thought," Tobias said dismissively. "Anyway, only a wooden stake, decapitation, or fire would kill me. But you're not a fire witch, and I see no weapons, so—"

"Yeah, yeah, I'm going to be on the ground a lot," I cut him off, not wanting to hear any more on how great vampires were.

Hans's lips twitched. "This is only your first lesson. You need to figure out how we magical beings move, how we fight. Later, you can learn how to defeat us."

Closing my eyes, I simply breathed for a second.

I wasn't used to being the new one, or bad at what I did. Ever since the Ringmaster had plucked me up off the streets, I had been one of the best thieves in his company. Of course, I knew now that was partially due to my hidden magic, but still, it sucked to be at the beginning.

"Fine." I huffed, opening my eyes. "Let's get this over with."

Hans nodded, his gaze shifting between me and the vampire. "Take ten paces back. I'll count to three, and then the sparring begins."

We did as he said, and the countdown started. As soon as the final number left the wizard's lips, Tobias was in front of me, knocking my feet out from under me.

My tailbone hit the floor, and the thin carpet did nothing to pad the pain shooting up my spine.

"Okay, what the actual hell am I supposed to do about that?" I threw an accusing glare at Hans.

My teacher shrugged. "Vampires move very fast. Next time, be ready. Anticipate him. Whatever will hurt you most, he'll do. Get into position again."

We did, and the second time, I fell forward instead of backward. The third, I dropped to my knees, my bones hitting the floor with a *crack*. I winced but didn't cry out, didn't let on that it hurt. I just hauled myself back up, and we kept going.

I earned myself half a dozen bruises before an idea struck.

As always, Tobias approached, fast as lightning, but this time, I had a plan. I knew how tall he was, where his eyes were, and I had two fingers perfect for poking.

The blur of his form came closer, and I raised my hand in time for my digits to meet soft flesh.

The vampire flew back, a snarl ripping from his throat as he glared at me. Though his expression was scary, and a shiver curled down my spine, I smiled back, not about to let Tobias know he was getting to me.

Hans let out a laugh. "Very human of you, but I like it. Again."

The elation of victory was short-lived as Tobias prowled toward me once more. Five more times, I fell, and five more times, I hauled myself back up. I didn't try eyeball-gouging a second time; the vampire would be ready for it. Instead, I wracked my brain, trying to figure out some new, unexpected way to beat him.

The bout started, and Tobias zoomed closer. My magic surged and, going with the flow, I pulled it into my hands.

A faint blue light pulsed out in front of me and, to my utter shock, the vampire went flying backward, stumbling over his leather loafers before falling on his ass.

Pride gushed inside me as the wizard let out a whoop.

"Awesome work! What did you do?"

"Honestly, I'm not sure."

He laughed. "Our magic can sometimes give us a boost if it thinks we're in danger. That's how kids protect themselves against threats. That you could pull so much so soon after learning how to call your power is a great sign."

Interesting. He hadn't spoken of magic like it could have its own mind before. But then again, I'd used power for years and never known it, so it must be somewhat instinctive.

"One more time," Hans said. "After, we break."

Tobias and I separated again. The space between us had grown by many paces since we'd started. This time, when he turned to face me, I stiffened and then shuddered. This was practice, but he looked like he was carved from marble, his face was so hard.

Tobias was taking my small victories super personally. Actually, come to think of it, he took most things regarding me personally. And I took his attitude more personally than normal, too.

Why do we grate on each other so much?

I shook my head, not even noticing when Hans counted down. Fortunately, at the end of it, Tobias didn't run toward me with the speed of a bullet. No, this time he *stalked*, like an animal hunting prey. Like a dominant wolf about to attack a challenger. Like a . . .

His eyes glowed red. His pupils were blown out. Wild.

Oh no.

This time wasn't like the others.

This time, I was in real danger.

CHAPTER FOURTEEN

TOBIAS

I PROWLED EVER CLOSER TO THE WITCH, MY PRETERNATURAL DRIVE urging me forward.

This is a huge mistake.

The rational thought—one of the few I'd had since we started this charade—popped into my head. But it fluttered away almost instantly as my instincts seized me again.

Hunt.

Seek.

Dominate.

I shook my head, the motion so small Meredith didn't even notice. Or if she did, it didn't show on her face.

Instead, her fear spiked the air, injecting it with a bitter apple scent, like poison meant to draw a rat.

Fear always smelled that way. Unpleasant, but in a way that made my mouth water. A faint aroma of magic followed, sweetening the bitterness. Honey.

Meredith was trying to call her power and failing. Still, the pushback made the dominant monster inside me roar.

I had to put an end to this before I went too far—before she got hurt, before I couldn't stop myself.

A second later, I was at her side, overwhelmed by the strange mixed aroma of jasmine and fresh spring pine that clung to the witch. It drove away the stench of fear, as well as the sweet smell of magic, leaving only the witch.

My heart thunked hard against my breastbone.

Meredith reached out, her palms landing on my shoulder as her small hands tried to push me back. I stood immobile, solid as a statue, hovering and staring. With every shift of her fingers, my muscles seized a little more. Thirst grew inside me, making my throat itch and burn.

Behind me, Hans shifted his stance. He had to have picked up on the change of atmosphere. But it was too late. Whatever was happening to me would not be undone, not even by a wizard.

I reached out, pulled the girl against me, and grabbed her head. Then, in a threat to end all threats, I tilted her neck and protracted my fangs.

"What the hell?!" Meredith shrieked.

"Tobias!" Hans barked, his accent thicker than normal. "This is training!"

The common sense washed over me like rain on oil as I brought my fangs to within centimeters of the delicate skin of her neck. The throbbing of her jugular as her heart pumped harder filled my ears. The warmth radiating from her enticed me, and my teeth touched soft, supple flesh.

"You win," Meredith breathed in surrender. "You win."

The desire to subjugate vanished. My fangs slid back into place, shrinking to nothing more than sharp, human-looking cuspids.

I loosened my grip, and she yanked her body away. Her

eyes, one blue and one green, flashed at me, accusing me of terrorizing her.

Meredith edged away, never breaking her glower. A wise move. No one should turn their back on a vampire who'd just tried to dominate them.

Suddenly, shame welled within me. Why had I done that? She was a new witch, a person who barely knew a vampire from a mage. I'd probably scared the living daylights out of her.

Though, truth be told, she didn't look scared; she looked fierce. Pissed off.

Hans positioned himself between us. His magic wasn't visible, but I could feel the intense heating of the air. This wizard was ready for anything. Ready for me to act out once again.

"We're done for the day." My tone came out harsher than I intended, thicker.

"No shit," Meredith snapped.

"I agree *you're* done," Hans said, training his eyes on me. "Meredith, stay here for a bit. I want to talk to you about a few things you can practice."

The wizard turned his back to me in clear dismissal. Fists clenched, I marched out of the room.

A short hallway led me into the atrium, and only then did I exhale the breath I had been holding.

None of this made any sense. I had trained with hundreds of new recruits over the years, and none had made me react like her.

My gaze trailed around the oblong room, the heart of S&S, sweeping over photos of the witches, wizards, vampires, mages, and shifters who had led the coven before. A few of whom I'd known. They'd all been tough teachers, but none would have ever acted out against an initiate like I just had.

It couldn't happen again. Meredith had taken the oath; she was part of the coven and protected.

A comrade, not an enemy.

My attention drifted to the upper levels. Headquarters was quiet for once. I suspected most people had left after the witch's initiation ceremony.

Most, but not all.

I climbed the staircase leading to the third floor. When I got there, I aimed my body in the direction of Luca's office.

The door was open—his usual practice, so people felt inclined to approach him whenever they wished—but still I knocked lightly before entering.

The moment I stepped inside, my lips parted in shock.

Luca lay on the navy couch, and his eyes fluttered open weakly, his gaze finding me. "Tobias. How's training going?"

"First things first." I closed the door behind me. "You look like hell. Are you okay?"

"I've felt better, but it's passing." He coughed. "I think I need to eat."

I doubted that whatever was going on with him was 'passing.' I'd seen death many times—both natural and not. The sheen of sweat on his forehead and the emptiness of his eyes whispered of something serious.

My conviction grew as the coven master stood and swayed.

"Did you pick up a flu?" I asked, not revealing my doubt. "You should see a healer. I can fetch one to come up?"

"I'm fine." Luca waved me off. "You didn't answer me."

"Because training shouldn't concern you right now."

"Answer me, Tobias."

I snorted, and my words came out on the back-end of a

resigned sigh. "The training went as well as could be expected."

It had gone as well as *I'd* expected. Though, I couldn't bring myself to admit what I'd done. Surely, Hans would tell the coven master, and I didn't want to be around when he did. It was mortifying.

"I need to be taken off her detail," I said resolutely.

"You're the best hunter we have. She is a seeker and will require training from the best to maximize her talents. Meredith needs to be able to fight and defend herself. Once word of her power gets out, she'll be in grave danger."

"Let Gunner train her."

I would never admit it out loud, but the wolf was nearly as good as me. *Nearly* being the operative word.

"Why are you doing this, Tobias? Skull and Bones has already hired the pair of you. If you train together, you'll know her powers best. And she will understand you better too."

Fine. He was forcing my hand.

"I tried to dominate her." I gritted the words out, hating every syllable, wishing I didn't have to admit it.

Dominating a person in the way I'd done was something newbloods did. When older vampires controlled another, it was because the person was a *true* threat, usually another vamp looking to steal power.

Meredith was neither of those things.

This time, Luca's eyebrows arched. "Interesting. Why?"

"I don't know." I averted my gaze, trying to compose myself and failing. "Something happened. After she won the hunt, something happened in me."

"I see." Luca shuffled to the table. Setting one hand on the furniture to steady himself, he poured a glass of water and downed it in one gulp. "Still, I can't allow it. You two will go on the hunt together for Skull and Bones. Meredith needs a mission exactly like the one they've offered. It's too perfect of a training exercise for her to pass up—simple, but not without its own sort of danger."

"Then you should send someone else with her. I'm not the only vampire in S&S. Even a shifter would be an adequate shield. Or Hans."

"While that's true," the mage allowed, "I'm in charge, and I want you to go with her."

"Why?"

There had to be a reason. Luca did not put his foot down without conviction.

"Whoever broke into the house last night was a vampire. Did you know that?"

My lips parted. I hadn't known. I'd heard about the break-in, but I'd stayed away from Hans's house, away from *her*. The bloodlust had been bad enough last night, outside the entrance to Skull and Bones . . . though not as bad as how training had gone.

Bloody hell, I was going mental.

I cleared my throat and drew myself up, trying to appear as if I wasn't a riotous mess inside each time I thought of the witch. "Are you sure?"

"Positive. I checked it out after Shay called, and had a suspicion. Harper collected blood that has since been analyzed in our lab. It's plain as day that a vampire broke in. A new one, I believe, as traces of humanity lingered in the sample."

My throat tightened. Older vampires were dangerous because they had experience that came with a long life. They also possessed vast raw strength and, usually, a lot of power.

But newbloods were dangerous too. They had little control and profound strength they didn't quite know how to harness. In addition, the drive for blood dictated their every move for the first month after they were changed. If their maker was reckless, so too would the newblood be. And if no maker stayed with them, that put anyone nearby in peril.

"During training, I need you to be on the lookout for the newblood who is after her. If you smell or see anyone fishy on campus, let us know. That's an order." Luca looked me in the eye. "Do you understand?"

It was one of the few things I did grasp, but that didn't mean I liked it. Or that I'd follow orders.

The mage didn't see how close I'd come to snapping. His underestimation was understandable; I typically remained cool, calm, collected. Even now, I was more detached than most could ever manage. And I'd keep it that way for as long as I could.

Some deemed me to be 'stiff,' but I preferred to call it poised.

Vampires were usually masters at distancing themselves. For a long time, we'd had to be, else we'd be hunted and killed. Lately, though, my composure had slackened. More specifically, whenever I was around the witch, my control slipped entirely.

The situation was wholly unacceptable, a matter I needed to remedy . . . even if it meant going against the authority of the coven master.

"Judging by the power I felt in her, she'll be ready within the week," Luca said, apparently taking my silence as resignation. "The mission doesn't seem too difficult, but it's a great test of aptitude. Mostly, I need you there to sense for the newblood, and to deal with him or her efficiently, if you must."

A week. A mere seven days was how long I had to come to grips with my need to dominate Meredith.

It didn't seem nearly long enough.

CHAPTER FIFTEEN

MEREDITH

MY MUSCLES ACHED AS I TRUDGED UP THE PATHWAY TO SHAY'S home with a heavy sack slung over my shoulder.

"Pick you up tomorrow at nine!" Hans called out the window of his Jeep Gladiator, which I learned on the ride he liked to trick out in his free time.

Though I preferred to walk, Hans told me that walking unaccompanied was a no-go for the time being. That would be the case until they had apprehended the person who had threatened me.

"Can't wait!" I called back, not meaning it in the slightest.

I could *totally* wait until my next training session. I could wait *years*. Sure, I was excited to be learning magic, and I certainly felt freer now that Luca had unbound my power, but after a day of learning only the basics, exhaustion gripped me to the core.

And that wasn't the worst of it. Tomorrow, I would have to see Tobias again.

I wasn't happy about that. During training, he had acted

crazy. Scary crazy. When the vampire had pressed his fangs to my neck, I hadn't been sure he'd stop.

Or if he even wanted to.

I shuddered.

Though I didn't like to think about it—let alone admit it to myself—something about Tobias's obvious threat excited me as much as it terrified me.

Did that make me crazy?

Probably, so I needed to keep that to myself.

I opened the front door, and a wash of heat caressed my skin as I entered the house. "Hello?"

Footsteps sounded on the floor above, and a second later, Shay appeared at the top of the stairs, beaming at me. "Rooms! How was your first day of training?"

Rooms?

My skin prickled at the strange feeling of inclusion, but I brushed it off and rolled with it. The nephilim marched to the beat of her own drum.

I set down the bag I'd been carrying, and it hit the tile floor with a *thunk*. Liberated, my shoulder groaned with relief. Hans had filled the sack to bursting with books. "It was draining, enlightening, and confusing. And a lot of other things, but those are the top three."

I didn't mention that Tobias had almost killed me. I needed to think more about what the hell that was all about.

"Sounds about right." Harper appeared from the kitchen, dusting flour off her hands. Some of the white powder coated her red hair too, making the usually put-together wolf appear almost normal.

"We're having homemade pizza tonight," Harper said. "I just finished with the dough. Want to clean up and assemble your own? I didn't want to assume your toppings."

"She looks tough," Shay said amusedly, "But Harper is like a mother hen in the kitchen. Everything has to be juuuust right."

My stomach growled, and the rest of me perked up a bit. Pizza was a top-three meal, right behind tacos and döner kebabs, which I'd fallen in love with in Germany. "Let me put this pack upstairs and I'll be right down."

"First girls' night!" Shay sang and did a little dance.

"Already happened," the wolf said flatly.

"Not really."

"So what do you call last night?" Harper challenged.

"Oh, that doesn't count. Mer showed up later, so this is our first *full* girls' night. We gotta do it up!"

My lips twitched as Harper grumbled and returned to the kitchen.

I still wasn't sure where I fit in with those two, but their dynamic amused me. Harper was as serious and thoughtful as Shay was carefree and spontaneous.

I scooped up the bag of books again and hustled upstairs to my room, then shut the door behind me. I pressed my back against the door, closed my eyes, and let out a long sigh.

"Long day?" a voice said.

My eyes popped open, and I looked around to find no one.

"Down here."

My attention snapped to the floor, and my hand flew up to cover my mouth. At my feet sat a cat, black, fluffy with glowing light-amber eyes.

Obviously, the voice couldn't have come from the animal, so I must have heard someone talking outside. Still, its presence alone was weird.

"What are you doing here, little guy? Do you belong to Shay or Harper?"

I didn't think so. I'd asked them if they had any pets last night, and they'd both said no. Besides, I couldn't see Harper —or *any* wolf shifter—having a cat as a pet. A crocodile was more Harper's speed.

"I don't belong to them," the cat replied.

This time, I saw its mouth move, and I swayed a little. Either I was hallucinating, or this was really happening.

"Are you alright?" the cat asked, his head tilting to the side.

Yup. This was totally happening.

Oh hell.

"Uh, maybe." I inched away from him, my arms beginning to ache from the bag. "I think you should probably leave, 'cause you're freaking me out. Plus, I'm allergic to cats, and this is my bedroom."

"You're not allergic to me," the cat said with a surety that had me questioning my own lifelong allergy.

"How do you know?" I asked.

And how was I not losing it right now? I was talking to a cat! This was the weirdest thing that had happened to me— and considering recent events, that was saying a lot.

"You're not allergic to me because I'm your familiar. Everything about me is compatible with you, Meredith Stone."

The cat just said my freaking name.

I blinked, trying to take it all in. When my stunned speechlessness continued, he stood and stretched.

"Clearly, you have never met a familiar before. I assure you, I'm an excellent companion. Not only that, but I can help you with your magic. Now that it's awakened, I can sense it— which is how I found you."

I shook my head. "Shay must be screwing with me. This has to be a joke."

"I assure you it's not," he said, crisply. "Let's go downstairs and talk to your roommates."

Oh sure, the first thing I wanted to do was run downstairs with a stray, talking cat and ask my new roommates if it was my familiar. They wouldn't think *that* was super crazy or anything.

But what other choice do I have?

He looked content to stay put; I supposed I could pick the cat up and set it on the roof overhang so it could find its own way down . . . but it had already snuck into the room once. What was to say it wouldn't come back?

Not to mention, this was clearly a *magical, talking* cat. So either my roommates had set this all up—though I didn't see how they could've—or this cat might actually be my familiar.

Needing a second to process, and to set down my hoard of books, I walked to the bed and tossed the bag of books on top of it. When I turned back around, the cat stared at me, waiting.

Maybe the magic is messing with me? If I just go about my business this will all disappear?

"I have to wash my face," I announced.

I walked to the bathroom and splashed some cold water on my face, hoping it would knock some sense into me and the animal would be gone when I returned.

But when I stepped back into my room the cat was still there, staring at me in a semi-creepy way.

Or maybe just a cat way.

This is really happening.

I sighed. "Okay, let's go downstairs. I guess."

I opened the door, and the cat trotted out into the hallway before me, head held high.

We descended the stairs, and with each step, my nerves

grew. Was this crazy? An illusion? Had the release of my magic screwed with my head?

Below, Shay and Harper bickered—something about pineapple on pizza. When I got to the kitchen, Shay turned, a chunk of pineapple in her hands.

"Rooms! Took you long enough. I—" She dropped the pineapple and let out a shriek. "Is that a familiar?"

The cat leapt onto the table, which was positioned at the far side of the open kitchen and dining space. "In the flesh."

"Harper! Can you even believe it?!"

"Yes. What I cannot believe is the cat having the audacity to jump on the table. Get down, you fleabag."

"That's rich, coming from the wolf," he retorted. "Everyone knows about your kind's rampant flea infestations."

Harper glowered at the animal and planted her hands on her hips. "Untrue. Now *get down*."

The cat dropped to the chair instead of the floor, and pinned Harper with a defiant stare.

The wolf must've decided it was not worth the fight, because she turned back around and began carefully placing toppings on a pizza, now muttering about felines *and* pineapples.

"Mer, this is *so* exciting." Shay squeaked. "Not all witches have a familiar, you know."

I eyed the creature. "To be honest, I was kind of hoping this was a joke."

"Excuse me?" the cat hissed, peeved.

Shay laughed. "Why?"

I didn't want to tell her that, for someone like me, someone who had always operated alone, having a familiar— or anyone who seemed attached to them—was sort of terrifying.

So I just shrugged. "I'm not good with animals."

"It is insulting that you think you'll have to care for me like a regular cat." The familiar sniffed.

"Oooo, you got a smart *and* cute one," Shay cooed as she walked toward the feline.

"I guess so. Do you have a name, cat?"

"I thought you'd never ask. It's quite rude to keep calling me 'cat,' you know."

Shay's lips twitched with amusement.

"Sorry," I said, barely refraining from rolling my eyes.

"All is forgiven. My name is Benedict."

"Benny!" Shay squealed.

The cat scowled—like, *really* scowled. "Benedict. There will be no shortening."

"Good luck with that one, litter lover." Harper scoffed. "Now, if you two are done gushing over the cat, can you help me finish with these toppings? You know I'm not touching that nasty-ass pineapple, Shay."

The nephilim snorted, but she did as the wolf asked, rising to wash her hands and top her pizza.

Needing a moment of normalcy before I spoke to the cat anymore—that was going to take some getting used to—I joined them. My gaze scanned the impressive lineup of toppings before I picked jalapeño, pepperoni, and pineapple.

I was firmly on Team Shay when it came to pineapple on pizza.

While our pizzas baked, Harper plucked a bottle of wine from a stand. She pointed the bottle at me. "I'm guessing after your training, this might be welcome?"

Honestly, I didn't even like red wine much, preferring white. But at this point, I'd drink from the bottle.

"What gave you that idea?"

"I saw Tobias leave headquarters. Looked like he had a stick shoved higher up his ass than normal."

The mention of the vampire's name sent my heart into overdrive and my lips into a frown.

I didn't usually go for the hot asshole type. To be fair, I rarely went for any type. My life to this point hadn't been conducive to relationships. But if it had, I still wouldn't go for an alpha-dick.

He was confusing me on the most basic levels.

"You're right. It was overwhelming. Yes, to the wine."

Harper set to filling three glasses, and we took up places in the living room, which was decorated with bright colors and triangular patterns that made it feel art-deco.

I took a sip and was surprised it tasted so good.

"Tell us what happened," Shay said.

As if I'd known them forever, and not just a few days, I did. The ease with which the story slipped from me was as shocking as finding a talking cat in my room, but I rolled with it.

When I was done, they said all the right things, cursing Tobias and totally siding with me. Neither seemed to know why he'd acted the way he had.

We were interrupted when the oven timer buzzed, and we went to retrieve and slice the pizzas. It smelled so heavenly, that I had to resist ripping off a piece of crust, my favorite part of a pie, and shoving it in my mouth. Once food filled our plates, we returned to the living room with our dinner and wine.

Benedict, who had been exploring the house during my story, joined us again. Shay perked up the moment he lay on the couch next to me, paws crossed.

"So, Benny, why are you coming into Mer's life now?"

Harper snorted out a laugh.

"BENEDICT."

"Right. So?" Shay pressed, looking unbothered by the correction.

The cat's eyes narrowed for a moment before he answered, "Meredith released her magic, allowing me to find her."

"Huh. I always thought a familiar would find their witch or wizard as soon as the familiar was born." Shay took a gargantuan bite of pizza. "From what I've heard, the familiar is usually younger."

I was amazed she could talk through the pizza, but I was equally intrigued by the comment.

"I did find her when she was younger," Benedict said. "But her parents told me I needed to disappear until she was ready. Which I assumed her to be by the unleashing of her magic."

The food turned to ash in my mouth.

My parents?!

I stared at the cat, my familiar—*Benedict*—waiting for him to elaborate on the parent bomb he had just dropped on me. But he didn't.

Surely, he would realize I was interested in more information? My familiar would *have* to know such a thing.

Right?

Apparently, I was dead wrong, because the next second, Benedict sat up from where he lay on the couch, turned his head away from us, and began giving himself a bath.

Harper wrinkled her nose. "*Ugh.*"

Shay punched her in the shoulder. "Don't act like you don't do that in your wolf form."

"Oh, I most certainly do *not*! I come home and take a shower after I shift. And even if I *did* do that, I would never do it on the couch!"

Shay rolled her eyes, but I remained fixated on what the cat had said. The cat who was apparently oblivious that he had information my heart desired.

"Beeenedict," I drew out the name, "you said my parents told you to disappear until I was ready for a familiar, and that you sensed my magic, and that's what told you to come back?"

He gave a little nod, the gesture so human. "I've caught hints of it now and again for years, which they said would happen. They told me that when I felt like someone was pulling my whiskers, that was when you would have come into your full power again, and only then should I find you. I have to admit, I'm glad the time has come. Being a comfort cat at the senior center was beginning to wear me out."

"Does that mean *they* blocked my magic?"

Benedict twisted to stare at me with those disconcerting, amber eyes. "Of course. Who else would do it?"

My lips parted. Well, I had no flipping idea!

"When?" I demanded.

"I believe they did so right before the—" For the first time, the cat looked like he didn't want to continue.

"The crash," I finished for him. "They blocked my magic before the crash. And they took away my memories, right? Before or after?"

Shay's hand flew to her mouth, her eyes wide with pity. I hated that look. It was why I never told people about my past. But in this case, that was unavoidable.

"The magic was before. The memories resulted from your mother's final spell. A witch's final spell is always their most powerful."

"But why take my memories?" Had my parents not wanted me to remember them? My throat tightened.

"They did not want you to be traceable. But fear not, now that your magic is back, the memories will return too."

"They haven't."

When Luca had unbound me I saw flashes of the past. While I'd eaten to gain my strength before training, I'd tried to corral those memories, but it hadn't worked. And after training, I'd been too exhausted to try again. I couldn't recall even a faint snapshot of what I'd seen.

"They will return slowly," Benedict amended. "Too much at once could be disastrous."

I downed the rest of my wine.

"Whoa, girl," Shay murmured, her tone about twenty times quieter than normal. "You okay?"

"Of course she's not okay," Harper said. "She learned that her parents bound her. Who in their right mind would be okay with that?"

"No one," the nephilim admitted. "I, as much as anyone, know how horrible it is to have your parents try to control you after you're grown."

I had no idea what she was talking about, but I wasn't ready to dig into their pasts. I was barely handling my own.

"You said they didn't want me to be traceable. Am I being hunted?" I asked Benedict.

"Yes. Since you were young, people have looked for you. Partially because you're a seeker—"

"So that's certain?" I asked, my breath thin.

"Yes," the cat said, so certain I didn't think to ask for proof.

"What else?" Shay asked, excitement seeming to make her vibrate. "You said *partially* cause she was a seeker."

"People will also look for her because of what else runs in Meredith's veins."

Again, I waited for him to elaborate.

"Oh, I can't tell you," Benedict added after a long moment of silence. "You must remember that bit on your own."

Shay groaned and stood. "Screw wine. I'm going to get the tequila, because I can already see this is going to be one hell of a night."

"Aren't familiars supposed to be helpful?" I accused, unable to hold in my frustration.

"We are. However, I made a vow to your parents, and I intend to keep it."

A full shot glass landed on the table before me. I grabbed it and slammed it back.

The tequila burned going down my throat, but I welcomed the pain. It was something solid and grounding while I bobbed in a sea of uncertainty.

"You can't even give me a hint?"

"No, but your parents assured me you would remember in due time. You have already discovered one secret—that you're a seeker."

"How do you know that?"

"I have my ways," he said smugly. "Anyhow, that's quite a big thing to be dealing with. It's not wise to give you another tidbit yet."

I wanted to press, but there were other, far more intriguing questions to be answered.

"Can you tell me about them?"

"That depends."

"Cats are *such* assholes," Harper muttered as she leaned back and sipped her wine. Unlike Shay and me, she still had half a glass of wine left.

"We're simply more discerning than other four-legged creatures," Benedict replied, not even bothering to look at the wolf.

"How about you ask me what you want to know, and if I can, I'll answer."

"Were they both supernatural?"

"Yes."

"That's all you're going to give her?" Shay said incredulously. "I called you smart before, but now I'm kind of leaning toward Harper's assessment. You do seem to be kind of a dick."

Benedict sighed. "As I said, your mother was a witch. Your father was also of your supernatural order, a wizard. Both were of distinguished bloodlines. That's all I can say."

My gaze trailed to the girls. "Okay. That's not a lot to go on. Are we, like, the witch version of the Rockefellers?"

He twitched an ear. "I took a vow that if broken would result in my death, so I truly can't say any more."

"I'm shocked Luca didn't notice something," Harper admitted. "Distinguished bloodlines are often extremely powerful in very specific ways, and Luca studies old families —knows most of them, too."

"He was busy, though," Shay pointed out.

Harper nodded. "True, there was a lot going on during the unbinding, and he was working hard. I'm sure he was focusing on not hurting you with his power."

"I wonder if that's why Tobias was in such a foul mood. I think he sensed something was different about me and didn't like it. Are there bloodlines that hunted vampires?" I gulped.

I sure hoped not, but it would explain his actions.

"Oh, Tobias is pissy about a lot of things," Shay said dismissively. "I mean, he might just not have liked your shirt."

"What's wrong with it?"

"So not flattering," Harper chimed in.

Damn! People here were judgy-judgersons about what I wore.

"Well, I'm going to ask him tomorrow during training. Maybe he can give me some answers. But until then . . ." I lifted my shot glass, which Shay filled. "I am going to grill you for information, Mr. Benedict."

The cat gave a resigned sigh. "This is going to be a long evening."

CHAPTER SIXTEEN

MEREDITH

"Serious question. How does magic exist, and no one has devised a hangover potion?" My head pounded as I stared at my roommates incredulously.

It seemed I was the only one in need of such a thing. They both looked unruffled, pink-cheeked and bushy-tailed as we walked to coven headquarters.

But how do these bitches look so good?!

At that exact moment, my right temple throbbed. I groaned. I was still holding out hope that this was all one mean joke.

"Should have laid off the tequila." Harper shrugged as we passed into the alley hiding the entrance to the coven's hall.

I glared at her, but I assumed it came out looking more like a wince when she only returned my stare. Didn't even blink.

Or maybe she really didn't give a shit; the girl was savage.

"No potion exists," the wolf confirmed after a moment. "Water and exercise are what you need."

"But you two look fine," I protested, "and Shay drank as much as me."

"Yeah, but I'm a nephilim."

"How does that help you?"

"My angel blood protects me from hangovers. I can still get drunk, but it's shorter-lived than what witches and humans experience. I was pretty much sober by the time we went to bed."

I barely remembered going to bed. Dammit, why had I stooped to drowning my sorrows and anxiety with alcohol?

"And I have a shifter's metabolism," Harper supplied. "Not to mention I wasn't a huge idiot like the pair of you." She approached the door of Shadows and Secrets and placed her hand over it, whispering the password.

After my attack, the coven had tightened security. Now, each magical order had a different way to enter the secret society's hall. Magic or passwords were the most common methods, the latter used by shifters. Once I could enter solo, I would do so by magic.

I groaned again as I weathered the sensation of a sledge-hammer slamming into the back of my head. "Well, *you* shouldn't have brought out the tequila." I scowled at Shay. "And *you*." My gaze sought my familiar. "You should have stopped me."

"That would take an act from the Goddess herself," Benedict muttered as the hall's door opened.

We had been getting a lot of strange looks, with the cat following us through Yale's campus—particularly when I'd answered a couple of his questions.

I didn't know if non-magical people could hear Benedict, but I wasn't making it easy on myself. I found it difficult not to look down at him as I talked. I needed to work on that, or people would think I was crazy and talking to myself.

"Aren't you supposed to be sympathetic to me?" I asked

him. "Or give me good advice? You're my familiar. Doesn't that mean something?"

"You're correct. Usually, it means we keep our people from doing stupid things." Benedict loped closer to the door. "But you were quite insistent last night. Who was I to deny you your idiotic binge?"

I glowered at him and filed into the hall of Shadows and Secrets behind the girls. "If *someone* hadn't dropped the parent bomb, I wouldn't have been so in need of a stiff drink."

He stared back at me, not at all sorry. "You had to find out one day."

"Cats have shitty timing," Harper said. "It's kind of their thing."

Benedict hissed, and I winced as the sound grated on my every raw nerve. Living with the pair of them would be interesting.

Our little group arrived in the atrium, and veered in the direction of the room Hans claimed for training the day before. I was about to open one of the double doors when Hans's voice called out my name.

I turned and saw the wizard marching toward me, a wide grin on his face.

"My student is early! I was worried when Shay called and said you wouldn't need a ride."

"I'm only here because of Harper," I muttered.

I would've blown off training this morning altogether, but the wolf shifter had dragged me out of bed and forced me to dress so I wouldn't miss a lesson.

Hans tilted his head. "You feeling okay?"

"She's hungover," Benedict announced too loudly for my headache.

The blond man's eyes widened as he took in the cat for the first time. "Where did this guy come from?"

Benedict strode up to Hans and sat with his fluffy tail curled over his feet. "The name is Benedict." Amber eyes glowed as if alit from within. "No shortening it or giving me cutesy nicknames. I am Meredith Stone's familiar."

Hans arched an eyebrow. "You kind of remind me of a vampire I know."

My lips pursed. He wasn't wrong. Like Tobias, Benedict was a little stiff.

"So, are you ready?" Hans asked, opening the door to the training hall and waving me inside.

"I guess. What are we going to work on?"

"Shielding first. Tobias will be here later, and we'll see if you can block him. As you know, vampires are freakishly fast, so it will be an excellent test. Until then, we'll work on pulling up your shield."

"Awesome," I muttered.

He could have said anything, and I still would've considered it beyond my capabilities. Right now, *blinking* too hard hurt.

Hans chuckled. "Memo to the wise, never try to outdrink a nephilim. Or a shifter, Goddess forbid."

"I wasn't trying to outdrink them," I grumbled. "But lesson learned."

Benedict jumped up onto the table and began grooming himself, which made me wrinkle my nose. He caught the gesture and stuck out his tongue. "Would you rather I walk around your house filthy? Sleep in your bed dirty?"

"I don't share my bed with animals. I wasn't able to tell you last night, but tonight will be different."

Benedict snorted. "If you do not wish for me to sleep in your bed, you must provide me with suitable sleeping arrangements. Memory foam, preferably."

I rolled my eyes. Stiff *and* a diva—how had I gotten so lucky? "I'll get right on that."

"Over here." Hans waved me to the center of the room.

With each step, death inched closer. When I reached the wizard, he took my hand.

"Feel this."

I gasped. For the first time all morning, something other than pain rippled through me. Hans's magic lit up my hands and traveled down my arms. It resonated as hard and protective. "What are you doing?"

"That's what a shield will feel like when you get it right. Sometimes it's easier to know if you're on the right track after you've experienced the correct sensation. Of course, pressing the shield out and making it take shape—something bigger than, say, a dinner plate—will feel a bit different. But we'll get to that later. First, try to mimic what I did."

He dropped my hand and took a step back to wait.

"This ought to be good," Benedict drawled.

Okay, I needed to talk to whoever assigned familiars; mine was a total dick.

Shaking off his fantastic lack of faith, I closed my eyes. But the temptation to fall asleep crashed over me, instant and almost irresistible, so I opened them again.

Needing to put my focus somewhere, I stared at my hands and tried to conduct the same feeling Hans had pushed through me.

I failed a dozen times, although I did manage to produce magic at each attempt. It was just nothing like what Hans had created.

For his part, Hans did his best to be supportive, even though I could tell he was getting annoyed. I bet he thought that if I wasn't hungover, I could do this . . . but I wasn't so sure. Things just weren't clicking.

After another failed attempt, I dropped my hands and tilted my chin to the sky, unable to hold back my frustration. "Are you sure this is basic for a seeker?"

"It is." Hans's expression softened a touch. "You might not conjure the strongest shield, like one a warder would create—those are basically impenetrable to anyone but other warders of the witching kind or mages. But you should be able to form some sort of protection for yourself. It's a necessary bit of magic to master before you go on your first mission."

I sighed and tried again.

And again.

And again.

I lost count of how many times I attempted to make a shield before I slumped to the ground and dropped my head into my hands. Tears welled in my eyes, though I wasn't sure if they were from my failure or my frustration with myself. Or from feeling out of control with the news of my parents.

What the hell was wrong with me? I was tougher than this.

Hans placed his hand on my shoulder. "Hey, it's okay. I'll admit, I thought it would have happened by now, but it's not unheard of for magic to be stubborn. Especially since you're so new."

He paused and, though I wasn't looking at him, I could sense him staring at me, trying to puzzle me out. "Is there something else going on besides you being hungover and tired?"

I hadn't told him about my parents' deaths and my so-called distinguished bloodline, not being ready to talk about it before I had more answers, but now I felt like I needed to explain myself.

"Last night, I learned about my parents," I blurted out. "That *they* bound me before they died, and took my memories. And my familiar has other secrets, but he's not telling me."

"I made *a vow*!" Benedict howled.

Hans took a step back, his gaze trailing from me to the cat and back. "I see. You might have a major emotional blockage."

"What does *that* mean?"

"We should go see the healers. They won't be able to clear this up completely, but they might make you feel lighter. Less frazzled. Then we can keep training." He looked uncomfortable, and I got the sense he was one of those guys who didn't know what to do with an emotional woman.

I sighed. It wasn't fair to pin this on him, anyway. He was my trainer, not my therapist. "If you think it will help."

Whatever I needed to do to ease the pain, I'd do it.

Hans helped me stand, and we headed for the double doors. We were almost there when they burst inward, and a man strode in, a wide grin spread on his face.

"Gunner," Hans said slowly. "What are you doing here?"

"Toby asked me to fill in for him."

"What?" The wizard's tone tightened. "He didn't clear this with me, and I'm in charge of Meredith's training."

Gunner's face fell.

At the sidelines, Benedict stared at him in the way he reserved for Harper. Belatedly, I recalled Gunner was a wolf too.

"He didn't?" Shock was evident in his tone. "He said he cleared it with you and Luca."

Hans clenched his teeth. "Nope, he sure didn't. Would you

mind taking Meredith to the healer's wing? I'm going to find Tobias—wherever the hell he's hiding."

"Probably the library!" Gunner called as Hans stormed out of the training room.

The wolf watched him go before turning back to me. "Those two are always going at it, but they're still usually pros. Toby didn't mention anything big happened."

Of course he hadn't divulged he'd threatened a new witch. Who would broadcast that? It screamed of cowardice.

As did running away.

Frustration curled in my gut, because even though I was annoyed Tobias had ditched training me when I had been hoping to prove myself today, something else was there too.

My shoulders tightened and my face dropped to the floor as I worked it out: I felt a little sad. Like I had wanted to see him.

I mentally bitch-slapped myself. Tobias treated me like prey, and I missed him?

No. Just no.

Gunner tilted his head toward the door. "Let's go. Hans is right. You need the healers. You look like hell."

I choked out a laugh. "You sure know how to make a girl feel good."

"He's a wolf. Don't expect things like that of him," Benedict called out, seemingly unable to help himself.

Gunner stared at the cat, shook his head, and chortled. Apparently, Benedict didn't ruffle his feathers like he did Harper's.

"Darlin', I'm a master at treatin' the ladies right." He grinned and his whole face lit up. Though I wasn't attracted to the wolf, I had to admit he was very handsome; ladies probably threw themselves at him. "But I bet if I tried to soothe *all* your pains, I'd have someone coming after me right quick. And I don't want to deal with that—no offense."

I blinked as he led me from the room. What had he meant by *that*?

CHAPTER SEVENTEEN

MEREDITH

"Good job today, Stony." Gunner held out his hand to help me up.

Though my first reaction was to hurl sarcasm, because I hadn't done well at all and we both knew it, I pushed down my attitude. Gunner was immune to my barbed replies, so there was no use in flinging them.

Instead, I gripped his hand, accepting the assistance. He hauled me up, and once I stood on my own two feet, I wobbled.

"You fight well," the shifter added. "A few more lessons, and you'll be able to hold your own against almost anyone. At least long enough to escape to safety."

I reviewed the day's training. Gunner had put me on the floor nearly every single round, much like Tobias had the day before. Envisioning the vampire made my stomach knot up.

"Can you help tomorrow?" Hans asked Gunner, his tone sour. He'd looked for Tobias for an hour and never found him —in fact, no one had seen him since my last lesson. "I can't rely on the vampire to be here."

"Probably," Gunner replied. "Let me talk to Luca. He might be sending me on a mission soon, but no word on that since the initiation ceremony."

"Let's go talk to him together," the wizard replied. "I need to fill him in on where she is at in training, anyway. Meredith, you can come too. The coven master would probably love to hear from you."

I might as well join—Shay hadn't gotten me a key to the house yet. That was on her list of things to do today. Until then, I'd have to wait for one of the girls—wherever they were —to be home to get in the house.

"Alright, then," Gunner drawled. "Let's go see that mage."

We left the training hall and climbed the stairs to Luca's floor. Benedict trailed behind, on cat time. When we reached Luca's office, the door was closed, so Hans knocked.

"Come in," a faint voice called out.

I cocked my head. Luca sounded different.

Hans opened the door, and my eyes popped open wide.

The coven master lay on the couch and he looked absolutely terrible, worse than the day before. Luca's olive skin had grayed, and sweat poured down his face.

"My man," Gunner said as we entered the room. "What's wrong?"

"Caught a bug," Luca croaked.

Gunner and Hans shared a look that told me they didn't believe that for a second. I shifted to stand by the wall-to-ceiling bookcase, feeling uncomfortable.

We shouldn't be here. We should let him rest.

"You sure it's not something else?" Hans asked after a prolonged silence. "Something magical?"

Were there magical diseases? Or was he referring to something else?

"I'm *fine*," the coven master insisted. "I've been active all day, and had to lie down for a bit, but I'm already feeling better."

One glance at Luca's face, and it was obvious he wasn't fine—not even close to it.

Hans had opened his mouth to say something when Benedict, who had been trailing lazily behind us, waltzed in.

The coven master's eyes widened. "How did a cat get in here?"

"I'm a *familiar*," Benedict sniped. He hated being thought of as a normal cat.

"Oh. I see." Luca's attention shifted to me. "Yours, I presume?"

"He showed up last night."

"Only powerful witches have familiars. The stronger the magic, the stronger the bonds between them. Did you know that?"

"I've learned."

Though I had my doubts. I didn't seem all that powerful.

Benedict jumped on top of a shelf, turned his butt to face Luca, and stretched, displaying his butthole. I rolled my eyes, and Luca's lips pursed at the obvious slight before he turned back to Hans.

"Fill me in on the day. I want to hear all about your training, Meredith. Hans, how'd she do?"

Now that he'd seen how bad off Luca was, my magical mentor looked reluctant to unload, but did as the coven master requested.

His rendition of the day kind of shocked me, because he was making it sound positive. Gunner backed him up, though. So although I felt like a complete loser for most of the day, I must have done better than I'd thought, which lifted my spirits.

"She's strong, and knows about fighting and blade-work already, but Meredith still needs to learn the right defensive and offensive moves against supernaturals," Hans said with a scowl. I suspected he was thinking about Tobias so often that day, much to my annoyance. "Her magic will take more time, though."

"We can't expect her to master everything all at once. But as long as Tobias is with her and she uses her seeking intuition, that should be enough for the Skull and Bones mission. I don't foresee this being a dangerous job."

Luca stopped and blinked, as if realizing something. "Where is Tobias? Gunner, you trained her today?"

He must really feel like shit if he just put two and two together.

The men didn't reply.

"Where did Tobias go?" the coven master demanded.

"A coven should be more organized," Benedict drawled.

Luca scowled but ignored my familiar, focusing only on my wizard mentor.

Hans sighed. "No idea. He sent Gunner in his place."

Luca turned to the shifter. "And you went along with it?"

Gunner raised his palms to the ceiling. "He said he needed to take a leave and you okayed it. I didn't even question it because Toby's pretty honest."

"I should have seen this coming." Luca muttered a few colorful curse words. "It's not your fault. He disobeyed an order, though. Thank you for stepping in. I'd appreciate it if you stayed on Meredith's training until Tobias returns. Your assignment isn't ready anyhow."

"Sure thing." Gunner took a step back. From the way he kept glancing at the door, it was apparent he wanted to get the hell out of there. I understood; though the coven master was ill, anger radiated off him, palpable across the room.

Luca caught our discomfort and exhaled slowly through his nostrils. "If that's all you wanted to talk about, you may go. But if you see Gabriel, would you send him up? I need to speak with him."

The guys agreed, and we left the office, Benedict once more trailing behind.

We made it halfway down the hallway before Gunner let out a low whistle.

"It surprised me when he lied to you." He nodded to Hans. "But Toby didn't even tell the coven master he was bailing. He's been acting weird since . . ." He looked at me.

"Since I arrived," I finished. "You can say it. He was a real jerk yesterday."

"I heard about that," Gunner said.

An uncomfortable moment passed between us, but then his face brightened. "You know what we need?"

"What, is this going to be some hick barn dance or something?" Hans asked sarcastically.

Gunner didn't take any offense; he never did. The wolf was fun and easy to like. He'd won me over even as I wrestled my hangover into submission. That was some serious charm.

"No square dancing, but we need to have a real welcome wagon for our girl!" Gunner beamed. "I got to meet her today, but lots of people still want to. Let's hit up the Ordinary and then the Gryphon."

I groaned. I'd been hungover the whole morning. Only the fact that I had been sweating out the toxins, and Hans had forced me to drink water, had eased the pain.

"I'd rather not party. I—"

"Did someone say 'party'?"

I twisted to find Shay jogging down the hallway.

"Rooms!" She waved madly.

Benedict scampered off, and though I liked Shay, I wished I could do the same.

"Hey. I don't want to go out," I reiterated, because clearly she'd only latched on to the word 'party.'

Shay threw her arm around me. "You had a rough morning, but this is a great idea! Everyone wants to meet you. I promise we won't stay out late. Come on, I wanna go and want you to go too! *Please* come!"

"*Please* come," Hans mimicked Shay, his voice high.

She stuck her tongue out at him. "Shove it, Hans."

Everyone waited for my answer, and although it was the last thing I wanted to do, it was refreshing and nice to have people want to be with me. It almost felt like I had friends— and that hadn't happened in a long time.

Finally, I caved. "A couple of drinks. That's it. I need to get some rest tonight."

Shay squealed and linked her arm through mine. "I need my beauty sleep, too. You won't regret it, though. The Ordinary has great food. I'll make calls as we go and tell people to meet us at the Gryphon after dinner."

THREE HOURS LATER, I WAS HAVING MORE FUN THAN I HAD bargained for. Shay had a way of making everything seem like a party.

"Anyone want another beer?" Gunner asked as he got up from the table. "It's on me."

I shook my head. "I'm switching to water, or I'll be hurting again tomorrow. You guys can really drink."

"Shifters have a higher metabolism," Gunner explained. "Plus, I like beer. Back home, I used to brew my own, but don't need to here. Good micros like these flow like water in New Haven. They're better than what I made by a mile."

He wasn't kidding. There were about a million taps, most of which I'd never seen. But then again, the Gryphon—our second venue of the night—had to cater to many types of people. Everyone from students to professor-types to townies and coven members were present. I caught many of the students eyeing our table of ten, probably sensing we were different.

Along with those S&S members I already knew, I'd met five others here. A fae with long, silver-white hair and unnerving silver eyes named Silas sat at the far end of the table. A pair of twins were among the group; both Dan and Gus were bear shifters and claimed to be whiz kids with tech. The last two were necromancers, and possibly dating. I got the sense that they were close, anyway. Sara, a cute strawberry blonde, had just returned from a mission, and Josiah was the one who'd used ravens to watch me and keep me safe.

"I can get you a soda instead," Gunner offered, trying to be hospitable.

"Nah, water please."

The shifter nodded and took a few more orders before he left.

Conversation resumed, only to be interrupted a minute later when someone else took Gunner's seat. I turned, expecting—okay, praying—to find Harper saying we needed to go home, but was met by a guy I didn't recognize.

He had short, blond hair and a square jawline. His clothes looked expensive, and his confident smile told me he was used to getting his way.

"Um, hi?" I said warily.

"Hey, gorgeous. So good to finally meet you."

"Right," I said, already rubbed the wrong way. "Who are you?"

All around the table, conversation quieted.

I shot a glance at Hans, and he shook his head slightly. I took that to mean this guy was not part of the coven, and I needed to guard my tongue.

"Bentley Sloan the Third. I'm a senior this term. I haven't seen you around. What year are you?"

"Incoming freshman. I enrolled late and am taking summer courses to make up for lost time."

I felt like I had to explain why I was already in New Haven because fall semester didn't start for a couple of weeks. Plus, I didn't think I looked like a freshman.

"Better late than never. I have a course to make up too. Yale is great, huh? What summer courses did you take?"

"Chem 101," Shay piped up, possibly thinking I wouldn't be familiar with the class nomenclature. I would have said biology, with no number, so she'd thought right. "That's where we met. We both needed to get a prerequisite out of the way."

Bentley spared Shay a glance. "I couldn't help but notice this table has the most beautiful ladies in the bar, and decided I would be an idiot not to come over and introduce myself. You should join me at my table, with my friends." His hand wrapped around my wrist, and he glanced at Shay again, then Harper and Sara. "You three are welcome, too."

Resisting the urge to slap him for touching me without permission, I removed my hand from his grip. "Thanks for the invite. But I—"

"Of course," Bentley smirked, interrupting my brush-off.

"We like to get to know the new kids. I can tell you all the Yale secrets."

"You especially like to get to know the fresh blood if they are hot and female," Hans inserted. "I notice you're only inviting the girls. What about the rest of us, Bentley?"

"Only got a few seats," he said unapologetically. "Come on, you *want* introductions to my friends. We have a lot of influence on campus."

I *wanted* to tell him he could shove his influence up his ass, but Harper caught my attention and shook her head. Apparently, she could tell I was about to throw some sass, and didn't approve. This guy might actually have influence.

With a name like Bentley Sloan the Third, I wasn't surprised.

"I'm good here," I told him curtly.

Bentley looked unimpressed as he stood. "Your loss."

Not likely, asshole.

He walked away, and I frowned. "Are all the Yale guys like this? 'Cause that was annoying and arrogant as hell."

"A good number of them," Harper admitted. "Especially the ones whose families have attended for generations. Bentley is one of those. He was also tapped for Skull and Bones last spring and immediately snotty about it." The wolf rolled her eyes. "You get used to it, unfortunately."

"Tapped?"

"Chosen. Every year, they choose fifteen juniors to join the society the following term."

"But I thought the secret societies knew about us?"

"They do, so Bentley will learn this year. Probably soon, unfortunately for us."

Gunner reappeared and began dispensing drinks before plopping back down. "Could hear that fool all the way across the bar. I guess that'll teach me to leave my seat. Next time, someone else has gotta get *me* a beer."

"Or you could lay off the sauce," Harper muttered.

Gunner grinned and winked at her.

I wasn't sure what was going on between the two of them, but there was definitely something. They'd been bantering all evening.

The conversation returned to normal. I tried to be involved, but I kept feeling eyes on me. A few times, I turned to look for the source. To my annoyance, Bentley watched me . . . but the sensation came from elsewhere. Somewhere deeper in the crowded bar.

I couldn't locate the person.

Maybe I was imagining things. Or it might be a ghost. The bar was old and gothic-looking, so a ghost might want to hang out here.

I shuddered and tried to focus on my coven members.

Half an hour later, my bladder alerted me it was time to pee. I excused myself and made my way to the bathroom. There was no line, thank God, so I went right in.

The moment I locked the door behind me, I exhaled. This was more socializing than I had done in years—and that was counting when I'd seduced the researcher in Egypt. Those academics could party, but there hadn't been as many of them.

I did my business and washed my hands, and when I opened the door to exit the bathroom, Bentley was in the hallway.

"I figured I would come by and say hi," he said. "Swing by our table. I saved you a spot."

"You waited out here for me?"

Creepy much?

"It was closer than going back to your table. Plus, those

guys don't like me." He grabbed my arm, his grip powerful and demanding, and I sensed he wanted more from me than to say hi to his friends.

I needed to set the record straight.

I yanked my arm away. "Keep your hands off me. I don't want to meet your friends. Now, leave me alone."

His face hardened. "You're hot, but a stone-cold bitch."

"Because I don't want to meet your friends? It's not my problem you invited yourself to my table and then tried to drag me someplace I didn't want to go. Maybe you're the bitch."

His face tightened, and he tried to back me into the wall. Too bad for him, my defenses were already up.

I slammed my heel down onto his foot. Bentley let out a howl and began hopping on the other foot.

I pressed my finger into his chest. "Don't touch me. Don't approach me. Don't talk to me, don't even *look* at me. I want nothing to do with you. Clear?"

He jerked his head down, his eyes burning with a mixture of anger and humiliation.

Done with Bentley's shit, I left him in the hallway. I was so ready to leave, ready to—

My blood froze.

A guy was exiting the bar. I could only see the back of him—the strong set of his shoulders straining the bulky bomber jacket he wore and the way his Terminator-style glasses perched on his head—but the resemblance was uncanny. That guy looked a hell of a lot like Denz.

CHAPTER EIGHTEEN

TOBIAS

I trailed down a dark, unnamed alley, not lost despite my many efforts to lose myself in the night.

It had been a full day since I'd left New Haven, and Meredith Stone was as fresh in my mind as if I had just seen her. Her scent of jasmine mixed with fresh spring pine clung in my nostrils, and if I listened hard enough, I swore I could hear her voice among the chattering Parisians.

A sigh gusted out of me. What on earth had drawn me here? I hadn't seen the City of Light for years. Even when Luca booked missions here, I didn't volunteer. I avoided this place.

Avoided *her*, the woman who could see me far too clearly.

So why, when I was in tumult over another female, did I return here, to my second home? It made no sense, and yet, here I stood on French soil.

I stopped at yet another intersection between two alleyways, an uncomfortable, narrow affair filled with a mix of the reek of urine and the temptation of expensive perfume—the downtrodden and the decadent. Humans spoke of a wage gap widening with the years, but it had always been a reality. The

Internet just made it more starkly apparent. Even in Paris, a romanticized city, there had always been a cringeworthy juxtaposition of wealth and poverty.

"*Monsieur?*" a male voice came from behind.

I twisted to find a short and pleasantly plump man. I'd bet he spent every morning devouring a croissant or two. A century ago, he would have been the exact type of human upon which I liked to feed.

Slightly chubby humans tended to have the best flavor.

But it had been a long time since I'd sipped from the vein, and this man didn't tempt me in the slightest. Nowadays, only one person tempted me, and I'd crossed an ocean to be free of her.

Not that it's worked.

"*Oui?*" I asked.

"*Vous êtes perdu?*"

This man was a rare Parisian who worried over lost tourists. What a surprise.

"*Non. Merci.*"

The man gave me a strange look, but left, throwing a couple of glances back my way. He didn't believe me.

Understandable. I'd lived here once, but I'd been in the States a long time. I now walked like an American. My attire was less chic than it used to be. My French even sounded off. I had lost my French *je ne sais quoi.*

But that didn't mean I didn't know Paris. Things here had changed, like every other place, but I still recognized every dark corner, every hidden bistro and bar where only creatures of the night crawled. The heart of the city continued to beat in a way that spoke to my heart, even as an outsider.

Having lingered long enough, I turned right and continued

to twist and turn through a few more alleys and streets before deciding it was time to settle for the evening.

I popped out of the maze onto a thoroughfare, if one could call it that nowadays. It wasn't even as wide as many suburban neighborhood streets in the United States. Regardless, my eyes sought a door I hoped had not changed, and I smiled.

A tavern I loved in my younger years was still there, with a green lantern hanging over its door, providing sanctuary to all who were not human.

I crossed the street and entered. A bell jingled, announcing me as my gaze raked the area.

Inside, the tavern looked the same as I remembered: dark and elegant. *Fleur de lis* wallpaper spoke of a long-forgotten era —one I wished to return to, if just for the evening.

The bartender waved, and I went to the marbled bar, choosing a high-backed stool on the end. He smelled like a shifter, which meant he had a good nose. I asked for a wine recommendation and after ordering a burgundy—because when in Paris, I always drank French wines—I closed my eyes and tried to lose myself in the atmosphere. The soft melody of a harp softened my shoulders, and slowly, my breathing deepened.

I was trying so hard to forget Meredith that when my past came up behind me, it caught me off guard.

"Tobias Blake Aston Laurent. I sensed you lurking around."

I stiffened. Few people would use my vampire family name. Fewer still smelled of roses and the faintest hint of basil. And almost no one had my devotion the way this woman did, though right now, I'd hoped to avoid her at all costs. She was far too perceptive. Some even said that she'd been a seer before she was turned by a royal vampire, and her gift remained though everything about my maker changed.

The sign of my house, the Royal House of Laurent—inked on me the day after my own change—itched, as if the bloody snake was flicking its tail.

I stifled a groan. *I should've expected this.*

The bartender's gaze lifted to me, his expression shielded. No doubt he'd met the femme fatale behind me; he was clever to heed her with caution. She had been the one to show me this place, many years ago.

I exhaled and turned, a forced smile on my face. "Giselle. A pleasure."

"Truly?" Giselle's green eyes glittered with amusement as she placed a hand on her hip.

She didn't look any different from when I'd seen her last. Her loose blonde curls still barely graced her collarbone. Her heart-shaped face remained unlined, as it would forevermore, and green eyes glimmered with life. Her tastes didn't seem to have changed either. My maker had always favored high-end fashion and luxury, which her dress and shoes reflected.

"Because it seems as if you've walked all over Paris— everywhere except by my apartment. Are you avoiding me, Tobias?"

Like the plague.

"Why would I be avoiding you?"

"I wondered as well. I thought, *'why would someone whom I've given the world to avoid me?'* I despise guessing games, so I figured I'd ask you myself."

My maker had never been one to beat around the bush. It was both refreshing and frustrating—particularly when I was on the receiving end.

"I'll admit I've been trying to get away, but not from you. In fact, I wasn't even sure you were here."

Nor did I wish to find out.

Her stance softened. My answer had appeased her somewhat. "I returned from Isila a month ago. It seems things are happening here that require my observance."

"Don't they always?"

"Indeed. What are you running from?"

"A woman I can't pin down."

"Some things never change."

I snorted. It had been an age since a woman had flummoxed me. I'd forgotten it was a common occurrence after I'd been turned. But Giselle had been there, guiding me back to sanity each time.

Even the time the woman's death had nearly ushered in my own.

"So, the high-and-mighty Laurents have a job for you, do they?" I asked, not wanting to talk to her about Meredith, nor dwell on the one I used to love. "How long were you gone this time?"

Her lips pursed, and before answering me, she called to the bartender, "Cabernet."

He winked and supplied her one immediately, as if he'd been waiting for her order.

"*Merci.*" My maker gave the shifter a coquettish smile that could stop traffic, and took up the stool next to me.

"Years ago, the Blood of Laurent caught wind of someone trying to gather important magical objects." Her tone was hesitant, as if she didn't want to share too much.

Giselle descended from royalty in Isila, thus making her a duchess—though she did not spend much time in Isila asserting her rights.

Her slender finger ringed her glass. "For a while now, I've been on the lookout for a septet of items entering the magical market."

A septet. Seven items . . . My hand tightened around my own glass, a reflex Giselle did not miss.

"Any idea what I'm talking about, Tobias?"

"Depends which magical object you are speaking of. There is no shortage of them in the world."

"Nor in Isila." She leaned on the marble countertop. "But I've already told you a bit of my secret. I'll let you chew that over for now it is time for you to tell me some of yours. I'll accept information about the woman, or the object you may, or may not, be hunting."

Damn. As ever, my sire knew, or suspected, my business too well. I stared down at my drink, not wanting to meet her eyes and unwittingly give away anything.

Giselle didn't usually offer people choices, but as her child, I was gifted more leniency. The thing was, I couldn't inform her about the Pearl of Hell, the object I believed she was referring to—or, at least one of the objects. I knew my cunning maker, and her appearance in that moment was just too perfect for me to believe otherwise. And I shouldn't tell her about Meredith, either. At least not everything about the young woman . . .

Historically, seekers drew attention, so eventually, Meredith's reputation would get out. When it did, other supernaturals would come looking for her.

But the witch was in the coven now, and we looked out for each other. Giselle must not learn about Meredith's powers before the witch was ready. No one could.

"Tobias, I grow impatient. Do I have to *make* you tell me? I prefer the information to come from you willingly, but I will take it if I must."

Bloody hell.

I dared to look her in the eye to see if she meant it.

All royal vampires—Laurent blood—could compel anyone but their maker and other siblings. The more distantly related a vampire was to an original royal, the more of a toss-up it was that they had the power of compulsion.

Giselle could compel anyone, save for the royal family and other close cousins. I was not as strong, but still possessed the ability. Recently, fewer vampires had been made with that power—a fact that our race was hiding from the other supernaturals. We did not want to admit our defects.

After studying Giselle for a moment, I deduced she wasn't bluffing. She'd compel me to learn what I knew. And if she compelled me, she might take too much, go too far.

I'd rather offer something on my own terms, controlling the information I gave, and reduce the likelihood of her prying into other matters. I would merely have to trust that S&S would protect the new witch until she could do so herself.

"The woman . . . Meredith. She's a witch and new to our coven."

There. It wasn't a lie, but it wasn't the whole truth either, because Meredith was much more than your average witch.

"Is that all?" Giselle said, eyebrow raised. "You don't fall for the regular sort. No girl-next-door or rule-followers for you. What's special about her?"

"I haven't fallen for *anyone* in many years," I replied, shoving down the memory of the woman I'd given myself to.

I so wished Giselle would drop this.

"I am evidence of your exceptional taste." For a moment, her lips curled up smugly. "You've always liked the *extraordinary* woman. Answer me. What's extraordinary about this Meredith?"

I chewed on the inside of my cheek and then shrugged. "Truth be told, I'm not sure. I've been acting strangely around her, protective but also dominant. I don't understand it."

Another half-truth. Being a seeker was special, but I also had been acting protective and dominant. Faintly *insane*. More like a teenage vampire than a mature adult.

Giselle leaned back on her stool, relaxed as ever. "I see. There's more crossover between here and Isila than I would have imagined."

"What do you mean?"

More than magical objects being hunted in both areas?

She rolled her neck out, as if trying to squeeze a little relaxation out of her day. "Magical orders are forming unions—choosing outside of their own order for partners."

"That's nothing special." Maybe three hundred years ago, it had been, but not since my change, and certainly not now. People dated and wed outside their supernatural orders all the time. "And it has nothing to do with me and Meredith."

"I think it does. These unions are stronger than most, the connections undeniable. And if you are here, your connection to this woman is strong."

"When you say undeniable?"

She arched an eyebrow. "Fated mates. Soulmates. *Blood-bound.* Whatever you want to call it."

My stomach swooped, and I shook my head. *Impossible.* Fated mates existed, but they were rare. People spoke of them as myths, legends, nowadays.

"It's true," she pressed, reading the disbelief on my face like a book. "Most recently, a fae prince learned a witch from your world was his soulmate."

I had forgotten about Kora, a fire witch in S&S who had fallen into the Faerie realm of Isila and met the Prince of the Spring Court. She'd married him and now lived in his palace. I'd never been close to Kora and hadn't realized the prince was her soulmate.

Still, that had to be an outlier. The fates had made an error, as Kora was a witch and the prince a fae. I wouldn't deny their bond, but I did not believe that because they were the exception that I too would find my mate outside the vampire order.

"You don't believe me," Giselle said, a statement, not a question.

"Are there others?"

"All I know is that one union can usher in many. If that happens, it will undoubtedly alter our magic and what we become."

A soulmate bond was incredibly powerful. All-encompassing. Such a bind to another soul terrified me. I'd never experienced it, but after what I'd barely lived through in the past, I was certain I wasn't up for it.

Not that it would be necessary. I did not believe that Meredith was my twin soul. To think that would be on par with believing one was a god, it was that rare. How ludicrous. Plus, she was far too aggravating to be my soulmate.

"We both know vampires don't have natural children like witches do," I reminded Giselle. "So even if Meredith was my soulmate, we could never have children. And if that's the case, I'd be doing her a disservice by even telling her that others are finding mates outside their magical order."

"You should ask her if she even wants them before you make assumptions. Not every woman longs for a child, you know."

"She has no idea of our connection, and I don't plan on telling her."

"Oh, of course, she has *no idea*, because you're the only one feeling something between you two. She's torturing you but experiencing none of that confusion herself." Giselle rolled her emerald eyes. "How typical of men. Be better, Tobias."

"She's new to this world, her magic has just been unbound," I countered. "She could be mistaking whatever is between us for many things."

"I assume she has two brain cells to rub together? If so, she has *some* idea."

I ignored her comment and raised a hand, signaling for the bartender. I needed another drink to drown out what I'd learned, and hopefully, anything else Giselle would tell me this evening. I sensed she did not plan to leave, though I hoped I was wrong.

A vampire can dream.

Another glass of red wine landed in front of me, and I raised it to my nose. The bouquet was extraordinary—as the shifter bartender had claimed it would be. One didn't get wines like this in New Haven. Not unless they had their own cellar.

Shockingly, Giselle had fallen into silence, too. Was she done shattering my reality for the evening? Or hopefully for the year—better yet, the decade.

I'd allowed my hopes to rise, when my maker turned her emerald-hard gaze on me.

"I realize I might have upended your plans to wallow in Paris for God-knows-how-long, but before you leave, I think there's something I should show you. It might have to do with this woman you find yourself drawn to, or it might not—but something is telling me it does."

I arched an eyebrow and tried to hide the anxiety building within me at the prospect of anything happening to Meredith. "I have no plans to leave."

"You're not being honest with yourself. About many things," Giselle said flatly. "Anyway, I possess information that might alter your course. But I cannot tell you anything here." Her gaze swept the small bar, the few others enjoying their drinks.

I frowned. All I'd wanted was to come to Paris to escape and get my head on straight. This place was a sanctuary. I'd traveled here as a sailor and adored the city. After I was turned, I came here as soon as I could travel without my maker.

But my plans were as damned as my soul. Fate, that fickle mistress, had other ideas.

My maker downed her wine, setting the glass on the table delicately, and called for the check. "Finish your glass, Tobias. I have something to show you and I won't take no for an answer."

CHAPTER NINETEEN

MEREDITH

My pulse raced.

Denz, my old partner in crime, had been *here.*

Or had he?

The person had left so fast, and I'd only seen his back. But those glasses . . . And the bomber jacket, and the way he'd left.

He'd touched the doorway up high, where most others did not. But Denz did that to steer clear of germs.

I shuddered. It had to have been him. *Did he see me?*

My gaze drifted to the table of coven members. Normal people were watching the supernaturals, stealing glances every few seconds like we wouldn't notice.

Together, we attracted human attention. Our otherness both drew them to us and frightened them. It was why when supernaturals gathered in groups, they often preferred to do so in more private places—like secret societies in the heart of Yale.

My gaze raked over the rest of the establishment. Our supernatural allure combined with the fact that our table wasn't far from the bar led me to believe Denz must have seen us. And if he did, he would've spotted me.

The guy largely sucked at tomb-raiding. I was faster and lighter of foot, so infiltration had always been my job. However, he was very observant, which was why he was often my watchdog.

Why hadn't he said anything when he saw me? Why hadn't he yelled at me for leaving him locked up in Egypt?

Only one answer made sense, and it made my stomach churn. If Denz was here watching me, that meant the Ringmaster wanted to keep tabs on me.

"Blazing balls of shit." I bolted across the bar, determined to catch up with Denz.

Before I reached the door, Hans intercepted me, eyes wide. "What's happening? Gunner smelled your panic."

I tilted my head. "Shifters can smell emotions?"

"Some. Alphas can, if the emotions are powerful. According to Gunner, yours are off the charts."

I let out a breath. "I saw my old raiding partner. Tobias and I left him in jail in Egypt. He slipped outside just now, but he had to have noticed us. Noticed me."

Hans turned toward the door. Glass expanded across the top half, allowing him to see outside a little bit. "He didn't say anything, and now he's gone?"

"Exactly. I have to find him," I insisted. "He's out of prison, obviously, and still works for the Ringmaster."

Denz owed less money than me, a fact he'd let slip one drunken night. Still, he'd be in the Ringmaster's employ for another year. Actually, our failure to complete our last job had probably *added* to his term of servitude.

My blood ran cold. He'd be pissed about that.

"I'm in debt to my old boss," I said because I wasn't sure if

Harper and Shay had told others besides Luca. Now it was time to let everyone in on my embarrassing secret. "Major debt, Hans, and he won't let that slide. He's a dangerous man."

"The coven has money. We'll pay whatever you owe," Hans assured me, not seeming surprised. So he already knew. My cheeks flushed with heat. "You don't have to worry, Meredith. The coven helps out its members."

"It might be too late," I admitted. "My old boss could have sent Denz to scout me. If he confirms I'm here, the Ringmaster will—" I stopped, not able to choke out the real lengths to which my old boss would go.

Shaking my head, I finished. No more secrets. Hans needed to know. "We need to clear this up fast. He hires assassins."

Hans swallowed, and his gaze shifted back to our table. "Gunner," he called, his voice slightly elevated.

Thanks to his keen shifter hearing, the wolf stood and marched in our direction. Harper, Shay, and Sara followed, not far behind.

"You okay?" Sara, the necromancer I'd met that night, whispered to me.

I nodded, though I didn't feel that way at all. I wanted to get on with it and find Denz.

"What's up?" Gunner leaned against the wall so we'd look like a group of people just casually hanging out.

"Meredith's old raiding partner stopped by and didn't say hello. We need to find him, or her boss might send assassins."

Gunner's gaze latched onto me. "Damn, girl. Everyone's trying to get you. First the shade, then that vampire, and now your old boss."

"Tell me about it. Antiquities theft has never been a safe profession, but this is ridiculous," I muttered.

"I'm up to track him down. You in, hot stuff?" Gunner threw Harper a flirty grin.

She rolled her eyes and ignored him, which only made him smile harder. From what I could tell, he loved getting her goat. Given how rigid Harper was, it wasn't that difficult.

"Can't I do this, though?" I asked. "I'm a seeker. I should be able to find him, right?"

Hans shook his head. "Seekers can easily find magical *objects*, as long as they haven't been obscured by a spell. People are a different matter. An image in your mind isn't going to cut it—and so many humans come in and out of this place, they'd obscure traces of other people. The only way it would be easier for you to find your old partner than a shifter is if you had some of Denz's hair or fingernails."

"Please say you don't," Shay cut in, sounding super grossed out.

My nose wrinkled. "We weren't into the whole exchanging-body-parts thing."

"Thank goodness. What does he look like?" Shay asked.

"Medium height, balding," I said. "He always wears those terminator-style glasses and tonight he had on a leather bomber jacket that was almost too small."

"So he'd kind of stand out," Shay said. "Not many bombers running around New Haven."

"No," I agreed. Then another thought struck that I hadn't considered before. "Wait, can I find something if someone is holding it? What are the limits?"

"According to books I've read, if an object is *inside* a person, you would not be able to find it."

"Like if they swallowed it?" I asked, grossed out by the thought.

"Yeah, or implanted it in their skin. Like a piercing or body mod type of thing," Harper replied. "But if it's in their pocket, or somewhere on their body, you'd be able to."

"Excluding enchantments on their body and other limits, of course," Hans replied. "No one knows too much about those."

"Why?"

"Because there hasn't been a seeker in so long," Harper replied, ginger brows pinching together. "Didn't anyone tell you how rare your kind is?"

I frowned, not appreciating her attitude. "Yeah, but—"

"The point is," Hans interrupted, probably sensing the spike in my tone, "in this instance, shifters are our best bet." The wizard nodded to Gunner and Harper. "Thankfully, these two have excellent noses. You really think you can find this guy?"

Gunner let out a bark of a laugh. But where he sounded optimistic, Harper looked skeptical.

Her arm swung behind her to encompass the bar. "Dude. There are tons of humans in here. We don't know his scent. Gunner may think he's a wolf god, but you have to give us something to go on."

I thought back to when I saw Denz leave, and pointed higher on the doorframe. "He touched this spot when he opened the door. He's always been a bit of a germaphobe, so he avoids handles as much as he can."

"Understandable," Shay piped up. "People are nasty."

Harper glanced around. "I don't want to sniff the door. Not here."

Gunner shrugged. "I'll do it."

The wolf shifter approached the door, and even though Harper had claimed she didn't want to, she went with him. The pair pretended to have a conversation, their nostrils aiming toward the door occasionally, twitching slightly.

Finally, Gunner nodded. "Let's go. But maybe not all of us." He looked at Sara. "You guys should stay. Have Dan or Gus scent the door and be on the lookout. If someone who matches Denz's description comes back, call us."

"Good thinking." Sara darted back to the table, relaying the message to the bear shifters who'd been watching.

The rest of us left the Gryphon and plunged into the streets of New Haven to find my old partner. The wolves led the way, scenting at the air. Shay, Hans, and I chatted, trying to detract from the wolves' intensity and make the crew look normal.

With each block, I kept my eyes peeled for Denz. He couldn't have gone too far; the guy wasn't in great shape, so I didn't foresee him running anywhere.

Then again, he wouldn't want me to catch him. If the Ringmaster was after me, Denz would have been told to be covert. And failure to comply would only lead to pain for my old partner.

Again, my stomach twisted uncomfortably.

Now, I had the backing of the coven, but the Ringmaster had always terrified me. He had friends in high places, and he wasn't opposed to torture. Or jumping straight to murder— though I was trying really hard not to think about either.

We'd gone five or six blocks when Gunner turned back to me, his eyebrows furrowed. "Are you sure this guy is human?"

The question hit me like I'd run into a brick wall. I hadn't even known *I* was a witch. How would I have realized if Denz was something else? Would he have told me?

No.

Denz and I worked jobs together, but we weren't friends.

Some things, like our pasts and how we'd come to the Ring-master, had never been discussed. It was too painful.

"She's too new to this to have any idea," Hans said, echoing my thoughts. "Did you lose the trail?"

"Yeah." Harper's keen gaze scanned all around. "It sort of thinned to nothing. I've experienced nothing like it."

I pivoted in place, taking in the area. We were in a small square on campus, an open and empty place at this time of night. Denz was nowhere in sight.

My troubled emotions amplified, threatening to burst out of me. I inhaled, pushing down the rising tumult as I tried to keep my head.

It was too much of a coincidence that my old partner had been in the same bar as me . . . and *very* telling that he had slipped out without saying anything. Clearly, he'd been tracking me, but wasn't quite ready to make a move.

Was I too late to pay up? My mouth dried up.

One thing was certain: I needed to watch my back.

CHAPTER TWENTY

TOBIAS

GISELLE HALTED BEFORE AN OLD APARTMENT BUILDING, ONE OF the classics of Paris that had likely once housed the poor who had no means to afford country homes. Now, it stood proud, transformed into many high-end flats for the ubërwealthy.

She entered the lobby, which was decorated in white marble, and threw a wave at the attendant.

He set down his *café*. *"Bonsoir, Mademoiselle Giselle."*

"Bonsoir, Armand." She beamed at him as we stuffed ourselves into the tiny elevator and rode up to her penthouse suite.

We stepped out, and the scent of black currant hit me in the face. Though vampires rarely appreciated artificial scents—they were too strong for our sensitive noses—Giselle had always loved black currant.

"Have you been here before, Tobias? I can't recall."

"That's a sure sign you own too many homes."

She rolled her eyes. "It's more of a sign that I don't remember the last time I saw my favorite child."

I snorted. "Don't tell Raphael or Serena."

"I tell Raphael he's my favorite child to mollify him. You know how moody he gets."

"And Serena?"

"She's the *smart* one." My maker gave me an amused look as she made her way to a table littered with papers. "But truly, you are the favored one—even when you're hiding from me."

I didn't respond, only joined her at the table. From a drawer beneath the wooden expanse, she pulled out what appeared to be a map. Unfurling it, she pinned down the edges.

My gaze scanned the parchment. It was an old-world map, but not so old it deserved to be in a museum. Probably something Giselle had had lying around for a hundred years, collecting dust.

"What's all this about?" I asked.

Her finger pressed down on the parchment, right on Egypt. "I told you people were looking for specific items, but not what. I sense you know what they are, which is good because I can't tell you outright anyhow. I'm bound by my royal vow. I can, however, tell you that there are seven, they were once held by angels, and an organization called the Ordo Aeternum is interested in acquiring all of them."

Seven items, created by angels. So yes, the *lapis caelesti*.

"There have been rumors of their interest in dark magical artifacts for centuries," I said. This wasn't news to me, nor anyone in S&S.

"And I can verify those rumors because for the last five years, I've been a double agent for that organization."

"Why are you playing spy?" I asked, treading lightly.

"The Royal Blood of Laurent wants certain items too. The same seven." She gave me a pointed look, making it quite clear we were talking about the same thing, albeit cryptically. "The king, in particular, is possessed with the idea. If they have to come down against the Ordo Aeternum to get them, they will."

I didn't think my blood could get any colder. My maker had always been loyal to her family, but perhaps helping them attain the seven celestial stones—or even one of them—was going too far.

"What do they want them for?" I asked when she didn't answer. "To create a new world order, like the Ordo Aeternum is rumored to desire? Doesn't the Blood of Laurent hold enough power?"

"They believe the time for those items to see the light is drawing closer. Signs are cropping up everywhere."

"Has an oracle proclaimed it?"

Oracles did not exist in this world—at least, not that I was aware of. Not because there weren't any, but because they hid. They were almost as highly sought after as seekers.

My pulse quickened. The idea of the Laurents coming after Meredith was even more frightening than the Ordo Aeternum searching for her.

"There is one in Isila. She spent her life traveling with the rogue fae bands of the Summer Court, but one gave her up and sold her to the highest bidder—which, unsurprisingly, was the Laurents." Giselle shrugged.

"Did you meet her on your last visit?" How long had this fae been captive?

"Before that. Years ago."

"Why am I just hearing of it then?"

"Before it didn't seem important, but now . . ." Giselle trailed off for a moment. "The oracle foresaw seven beings holding the angels' creations and keeping them safe. All have been born."

She patted the map for a moment, as if considering what to say next. Then Giselle's green eyes turned on me. "You don't want to admit it yet, but it is clear to me you care about this woman. And she probably has something to do with all this, because as I said, you only have eyes for exceptional women." Giselle swallowed. "If I'm right, I want you to know so you can keep her safe. I might not be around to help you if anything should happen to her. I wish to protect you. As best I can."

My skin grew cold at the reminder of the past. How my maker had been the only one able to pull me from the depths of my despair.

"Why would you guess we're after one of those items?"

"The Ordo Aeternum has eyes *everywhere*, Tobias." She paused. "Regarding the Laurents, you will tell no one what you've learned here."

"As you wish." No child wanted to go against the will of their sire, for to do so was very painful. "Are you working with the Ordo Aeternum for the foreseeable future?"

Giselle's gaze trailed back down to the map. Only then did I notice an aggressively circled red dot right where her finger had been. It was near Cairo, the same city magic had radiated from when the Pearl of Hell was unearthed. The same place I had found Meredith.

Again, a sensation of dread washed through me.

My attention ran over the rest of the map, spying at least two dozen other dots, though some had been crossed out.

"At the rate we're going, I will be with them for a while." She looked to the map. "I brought you here for privacy—they really do have ears everywhere—and so you could see how dedicated they are to the search. It is a sort of mania in the Order. And if you've put two and two together, like I suspect you have, you now know they realize one of the septet was in Cairo."

"Of course they do. They took it, didn't they?"

"Actually, no."

What?

"Did the Laurents actually get their hands on it?"

And if so, why are you just telling me?!

"But that makes no sense. Who else is searching? We know of no other person or group interested in the celestial stones."

I paused at the slip up, but soon realized how little it mattered. We both knew what we were talking about. If anything, the absolute confirmation that came with an answer, or none, would be welcome.

"We're not sure," Giselle replied, eyebrows arched at my slip up, but indulging me with information all the same. "The Order got a tip from an anonymous source." She stared at me intently. "The OA checked out the site later. Whoever took the item left a calling card."

She picked up a pencil and began to sketch a symbol, starting with an upside-down triangle with an X drawn from the top two corners until the lines of the X strayed outside the confines of the shape. Giselle then moved on to the singular bottom point of the triangle, extending those lines a bit past the tip and curling them outward. Finally, she drew a small V to intersect the triangle's extensions. When she set her pencil down, I shook my head in disbelief.

"The Sigil of Lucifer? I haven't seen that in ages. What does it mean in this context?"

"We're not certain, but surely an ancient Egyptian did not carve it into the tomb's entrance."

No. Whoever did it must have done so after they knocked out Denz. And before Meredith surfaced from the tomb.

I looked my maker in the eye. "Why did you tell me all this?"

A soft breath left her. "I can't speak in specifics, but I don't always agree with my family. And I certainly do not support the Ordo Aeternum, though I will pretend because my family bid me to do so. Therefore, I must act in their interests, ultimately, I want to keep you safe. I joked earlier, but you really are my favorite child. My greatest wish is to keep the royals of Isila out of this realm and away from any of my children."

Her lips curled up. "And by extension, I care for the woman who seems to mean a lot to you."

"Of course she does," I said, though the witch disconcerted me more than anything. "She is a colleague. I should return to New Haven." My hand scrubbed the back of my neck. "My coven master will want to be filled in."

Giselle's lips twitched. "You do that, Tobias." She gestured to the heavily-circled map. "Obviously, the Order Aeternum isn't sure where to go next, but that doesn't mean we won't figure it out. And just know, if you and I see each other while I'm working for the Ordo Aeternum on behalf of the Laurents, I will have to make the fight appear realistic."

"I understand I'm on my own."

A sense of disquiet spider-walked down my spine as Giselle's green eyes latched on to me like those of a hawk.

Being at odds with my maker, and with the Blood of Laurent, was a terrifying prospect.

CHAPTER TWENTY-ONE

MEREDITH

I pulled back the curtains and peered outside for the tenth time that morning.

"You're beginning to look a *touch* crazy," Benedict drawled from where he lounged on his new memory-foam cat bed, complete with a built-in pillow. "No one has spotted him since that night."

"Him who?"

There were two hims on my mind, and I hated to think the cat knew one of them.

"Denz, of course."

A huff parted my lips, and I pulled the curtain firmly closed. "I know that, but that doesn't mean he isn't around, waiting."

"You claimed he was not stealthy. And that you never got a good look at his face. What if it wasn't actually him?"

Denz wasn't stealthy, that was true. That was one reason I had a hard time believing it was him at the bar, watching me while I was oblivious. As for only seeing his back . . . It was another claim I couldn't fight.

Was I seeing things? Or was Benedict trying to get a rise out of me? He did have a track record for being contrary.

"Are you calling me paranoid?" I asked the cat as I swept into my bathroom.

"Never. You have a lot on your mind, and you're clearly scared that the Ringmaster will find you. I don't think you're paranoid, but fear can make us think differently. So do you think perhaps you imagined Denz because you're on edge?"

"I don't know. The Ringmaster doesn't mind playing the long game." I sighed, running my brush through my long, brown hair. "Whether I did or didn't, you're right."

"I always am."

I ignored him. "I can't keep living like this. It's only been two days since I saw Denz, and I'm exhausted from keeping watch."

"As am I. You woke me up three times last night with your pacing, looking out the window, and tossing and turning."

I rolled my eyes and set down my brush to pluck eye-brightener out of my makeup bag. Gently, I applied it to the dark circles beneath my eyes.

"I'm sure you'll make up for it today, lazing about here." Benedict usually came to the coven's hall with me and snoozed in a patch of sun while I trained. But I wouldn't be doing that, at least not right away. "You can stay in your outrageously priced bed while I'm at Yale's orientation schmoozing with people who think I'm like them."

"Sounds awful." Benedict hopped up onto the counter, a look of disgust on his feline face. "I've had my fill of non-magicals for a lifetime. All the baby talk is nauseating. Will you be training afterward?"

"Hans said to swing by after orientation, but he also said not to rush. Apparently, it's important for me to be seen on campus." So important, Luca had insisted I skip morning training, when normally that wouldn't have flown. "I'll probably go by the hall at—"

"*Rooms!*" Shay shouted from the bottom of the stairs. "Hurry up! We'll be late!"

"Coming!" I turned back to the cat. "I'll be at the hall later, but don't feel like you have to go. The window is open if you want to slip out, but like I said, no pressure."

I applied a quick sheen of lip gloss before snapping my cross-body bag up off the floor and rushing out of my bedroom.

Harper and Shay were both waiting for me at the bottom of the stairs. Harper wore jeans, a tank, and an emerald cardigan to complement her flaming locks. Shay had opted for a red maxi dress and sandals—the girl was still clinging to summer, and luckily, the weather was obliging today.

"That's what you're wearing?" Harper asked, eyebrows pinched together.

"What? You can't go wrong with jeans." I gestured at my all-black attire. "And this is a crop top. Those are in, right?"

"You look so goth."

"I prefer the term 'rocker,'" I corrected her.

"You'll stand out, for sure."

"Luca wants us to be noticed, so that's a good thing," Shay reminded her. "And I think you look cute. I'd do a red lip, but whatever."

"Didn't have time to do it properly," I said, though I totally agreed. I loved a good red lip. "Aren't we worried about being late?"

"Yes." Harper turned. "Let's go."

"Be good, Benny!" Shay called out.

As the door shut behind us, the cat loosed a long hiss.

Shay needed to watch it with the nicknames, or she'd come home to her bed in tatters one day.

The moment we stepped outside, my gaze shifted right, then left. I exhaled. No one even remotely resembling Denz was around. Our little street was quiet, like usual.

"Still worried?" Shay asked softly.

My cheeks warmed, a little embarrassed she'd caught me in a weak moment. "I know Luca had a team do a thorough search, but that guy just looked so much like Denz."

"We're going to take care of you." Shay's insistence tied my stomach in knots. I wasn't used to others looking out for me, and I still wasn't sure how to handle it. "If we see anyone even slightly resembling the picture you showed us, you better believe he'll be locked in the coven's dungeon."

"*Dungeon*?" I sputtered.

"A repurposed basement where we keep enemies until they can be transported to a proper holding facility," Harper said matter-of-factly. "Except once, a coven member who had been possessed stayed there until an exorcism was done."

I gaped.

"You haven't seen all of our tomb yet."

I hadn't thought that I had, but a dungeon felt so Old World, so . . . dark.

"When you say 'proper holding facilities,' do you mean a magical prison?" I asked.

"That or a form of stasis—like being locked in a block of magic." Harper didn't blink, though both ideas made me shudder.

"In our world, punishments are more severe, because when supernaturals use their power for bad, they can cause major harm," Shay explained. "Not that humans can't, but it's just different."

"Right."

I stopped the conversation there and shrugged off the chill gripping my spine as we made our way closer to campus.

The sounds of students hit my ears when we were still a block away. For the last ten minutes, people had been streaming around us or past us, having already gotten their fill of orientation—even though it started only a half hour ago.

I inhaled deeply, centering myself before I had to be around a metric-shitload of people.

"You bluebooked already, right?" Shay asked. "Did your NetID work?"

Luca had pulled some serious strings to get me into the school and registered through the class catalog site in a few short days—an impressive feat, considering he still looked like hell.

"Yup. I'm signed up for four intro classes and one history elective. Women Who Ruled."

I *loved* the sound of that last one.

"You don't have to start with all the intro stuff, you know," Harper said. "You can take others if you want."

"I know."

She was being kind, thinking perhaps I didn't realize the level of flexibility I had since I was new to college life. The thing was, it had been a long time since I'd gone to school, and I was now going to be attending *Yale*. Though I was a confident woman, and smart in my own way, I was totally feeling the imposter syndrome.

"If they're too easy, she can switch later." Shay looped her arm through mine.

I smiled. "We'll see."

We turned the corner, and suddenly came face-to-face with mobs of students, all bright-eyed as they checked out the tables scattered across the lawn, greeted old friends, or dashed inside beautiful gothic buildings for major-specific meetups. They all looked so ready for the term to begin in a week. So like they belonged.

My stomach pitted. These people walking the aisles on the green, manning the tables, handing out bags of buttery popcorn, all looked different from me. And though I hadn't met a single one, I knew they saw the world differently too. The only people who could really relate to me were those who had worked for the Ringmaster.

Case in point, I was looking for Denz, a man surely sent to find my location and pass it on to a killer.

"Where to?" I asked, trying to shove down my fear.

"It doesn't matter," Shay said. "Let's dive in."

She sashayed forward, and Harper and I trailed behind. Despite there being many people around, eyes snagged on us, unable to resist the lure of a witch, a wolf, and a nephilim together.

The tables outside advertised campus activities. We trailed from one table to the next, and a half hour later my shoulders were just starting to loosen, when Shay announced she needed to use the restroom.

"I'll go too," Harper said.

"I'll stay out here. Talk to some people."

The more we were seen, the sooner we could leave—or at least, that's how I hoped this worked.

"Sounds good." Shay said. "We don't need to make a million connections, just be memorable. Having people know we go to Yale is a good cover."

"Right." I eyed a table cluttered with rocks and tiny shovels; the archeology club. A natural fit, considering my past. "I'm going to check that out. See you soon."

The pair left, and though there were a ton of people around, the moment they were gone, I felt more exposed. And strangely, though the stares should have lessened, I sensed someone watching me.

For one vulnerable moment, I considered chasing after my roommates, but didn't want to look like a chickenshit who couldn't handle being alone. I was not that kind of girl. I *could* handle this on my own. They wouldn't always be around to babysit me.

Even as I gave myself a pep talk, I once again scoured the green for Denz. As ever, he wasn't there.

And yet, the sensation of being watched remained, tightening my chest.

I need a distraction.

I strolled to the table I'd spotted earlier. Surely, Yale's archeology club would be able to teach a girl who dabbled in ancient civilizations and classics a thing or two.

"Hey." A young man with buck teeth and a strong jawline beamed at my approach. "Are you interested in archeology?"

"I am." Images of the latest tomb I'd raided flashed through my mind. "I like the quirkier stuff."

If one could call cursed necklaces 'quirky'.

"Cool." He picked up a pamphlet, handing it to me. "Then you might like our club. Let me give you the rundown."

The young man proceeded to talk my ears off about the days of the week the archeology club met and their yearly 'digs,' which involved going into the nearby hills and excavating.

"You don't try to go on real digs, like in Egypt?"

The man chuckled. "Some do. They're Anthro majors,

though. We're a hobbyist club, so we mostly do local stuff. Sometimes we find artifacts from colonial times."

Huh. Kinda lame.

I didn't want to waste my time digging into the side of a hill on the off-chance I might find something.

I held up the pamphlet. "Thanks for this. I'll think about it."

"Hope to see you at the first meeting!"

I turned and threw him a wave over my shoulder as I walked back toward where the girls had left me. Harper and Shay hadn't returned. Were the bathrooms a mile away or something?

Before I could investigate, I spotted a woman with reddish-blonde hair waving at me. I squinted, taking in the woman and the black man she strolled alongside. Finally, recognition dawned over me. They were two necromancers from my coven, one of whom could see through the eyes of ravens. I'd met them at the Gryphon the night I thought I saw Denz.

"Hey!" I called out.

Sara and Josiah veered off the path they'd been on and came over, hand in hand. So I had been right that they were dating!

"How's orientation?" Sara asked. "I remember when I did this. I kinda miss it."

"Good," I said simply.

Sara's lips curled up. "Are you okay? After the Gryphon?"

Totally not.

"Yeah," I lied. "People are looking for him."

"We are," Josiah assured me.

"So you don't go to classes?" I asked, trying to avoid the topic of Denz—and genuinely curious. Not all coven members did, but they looked about my age.

"I did last year but graduated," Sara said. "I'm working in a lab now for my cover. Joe works there too." She nudged the other necromancer and grinned. They were cute together.

"Speaking of the lab. Sorry we can't stay," Josiah said, looking at his watch. "My timer is about to go off. We gotta run. Have fun with this." He waved his hand in the direction of orientation.

"Sure," I said. "See ya later."

They left and though I'd still wanted to hide my past from them, the strange feeling of really belonging to a group washed over me. This was all so knew to me. Before coming to New Haven, I couldn't remember just bumping into someone I knew randomly.

All this newness was so weird. I pulled in a long breath, letting it go slowly as I turned back to the sea of tables and scanned for my roommates, who were still nowhere to be seen.

Not ready to try another table, I decided it was time for a break. Spotting a large oak at the far end of the green, I strolled over to it, shooting the girls a text so they could find me when they came back.

I leaned against the tree and slid down to sit on my rear. It was far away enough from the tables and hubbub that I felt somewhat alone.

A long exhale parted my lips. *Finally, some peace and—*

"Look what the alleycat dragged in," a posh voice drawled, making me shudder. "I could tell it was you from a mile away by your trampy walk."

I glanced up to find none other than dickwad Bentley looming over me, his eyes narrowed with disgust.

I groaned. "What do you want?"

"That's not how you should speak to your betters."

"I'll keep that in mind when I see someone fitting that description."

"Someone should teach you some manners, freshman." Bentley thrust out his hand to grab for me.

"What the hell, man?" I tried to bat his hand away, but he was quick.

He placed a firm palm on my shoulder, pressing me down as he lowered to my level. When he'd settled into his crouch, he knelt over my extended legs, his face separated from mine by mere inches.

"Hitting your superiors isn't very nice. It was Meredith, wasn't it?"

I snorted. "As if you could forget my name. Now let me go, or I'll scream."

He chuckled humorlessly. "You wouldn't. I can tell you're not that kind of girl."

Dammit, he was right, I wasn't the screaming type. Not unless something really scared the crap out of me. This interaction didn't qualify, although I was certain I wouldn't be strong enough to push him away.

"Now, let's talk about the stunt you pulled at the bar, Meredith." He licked his lips. "Your little tantrum could have really hurt me . . . and you don't want to do that. You see, my father is a powerful man, and we have endless resources."

I stiffened, recalling his last name was Sloan—the same as a very influential senator from New York. One running for president soon.

Even if S&S was as powerful as I thought, taking on a senator might be a whole other matter.

"I see you've heard of my family," Bentley smirked. "Good. Now, let's discuss how you can right your wrongs."

He cupped his crotch with his free hand, and his lips curled into an icy smile that didn't reach his eyes.

I nearly vomited. "You've got to be screwing with me."

"Only if you ask nicely."

"Absolutely not," I spat back. "And I don't apologize. What would your father think if he heard you followed women to the bathroom like a psycho?"

Bentley's expression hardened for a moment, before the cruel smile slipped back over his face. "You didn't give me a chance. I invited you to sit with us, and you didn't even consider it. Everyone deserves a chance, don't they?"

"Actually no."

Bentley's lips curled up a little more. "Agree to disagree. And I *know*," his hand slipped down from my shoulder, inching toward my breast, "I want another chance with you, Meredith. Let me take you out, then we can discuss how you'll treat me. And how I'll treat you, if you're a good girl."

I slapped his wandering hand away and spit in his face. "Let me go! Now!"

Both of Bentley's hands slammed to my shoulders to press me back against the oak.

Would anyone see this? Immediately, I knew they wouldn't. I'd come over here because it was quiet and secluded, and from the way he was crouched, Bentley probably looked like he was about to kiss me, not threaten me. If anyone saw us, it was likely they'd think we wanted privacy.

Ew.

"Now listen here, you little bitch," he growled. "You don't want me as an enemy."

Suddenly, my magic flickered to life inside me, and I gasped as my heart began to beat faster.

My power had never done that before, and I truly didn't

know what to make of it. Not until I recalled Hans telling me that magic might act on its own accord to save a person.

Not now, I begged, desperate to make it stop, even though I'd like nothing more than to fling Bentley across the green.

His shock and humiliation would bring me great satisfaction, but if my magic evoked it, that would probably only cause a headache for S&S. Even if Bentley was a bonesman and would learn about magic users this year, that was in a totally different context, one that would bind him to secrecy.

Alas, my power was as stubborn as me, and didn't listen.

The sensation of warmth, of strength, built inside me until I worried it would burst from me. Then the air began to hum softly.

Bentley noticed a shift. He hadn't let go of me, but his gaze darted from side to side, as if looking for what could be causing the disturbance.

"What the hell are you doing, slut?" he whispered.

"Let me go," I warned. "If you don't, you might get hurt."

"I doubt that very mu—*Hey!*"

Suddenly, Bentley Sloan the Third was lifted from my shoulders and soaring backward fifteen feet to land on his ass on the ground. His eyes blazed up at the person who'd pulled him off of me, and my gaze followed.

A sharp breath filled my lungs as I locked eyes with Tobias, who looked about ready to kill the senator's son.

I hadn't seen the moody vampire since our training session, the day he'd pressed his fangs to my skin. Though I'd heard he was around again and had taken a meeting with Luca, he seemed to be avoiding me.

So why was he here now?

"She said leave her alone." Tobias's voice rumbled in a way that made the hair on my arms stand up.

If Bentley wasn't such an idiot, he'd already be running. But he wasn't sprinting away, which made me think he wasn't that smart at all.

Maybe someone had pulled strings to get him into Yale too.

"You'll be hearing from my lawyer." Bentley thrust a finger at the vampire. "No one lays a hand on me that way."

Tobias barked out an unamused laugh, and for one terrifying moment, his emerald eyes glowed.

The outrage on Bentley's face dipped into fear. "What's wrong with you, man?"

"You don't want to know," Tobias said. "Now, the lady said to leave her alone. I suggest running along to cry to your father now." He made a dismissive hand gesture as if Bentley was nothing more than a child.

"What are you, her weird older brother or something?" Bentley scowled.

"I'm much scarier," Tobias said. "Now go. Unless you want me to hurl you into the Beinecke?"

Something in his tone must have finally gotten through Bentley's thick skull because he stood and began to back away.

As he did so, he threw me another glance. "This isn't over."

"Yes, it is," Tobias snarled.

Bentley whirled and, picking up his pace, strode across the green, not looking back again.

I exhaled, watching him retreat. Tobias did the same, and in that second, I was able to pull myself together enough to face the other man who, just days ago, had tried to scare me.

He'd *dared* to press his fangs to my neck, and then *poof!* Disappeared!

So when he turned and looked at me, smiling as if nothing had happened between us, I was surprised. But I didn't show it. Didn't miss a beat.

Not even when he held out his hand to help me up.

I refused the assist and rose to my feet on my own accord. Tilting my chin up, I asked, "What are you doing here, Tobias? And why do you think I need your help?"

CHAPTER TWENTY-TWO

TOBIAS

A muscle ticked in my jaw as I stared down at Meredith. The way her eyes blazed, one would have thought she was a fire witch, not a seeker. She had guts.

And she smelled bloody irresistible.

Luckily for her, I'd downed a liter of blood before searching for her, knowing she might invite my hunger again. So far, my preemptive snack was working. My desires to hunt, to dominate, were quelled.

I still wanted to put her in her place, but that was the dominance in me calling—a natural occurrence in all apex predators. But I was more than a predator. I could control my impulses.

And with her, I would get great practice in doing so.

"Don't vampires have good hearing?" Meredith snapped.

"Excellent."

"Then answer me. Why butt in? Did it look like I needed your help?"

"There's no shame in needing help, Stone," I dodged the question.

Was I sure she would have handled Bentley eventually?

Yes.

Had I been able to hold back my instincts to protect the witch?

No. The urge to hunt and dominate were lessened, but not the desire to shield her, which made no sense. And yet, here I was.

The witch's eyes narrowed. "For the record, I had it handled. And even if I didn't, I don't think *you* should be the one helping me. You threatened me too!"

Inwardly, I cringed. "About my actions the other day . . ."

"When you pressed your fangs to my neck?"

"Yes, that." I inhaled slowly. "I regret scaring you. I apologize."

For a moment, she stared at me, fire still blazing in those blue and green eyes.

"It was uncalled for," I added, feeling uncharacteristically unsure of how to proceed. "I can't even explain why I did it."

Giselle had given one theory, but I still didn't believe it. More than that, if it was true, Meredith didn't need to know. Vampires and witches—or any type of mortal—didn't belong together. I'd ventured down that path once, and it hadn't ended well.

"Fine. I accept your apology. And I do appreciate you tossing that little shit to the ground. Though I still think I could have handled him. Now, please get out of my way. I need to go find Shay and Harper."

She tried to push past me, but I shifted to stand in front of her.

"Wait. I didn't just happen upon you. I have a message."

"Spit it out, then."

"Luca says it's time for your first mission. We're to report to the Skull and Bones tomb."

Her eyebrows pinched together. "Like, right now?"

"Yes."

"Are they always on such short notice?"

"No, but this one is."

She huffed. "Fine. I still have to tell the girls, though. I don't think they've checked their phones."

I lifted my gaze to the tables across the green. Immediately, I spotted the red-haired wolf and the brunette nephilim. They did seem to be searching for Meredith among the chaos of new students.

"There they are." I pointed. "Be quick about it."

"How about we cool it on the commands," Meredith said, walking toward her friends and waving.

The pair saw her and met the witch halfway. I knew the moment Meredith mentioned her mission because Shay clapped her hands together.

Then Meredith jerked a thumb in my direction, and the girls peered around her. Harper nodded, while Shay narrowed her eyes at me.

Apparently, the excitable nephilim had heard about our training session. Thankfully, the unlikely pair didn't follow Meredith back over.

When she stood before me once again, she shoved her hands into her pockets. "Ready."

"Very well."

We strode through campus until we made our way onto the streets of New Haven. Though I was used to long silences, and usually relished them, with each step, I sensed the tension in Meredith rise. Presumed it would soon bubble over.

We'd turned onto High Street, when she reached a boiling point, stopping and whirling to face me.

"Where did you go?" she demanded.

"Pardon me?"

"You left."

"How do you know?"

She blinked, the effect surprisingly innocent and soft, a chink in the armor Meredith usually wore.

A protective instinct deep inside me stirred. Hastily, I pushed it down.

Feeling this way toward her was absolutely ridiculous. We barely knew one another. Not to mention, I was dealing with a *witch*—a new one, yes, but even before she was apprised of her powers, she was a woman fully capable of caring for herself.

As she'd insisted earlier, Meredith was no damsel in distress. She might be a Stone, but steel twisted through her veins, I was sure of it.

"Shay told me you returned yesterday," she said finally. Sharply. "Which means you left."

"I was in Paris," I replied.

"Why?"

"Some places just call to me. As it turned out, the choice was fortuitous."

"Why do you say that?" For a moment, it almost sounded like she forgot she was annoyed.

"I learned the Ordo Aeternum did not take the Pearl."

"How can you be sure?"

"A trusted source."

"You're not going to tell me who, are you?"

I shook my head. "Luca knows the pertinent details they've given us, and he'll pass them along in due time. But my source stays a secret."

Giselle had given us information freely, but she was my maker, someone I cared for, even if I preferred to avoid her because she saw me too clearly. Families, even vampire ones, were complicated, but I would not compromise Giselle's position as an agent for the OA.

"A source in Paris," Meredith mused. "Are you, like, a vampire lord with mistresses?"

My gaze slid to her. Sometimes she said the strangest things. "No. Where did you think I went?"

My lips twitched up as her lips compressed.

"Not that I dwelled on it much." The witch glanced away as if she couldn't care less. "But if I did, I would have guessed you'd holed up at home. Took to your coffin or whatever."

"We don't sleep in coffins. But in a sense, I was home," I admitted as we approached the Skull and Bones Hall. "Here we are."

She kept pace with me down the walk and as I climbed the steps to the door, which opened before we could knock.

A man wearing slacks and a sweater appeared, and at my side, Meredith squinted, probably shocked he wasn't in a robe and mask.

I smirked. The bonesmen liked theatrics, but that had been a bit much, even for them.

"The bonesmen welcome those of Shadows and Secrets," the man said. "Follow me."

I'd been in this tomb a handful of times, though never by the path the bonesman led us through now. We strode down a windowless hallway smelling strongly of dust, going all the way to the end, where the man knocked on a door.

"Enter."

Our escort opened the door and gestured for us to go in.

When we did, Luca was already waiting for us in a vast study with a desk off to the side.

He didn't always insert himself on missions, but this was Meredith's first true test as a dark artifacts hunter, and he was still angry at me for disappearing, so he'd insisted on being present.

Normally, I would have despised being babysat, but in this environment, it made sense. Luca was the coven master of an influential organization, and if the bonesmen respected anything, it was power.

The mage sat across the table from an older gentleman, two empty chairs flanking him. On the other side of the room, a pool table stood, balls scattered over its surface as if our meeting was interrupting a rack.

Bloody bonesmen, always playing games.

Their members were among society's most prestigious citizens. One would think they always had serious matters on their minds, but really, the men and women of the Brotherhood of Death dallied about quite a bit.

Or tempted trouble, which was likely why we were here.

"Welcome." The elder rose and inclined his head. "I'm Gerard, an alumnus of the brotherhood who will soon be helping the new members transition into Skull and Bones. As I'm already here, I've been asked to handle this matter as well. And who might I have the pleasure of speaking with today?"

"Meredith," the witch said.

"Tobias. Vampire."

"Oh, and I'm a witch," Meredith added, the apples of her cheeks coloring a delicious pink as blood flooded the area.

I avoided inhaling, knowing that her scent would have grown stronger.

"It's good to meet you," Gerard replied with a kind smile. "Please, sit."

I gestured for Meredith to lead. She did, choosing the seat to the left of Luca. I took his right, settling into the leather and wood chair.

Luca nodded at both of us, and when our gazes caught, I noticed he appeared to have regained his health a bit. There was no sheen of sweat on his face, though his skin still had not returned to its normal warm, olive glow.

Odd; when I'd seen him earlier, he'd still appeared ill.

Softly, I inhaled, and all became clear. A bouquet of herbs—pungent and medicinal—lingered around Luca. I suspected he'd ingested a potion to make him feel and look better.

The leaders of the secret societies did not enjoy showing their weaknesses. While Luca was more powerful than all of the humans in this society combined, he was no different in that respect.

Not that I could blame him. The face we wore for the outside world determined how they treated us. As this was a business meeting, Luca would want Shadows and Secrets to retain as much authority as possible.

Gerard lowered himself slowly into his seat, the wood creaking beneath his weight. "Skull and Bones thanks you for entertaining this job. It's been quite an embarrassment for our tomb, and we're hopeful you'll retrieve our stolen item quickly."

"We'll do our best," Luca replied. "As you know, Meredith is new to Shadows and Secrets, but skilled. You and I have already negotiated a fee based on her abilities, so now we discuss what is expected of my team. The item is magical in nature, no?"

"It is, and it is relatively weak." He gulped. "But actually, this is a different item from the one we discussed." The man's voice took on a sheepish tone. "We've had another break-in just last night and this item takes precedence."

"Oh?" Luca's eyebrows rose.

"Will we have to renegotiate a fee?" Gerard asked. "I can do so."

"Perhaps. Tell us about this newly stolen item. Who do you believe took it? Might it be a reciprocation of your notorious crookery? As you suggested the other item was?"

Gerard's lips twitched. "We do enjoy claiming other societies' relics. Never yours, of course . . . But we're not sure who took this one. As I said, the item disappeared in the night, and the thief left not a trace."

"Humans normally leave *some* trail behind," I mused.

"Agreed. So you believe the thief is supernatural?" Luca asked the older man.

"That crossed our minds," Gerard admitted.

"All the more reason to employ us. Still, we won't rule out other societies. We all have connections and means to perform the extraordinary, and they may be seeking revenge for items taken from their tombs."

"Precisely." Gerard's gaze flickered uncomfortably to Meredith. "Though, I do hope it's not another society. If word got out what our item could do, it would embarrass the brotherhood."

"What can it do?" I asked.

Meredith had been quiet so far, which came as somewhat of a shock. She wasn't shy—but then again, she might not know which questions to ask.

Again, Gerard's attention darted to her, and she finally spoke up.

"There's nothing you can say that will surprise me. I've seen some real shit, so tell it how it is."

The man swallowed. "Better I show you. Come with me." He stood and walked to the far side of the room, past the pool table.

We followed, and I wasn't the least bit surprised when he pressed the wall inward and a hidden door opened.

I had to duck as we trailed Gerard through a low-ceilinged hallway, which thankfully was not long. Then we exited into a dark room that smelled even mustier than the corridors. The small space was lit only by candles sitting in wall sconces.

Candlelight. How cliché of them.

As if they couldn't afford proper lighting.

"This is what I wanted to show you." Gerard ambled to an island and gestured down.

When we reached the table, I blinked.

"Gross," Meredith whispered, though she didn't back away. "Why the hell do you have that?"

I, too, was surprised. We weren't looking at an island at all, but rather, a glass-topped coffin of sorts, out in the open for the bonesmen to see.

A skeleton stared back at us, nearly complete, save for the missing femur bone.

"Who is it? And where's her leg?" I asked.

"The leg-bone is what we wish for you to find. It belonged to Madame de Pompadour, Louis XV's mistress."

"And why is it here?" I asked, astonished the rumors were true.

It was said her skeleton protected founding papers and other documents, though I didn't think that bit was right. I saw no papers in this room.

"She was moved here," Gerard said. "After the theft."

"Not what I mean," I said, sensing he was dodging. "You told us the item was magical. But I don't see what's magical about a king's mistress's femur."

Gerard cleared his throat. "Her bones are enchanted to increase the virility of our members."

"I see," I said. It became crystal clear why this bone took president over their other stolen item.

No bonesmen wanted *that* secret to get out; least of all the oldest ones, who likely could no longer get it up. That would be quite embarrassing.

"Meredith will need to take another bone with her to find the missing piece," Luca said, his gaze still on the skeleton. "A small, portable one."

"But it *will* be returned," Gerard said, his tone a command.

"Of course. It will merely help her. She's new to understanding her magic—though she might be able to seek without another bone, if you want to take that risk."

"I want no risk, only for the femur to be returned quickly. Is that all you need?"

Luca and I turned to Meredith. Though I would hunt with her, protect her as she worked, truly this was her test.

She swallowed, her eyes locked on the skeleton with a macabre interest. "A finger bone should do."

Gerard pressed a button on the side of the table. The glass lifted, and he reached inside, plucking the longest bone of the right hand, a metacarpal, from where it rested. Reverently, he handed it to Meredith, who looked like she might be ill at any moment.

"Thanks." She held the bone gingerly between two fingers. "Can I?" The witch gestured to her bag in a way that made me stifle a laugh.

She was clearly disgusted but trying to be polite.

"Of course, but do be careful with it."

She nodded and tucked the ivory rod away.

"If that's all, we should get going," Luca said. "They'll start the search tonight."

"Skull and Bones appreciates your assistance."

We left the hidden chamber, filing back into the study. Once Gerard sealed the doorway behind us, he strode to the exit of the room and opened the door.

"Please, show our guests out."

Apparently someone had been waiting there the whole time.

Well, they're going to have to keep waiting a moment longer.

Luca and Meredith made to leave, but I hung back.

The coven master noticed as they passed the desk. "Tobias?"

"If Gerard wouldn't mind, I'd like to have a private word with him."

Luca's eyes widened, but he said nothing—a testament to how much he trusted me, even if I had been a pain in his arse of late. "Very well. Gerard?"

He nodded. "Of course. I'll have someone else show Tobias out."

"I'll be in touch about retrieving the original item later." Luca inclined his head, and the door shut behind him and Meredith.

Once we were alone, Gerard turned to me. "Is this about the job? The change in targets?"

"No. One of your newest additions."

Meredith might kill me for this, but that only mattered if she found out . . . which she wouldn't.

"Oh? Do tell."

"He's harassing our members. Specifically, my partner. I caught him doing so today, in broad daylight, and expect him to be reprimanded."

"Of course, I'll take care of it personally. Who was it?"

"Bentley Sloan."

Gerard's face grew stony, conflicted.

Sloan was from a respected political family, but I didn't give a damn about that. Bentley was an elitist bastard who needed to be taught a lesson. I'd watched Meredith since she'd arrived at orientation, lurked in the shadows so she didn't know, and the moment Bentley had arrived, two things happened: she became angry, and, for a moment, scared.

Not that she'd admit it.

Not that I'd expect her to.

Still, I wouldn't have some tosser rich boy frightening members of my coven.

But while I didn't care who Bentley's family was, Gerard did. I could see it in his eyes, in the stiff way he held himself when confronted with the idea of putting a person with influential ties in their place.

"We will inform him that such behavior is unbecoming to those in the brotherhood," Gerard assured me, though there was a lack of conviction in his tone.

A bit more pressure would need to be applied to ensure he did the right thing.

"Make sure you get him in line." My eyes pinned him in a way that would make most mortals tremble. Though the old man did not, he did avert his gaze, recognizing my dominance. "If you don't, *I'll* make sure he understands. And you might not like my methods—few mortals do."

Slowly, I extended my fangs.

The old man's face blanched.

In this tomb, members of my coven acted as humans, but he knew what I really was, and he'd received my message loud and clear.

Turning to the exit, I told him, "I'll show myself out."

CHAPTER TWENTY-THREE

MEREDITH

The plan was to wait until nightfall to begin the search.

Apparently, the Brotherhood of Death was notorious for 'crookery,' the term they used for stealing from other societies. Or even Yale!

Some people's kids . . .

To Luca, it felt all too likely that someone from Scroll and Key, or Wolf's Head, or any of the other landed societies, had gotten into Skull and Bones's tomb and taken the femur.

I found the practice absurd, but I didn't disagree with the coven master. People did weird things and purchased odd relics to gain the slightest semblance of power. To the Brotherhood of Death, power lay within the bones of a deceased king's mistress.

These people weren't that different from the Ringmaster's clients.

"Couldn't they have charmed anything else to have the same effects?" I twirled the finger bone I'd taken between my own fingers as I stared at it. The thing was small, birdlike. Madame de Pompadour must have been tiny.

"Anything," Luca agreed from where he sat across from me.

The lounging area in his office boasted straight-backed leather armchairs that were more comfortable than they appeared. Though, one look at Tobias and you wouldn't know it. The vampire was as stiff as ever, lifting a glass of blood to his lips.

He was on his third glass since we'd congregated in Luca's office an hour before. Did vampires really need this much blood for sustenance?

"One would think a pin or something innocuous would be better," I muttered, my eyes fixed once more on the bone. "And more mobile than a whole freakin' body."

"She was a mistress," Tobias interjected. "Reportedly, an excellent one. It's the symbology of the thing, Stone. Bonesmen love symbology."

"Guess so. Seems impractical, though."

"Couldn't agree more." Luca stood and moved away from the seating area. His gait was slower now than at the Brotherhood of Death's tomb, almost shuffling.

Once the coven master reached the window, he pulled back a navy curtain. The sun was nearly gone, and the street lights illuminated his face, revealing a sheen of sweat on his brow.

Whatever illness had come over him, his condition seemed to be touch and go.

"Darkness will be upon us soon," Luca said. "Let's get you prepared."

"Prepared?" I'd already changed into a different all-black outfit, and shoes suitable for running—should we need to resort to that.

"Just one more thing." Luca moved to his bookshelf and

opened one of the drawers in the bottom half of the piece. "Which would you like, Meredith?"

I rose to join him. As I got closer, a soft inhale filled my lungs.

A dozen or more daggers lined the drawer. Some blades were super elaborate, others simple.

My gaze went to one somewhere in the middle of the lineup, to a sleek stiletto. A crescent moon sat on the pommel, an emerald the same shade of Tobias's eyes winking in the curve of the moon.

Tobias's eyes?

I wrinkled my nose as I caught myself.

Correction . . . My birthstone.

"That one." I pointed to the dagger with the moon.

"Perfect for a witch," Luca said with a smile. "I trust you know how to use it?"

"Absolutely."

What good tomb-raider didn't know how to use a weapon? I could fire guns as well, and was a decent shot, but for my usual jobs blades were more useful. Quieter. Easier to conceal. And more versatile.

"Perfect."

Luca pulled open the drawer below the top one and grasped a belt and sheath. He handed them over, and I slid the sheath onto the belt. Once secure around my waist, I placed the dagger in the scabbard.

"Why do I need a vampire escort if I'm going to be armed? Or why do I need a blade if I have a vampire?"

"The vampire who broke into Hans's home was a newblood," Tobias said, his gaze still on his glass of blood. He'd barely bothered to look at me since we'd arrived. "It's unlikely he or she will be as strong as me, but they're fast." The admission sounded like it pained him.

"And we don't know if the vampire is working alone," he added. "It could be a whole clan looking for you. In that case, though I can take down many, you should be armed to protect yourself."

"Alright then." My mouth dried up at the idea of multiple vampires hunting us. I still believed the Ringmaster had sent them, even if he'd sent Denz too.

How large was my old boss's supernatural network? And how had I not known about it before?

"Now I know why you insisted on a long jacket," I said, patting the blade at my side and trying to shrug off thoughts of the Ringmaster.

"We've done this a time or two." Luca winked, but the gesture lacked energy. "I'll be waiting for a report."

"Hopefully it won't take long," Tobias said, his voice further away than before.

I twisted to find him waiting by the door. Man, vampires were freaky quiet when they moved.

His gaze bore into me. Though he looked like he couldn't wait to get this over with, the depth of his attention still raised goosebumps on my arms. "Let's go, Stone."

"Good luck," Luca said.

"Thanks." I pulled on the jacket I'd borrowed from Shay, tucking the finger bone in its pocket, and followed the vampire.

Few people were in the hall, but those who were wished me luck. They all knew we were going on a mission, if not what it was.

When we finally got outside, I exhaled. Most people in the

coven were nice, but I was still acclimating to being around so many faces daily.

Then again, when the semester started, it would only get worse, so I'd better get used to it fast.

"Which way?" Tobias grunted. He hadn't said a word to anyone else as we walked through the hall. He also hadn't looked at me, apparently preferring to walk ahead like he had a stick up his butt.

I didn't know what the vampire's problem was, but as long as it didn't affect the mission—my moment to prove myself so I could move on to seeking the Pearl of Hell—I didn't really care.

"Aren't we supposed to swing by the other secret societies' tombs?"

"We are."

"You know where they are, right?"

"I do, but testing your power is paramount."

My lips parted in shock. "You want me to use my magic to lead us there?"

"You can't, can you?"

My nose scrunched up. "No," I admitted. "Everything I've found, I've always had a general location or locations to search in. The Ringmaster sent me places, and the boundaries Luca gave us to find the grimoire weren't that wide."

His eyebrows arched, but he said nothing about the competition.

Speaking of . . .

"Are you ever going to say you're sorry?" I asked, and didn't miss when his eyes widened in surprise.

"For what happened during training? I already did."

"Sure, but what about how you acted like a dick when we were supposed to find the grimoire?" I crossed my arms over my chest. We still stood outside the coven hall, and though I didn't really need this apology, something in me couldn't let it go. For reasons I couldn't understand, but usually blamed on me being a stubborn-ass Taurus, I had to dig my heels in.

Maybe, as we set out for our job, I just wanted him to know I wouldn't be pushed over.

A muscle feathered in the vampire's jaw. "I will admit my actions during your test were unsportsmanlike and unprofessional. I apologize for that day."

I cocked my head, waiting, and Tobias stared back at me, his emerald eyes blazing as if alit from within.

I'd gotten my apology, but it didn't feel fulfilling. Something else was there, missing, something he wasn't saying. Tobias held back, and it clearly had to do with me, I desperately wanted to know why.

"We should be off," he said finally, charging past me.

He marched down the street, tension lining his shoulders, and his steps heavier than usual.

"Coming, Stone? The bonesmen have already paid, and you need to prove your worth."

I didn't respond, just dashed after him, not sure if I wanted to get to the bottom of the mystery of Tobias Aston or not.

Two hours later, frustration threatened to bubble out of me.

So far, no magical pulse from the other landed societies had struck me. Not from Scroll and Key. Not from Book and Snake. Not from Wolf's Head.

With each failure, Tobias's jaw clenched a little tighter. He might have apologized, but it was clear he didn't want to be near me anymore.

Though the vampire infuriated me, I couldn't deny I felt chemistry there, was drawn to him as much as I wanted to push him away. I did my best to ignore the confusing back and forth. It didn't serve me, especially not when I needed to focus.

"Where's the next hall?" I asked wearily.

What would we do if it wasn't any of them? Where would we go from there? I wasn't sure, but the mission would probably take longer than Luca believed. Though he had not said as much, I got the sense he'd wanted this done tonight.

"Manuscript is the next society on the list," he said, turning east. "Berzelius is one of the last tombs we haven't seen. If it's not there, we'll have to explore other options."

"As in?"

"The bone might no longer be in New Haven. A secret society may not be the culprit."

"Which means it could be anywhere."

I eyed Tobias sidelong when he said nothing in response, and suppressed the groan working its way up my throat. I couldn't take that sort of tension. If I had to take a plane with him to China or something, I'd probably stab myself in the eye.

"Then let's pray to the gods and goddesses or whatever you magical people believe in, that it's at Manuscript. Berzelius . . . " I shook my head. "What kind of silly names are those, anyway?"

Again, he didn't reply, only turned left, leading me to the society's hall. On the way, we passed an archeology building and a vast green space that probably belonged to Yale—much like seemingly everything else around here—and then took another turn. When we found our way onto Temple Street, something beneath my skin began to warm and itch.

I sucked in a soft breath, which made Tobias turn.

"Problem?" He studied me with an unnerving gaze.

"No," I said, not wanting to divulge my thoughts yet.

My magic wasn't totally new, but this level of sensitivity to it was. It didn't happen when I trained with Hans, and I suspected it was because while I used power then, I wasn't searching for things. Just learning how to do basic spells and protect myself—stuff every capable witch should know, or so Hans claimed.

Was this how my 'intuition,' as I'd so often thought of it before, would have worked had it been totally free to flow through my veins?

"This way, then." Tobias turned back around.

I spotted the tomb before he pointed it out. Like the Skull and Bones headquarters, it was windowless. Berzelius was also white and largely unadorned. It didn't fit in with the rest of the city, which I was quickly learning was something those who constructed tomb halls desired.

"How warm and cozy," I said as we walked up to the entrance.

"Berzelius is meant to house secrets."

"I was being sarcastic. Heard of that in the thousand years you've been alive?"

He looked like he wanted to correct me. Perhaps the number of years he'd been living was on the tip of his tongue, but somehow Tobias held off and nodded to the building. "What do you sense?"

I closed my eyes, tuning in. The subtle heat under the surface of my skin was still there. Now tingles coupled the burn.

My hand dipped into the pocket where I kept the finger bone. When my skin touched the remains of Madame de Pompadour, the tingling intensified.

I was on to something. But for some reason, I didn't feel like the pull was coming from the building in front of us.

I let out a low hum before opening my eyes again and turning to the vampire. He watched me closely enough for me to jerk back a touch, but I corrected quickly. "I do sense something, but it might be around the back? I don't know, the directionality is off."

"We'll circle it. As much as we can." Tobias scanned the area, which was not as busy as other parts of the city around campus. "If you feel differently as we explore, we will figure out how to get inside."

Though I didn't know a thing about this hall, I'd wriggled into secure places before, and I was sure Tobias had too. If Manuscript had taken the bone, we'd get it back.

But the more we explored, the less sure I became we were in the right place. Once we neared the back of the tomb, the tingles vanished. Even when I touched the finger, nothing happened.

"We're getting further away." I frowned, gaze raking over the white stone. "It was stronger at the front."

"I doubt they'd keep it by the door," Tobias said, and for the first time that night, his tone was a little less chilly.

But I still stiffened. "Do you doubt my abilities?"

"It's not that," he replied. "Perhaps we should go back to the front. You can see if you still feel whatever you sense there."

I nodded, slightly annoyed. It certainly sounded like he doubted me.

This mission couldn't end soon enough.

We walked around to the front of Berzelius, and again, the pricking sensation surged. My eyebrows knitted together, and following a hunch, I spun on my heel and stared across the street. A small, triangular park, just a place to rest one's feet, was located between two streets.

Surely no one would leave an item belonging to a secret society out in the open? Not only was it magical, but Skull and Bones had money. If it wasn't another society that took it, but rather, someone needing money, they wouldn't get it if something happened to the bone.

"What else is around here?" I asked, scanning the surroundings. "In this direction." I pointed to the park.

"What do you mean?"

"Like, buildings."

"Let's see, there are shops, restaurants, a lab, a museum, the archeology building . . . all sorts of things."

I mulled that over. We'd passed the archeology building on the way here. While it might be the perfect place to hide a bone, I hadn't felt a spike in my intuition, or anything else, that hinted I was on track.

"The museum," I said because it felt right. "Let's go that way."

Tobias arched an eyebrow. "Why would someone place anything there?"

I crossed my arms over my chest. "I don't know, Tobias. I'm not a criminal mastermind."

"You sure?"

My teeth ground together. If he knew why I worked for the Ringmaster, he would feel so bad right now. Or, most normal people would. A vampire with an iced-over heart probably wouldn't care.

"Just show me the way," I gritted out.

CHAPTER TWENTY-THREE

The vampire scowled and turned his back on me.

CHAPTER TWENTY-FOUR

MEREDITH

WE REMAINED SILENT AS WE STALKED DOWN THE STREET. THOUGH I really wanted to give Tobias a piece of my mind, I was practiced in pushing down my emotions when it counted, and this was one of those times.

I needed to find the femur bone of Madame de Pompadour to prove to Luca my power was developing and that as soon as signs of someone using the Pearl began to show, I should be sent to find the gem.

But I'd never had to seek an item without already having a decent idea of where it was. A tomb. A rich dude's vault. A warlord's mansion. Within a few blocks of Yale.

I didn't have the vaguest idea where the femur bone was. Nothing other than the magic in my veins, pushing me forward. And my annoyance with the vampire would only cloud my abilities, so down it went, into the recesses of my being.

I released a heated exhale through my nostrils. Tobias turned slightly, eyeing me as if I were a bug on the bottom of his shoe.

"Well? Feel anything?" he prompted when it was clear I wasn't going to say a word.

We were on the other side of Temple Street now, still across from the small park but on another side of the triangle. With each step, the electrification of my nerve endings intensified. In my pocket, the token from Madame Pompadour burned, so I wrapped my fingers around the bone. A jolt ran up my arm, shooting down my spine like lightning. From behind my breastbone, magic pulled me forward, in a clear direction.

"Yeah. That way." I pointed, marveling at the new intensity in my seeking powers. "What's that building?"

Though street lights illuminated the area, we were still too far away for me to make out a sign. If there even was one.

"The large one?" Tobias asked, following my gaze.

I nodded.

"That's the New Haven Museum."

"I think the sensation is coming from there. Let's get closer."

Our pace picked up, and as we neared the museum—a large, brick, colonial-style building with white trim—the feeling of someone hooking me by the ribs and pulling me grew. This was the place.

If tomb-raiding had felt like this before, I wouldn't have been able to deny my power. Even just the tingling had been a lot, but the hooking sensation was undeniable.

"It's in there," I confirmed.

Tobias's dark eyebrows knitted together. "Which makes little sense."

"Why?"

"This isn't like the Peabody. Or the Smithsonian. A bone would be out of place in this particular establishment. It focuses more on the history of New Haven and art. Not archeology. There would be no hiding it in plain sight, so it would have to be in an office, and that seems unlikely."

"I'm sure it's in there," I insisted. "Maybe whoever took it is an employee with a vendetta against Skull and Bones. Have they ever stolen from this place?"

Tobias shrugged. "It's possible. They do love their pranks. But getting on the wrong side of the Brotherhood of Death would be dim."

It was funny how the bonesmen stole for shits and giggles while I did so to afford a place to survive and, eventually, buy my freedom.

Suddenly, I didn't feel quite as bad about being a tomb-raider.

"Do you think the lock is difficult to pick?" I left Tobias standing on the sidewalk as I climbed the few steps to the door.

"Perhaps we should try around the back?" he replied, striding to keep pace.

"Perhaps," I said, but didn't break my step. I wanted to check out the easiest option first. "Hide behind the columns if you're worried. I'll be quick."

Tobias grunted, but as I neared the door, he did as I requested. The warming and the strangely pleasant stinging of my skin was so strong, it made me want to scratch an itch, but I refrained and hoped that once I found what I was looking for, it would go away.

Before my magic was unbound, I'd always had some vague sense of intuition leading me. This was much stronger, a sensation I couldn't ignore no matter how hard I tried.

One glance at the lock confirmed I could probably pick it; I was no novice in this area. However, I also spotted cameras, and if there were cameras, the door was likely alarmed.

But that didn't mean all the entrances were.

"This is a last resort." I turned back to the vampire, whose shoulders were so stiff they resembled stone.

"You don't say?" he snapped. "Who would have thought busting through the front door in plain view of humans would be a last resort?"

"Oh, shut up." I gazed upward, doing my best to ignore the smugness rolling off of him. "How do you feel about scaling the building? Did they teach you that in vamp school?"

The idea of a vampire school struck me as ludicrous and almost made me laugh . . . until I realized it was no crazier than the coven I'd pledged myself to. Just when I thought I was slipping easily into this world, something like that would make it clear I hadn't accepted it as deeply as I believed.

"Not in school," Tobias muttered, his eyes trailing upward. "But you're probably correct that a window is our best bet. I doubt they're all alarmed. Certainly not the ones at the top."

"And you can get in?" Given enough time, I probably could figure out a way in myself, but if Tobias could use his super vampy strength and stealth for this and let me in a more mundane way, then all the better.

"I always find a way. Follow me."

Before I could respond, he was off, stalking toward the side of the museum where the streetlights could not reach.

We rounded the corner and strode toward the back of the building, finding ourselves in a small parking lot. Without the streetlights, it was even darker back here. Darker and secluded. If we could break-in through one of the windows, no one would see us.

"There," Tobias said, pointing upward. "The circle is our best bet."

I squinted and my mouth fell open. He was pointing to a window meant purely for decoration. One that had been placed three-stories high, and was smaller than the rest. Could he even fit through that hole?

"Okay, sure, but you're going to have to get up there. Not to mention, I don't think you'll fit."

"You'd be surprised what places I've gotten myself into," Tobias replied, not at all worried. "We'll have to break the glass, but it's our best bet."

I stopped and cast a glance around, as if searching for an answer to my unasked question. "How did the person who took the bone get in?"

"I suspect they came in during business hours. The museum isn't busy all the time."

How in the world someone just waltzed in and hid a leg-bone was beyond me, but weirder things had happened. Like this. Or my talking cat. Or basically anything from the last week.

"You're amenable?" Tobias pressed, turning to me. He didn't look pissed off. More like excited.

A tiny bit of the ice I harbored inside regarding him melted.

"Yeah, but how am *I* going to get up there?"

He turned around, showing me his back. "Climb on."

"You've got to be joking," I replied, glowering at his back.

"If any windows on this building are not censored, it's that one. If I get you in any other way, an alarm will sound. The coven can get its members out of jams, but it's really best to draw as little attention as possible."

My throat tightened as I broke my stare-off with the back of his head and allowed my gaze to drift up. Although I was in shape, there was no way in hell I'd be able to scale this wall.

"Meredith, we're wasting time. Are you sure the bone is in there?"

I was, dammit. And I was also sure this was the best way to get inside—certainly the most undetectable.

"Fine, but let it be known I do *not* like being treated like a child," I muttered.

"Noted."

Tobias bent at his knees, making it easier for me to wrap my arms around his neck. Then I jumped up, and the moment my legs circled his hips, a jolt of electricity shot through me.

I drew in a soft breath, and beneath me, Tobias stiffened.

Did he feel that too?

"Are you alright?" he asked after a moment, his tone a touch raspy.

I swallowed. "Yeah. You . . . shocked me."

Sure, that was what it was.

"Apologies. Secure yourself."

"How's this?" I tightened my grip around his shoulders and waist. "Too hard?"

"You can't hurt me." The way he said it made me think he wasn't so sure about that. "Ready?"

"I am."

The moment the words left my mouth, Tobias was at the wall, scaling it like a damned squirrel climbing a tree. My breath hitched, but I forced down any sounds of fear, not about to allow Tobias to hear them.

Within a minute, he'd made it to the top. As the vampire shimmied right, I hung on ever tighter.

Tobias reached the window and made a fist with one hand, leaving him—and me—attached to the wall by one hand. With a single blow, he shattered not only the glass, but the wood that held the smaller panes together in a loose lattice.

Blood dripped down his arm as he ripped the wood out and continued breaking glass until only the tiniest bits remained on the circumference of the circular window.

"That's the best I can do. Be careful of your hands and shins as you go in."

I gaped. I totally hadn't thought this through. Of *course* I'd have to go inside first. We couldn't fit through together, and there was no way I'd be able to cling to the side of this building without him.

But what if there was a thirty-foot drop on the other side? The memory of Denz slackening his grip on the rope in the shaft came back to me. I'd only fallen a couple of feet, and that had been terrifying.

My stomach pitted. "I don't know if I can."

"It's the only way, Meredith. If you can't get down, hang from the windowsill and hold on. I'll assist once inside."

He said it with such self-assurance, it almost erased my doubt. Almost.

"Do you know what the other side looks like?" I pressed.

"I don't. We have to trust we can figure it out. Not delivering on this mission is not an option."

No, it wasn't. And the faster I succeeded in a real mission, the faster I'd gain Luca's trust and get to search for the Pearl of Hell and right my wrongs.

Crap. Okay. Fine.

"Can you scoot below the hole, and I'll climb over you?"

Tobias positioned himself as requested without so much as a peep. No dry, witty remarks. He must have sensed my hesitation.

"Okay, I'm going to have to step on your shoulders."

"Do what you must. I can handle it."

I swallowed thickly as doubt clawed at my heart. "Are you sure we're going to be able to get down on the other side?"

"I will see to it."

Ugh. Again, with the confidence. It left me with no way to deliberate without sounding weak, so I took a deep breath and prepared to climb.

My hand trembled as it left the safety of Tobias's body to reach for the window. I latched onto the wood, avoiding the broken glass, and then pulled up. Only when I was sure I was up as far as I could go did I unravel my leg.

Quickly, I kicked and scurried my way upward, feeling the influence of gravity but fighting against it. Tobias helped, one hand pushing at my foot. My heart raced, and the next thing I knew, I plunged through the window, eyes wide and hands flailing. Somehow, I managed to keep my lips clamped tightly shut as I fell and when I hit wood a moment later, I gasped.

"Thank God," I wheezed, tempted to kiss the ground that had saved me from an imaginary free-fall.

I rolled over and looked around. We had entered into an office. Considering the piles of papers and cheap-looking furniture, it might belong to an intern.

"Watch out!" Tobias called from above. A second later, he hopped through the window with far more grace than I had.

He didn't miss a beat, approaching me with a hand extended to help me up.

I almost accepted his assistance, but drew back. My palms were bloody. I hadn't even noticed the glass shards cutting me.

"We have to bind them," Tobias said, his pitch elevated.

Something in his tone made me lift my gaze. His pupils were enormous, wild. I'd seen that expression before, the day we'd trained. The day he'd grazed my neck with his fangs.

"Are you okay?" I whispered, more scared for myself than him as I got to my feet.

"Fine. I ate at headquarters. It's just . . ." He trailed off, as if fighting a force deep inside himself. "Here." He stomped over to an open box and pulled a New Haven Museum t-shirt from its depths.

The next second, the shirt was torn to shreds, and the white cotton wrapped around my hands.

"Thanks," I murmured, noticing how the vampire's pupils shrank the moment my wounds were covered.

The blood he'd drunk in Luca's office hadn't affected him at all. Why did mine? Did my magic have something to do with it?

"Tune into your power," he replied curtly, his eyes on anywhere but me. "Do you still sense the bone?"

Though fear and apprehension zinged through me, it was easy to sense my power seeking the item.

"It's here. Close."

"Good. Let's find it."

Tobias moved to the door, showing himself out. I followed, careful to keep my distance.

He'd helped me get inside, allowed me to use him as a human ladder, and bound my cuts. He said he'd fed, and he'd held himself together, though my blood clearly affected him. All of those actions screamed I could trust him.

And yet, from the stiff way he walked, I wasn't sure I could trust Tobias not to lash out at me. To threaten me. To sink his fangs into my neck and drink.

No, I couldn't trust the vampire.

Not while I still had blood in my veins.

CHAPTER TWENTY-FIVE

TOBIAS

The scent of Meredith's blood never stopped flooding my nostrils, teasing my senses. We stopped only when we spotted the first blinking red light of a camera in a main hallway.

"What are we going to do? I didn't come prepared." She gestured to herself, which I took to mean that she normally wore disguises when infiltrating places guarded with such technology. "The tug of magic is coming from downstairs, so we need to get past that."

"Hold on," I answered. "Stay around this corner."

Vampiric speed made me unidentifiable on film, and my kind could jump quite high. As such, reaching the camera was not an issue, and neither was smashing it to bits.

After the first camera was taken care of, I darted down two more corridors, searching for more flashing red lights. Surprisingly, there were fewer than would have been prudent.

Then again, this isn't the Louvre.

I smashed each recording device, ending with the one at the top of the stairs, confident that would be the last one until we descended to the first floor.

"What was that about?" Meredith asked when I returned.

"The cameras are no longer an issue," I replied, trying to ignore the scent of her blood on her skin, and wishing I could distance myself. "There will likely be more downstairs, but probably not too many. I suspect the museum is in need of funding."

She arched an eyebrow but left her hiding spot.

When we passed by the first site of destruction, her eyes widened, but she said nothing and led me down a stairwell. At the bottom, I dispatched one more camera.

"This way," Meredith murmured, eyes wandering the area.

We crept past the often-photographed rotunda and into a photography exhibit.

"I think it's in there."

"Hold on."

I peeked inside, found one camera near the entrance, and took care of it.

"Sucks that they don't have funding and we're destroying their shit," Meredith said when I returned.

"The coven will make a sizable donation next week. If the femur is here, so will Skull and Bones."

It was all part of our contract with our clients.

She snorted delicately. "Of course they will."

"If you're done worrying about trivial matters." I gestured into the room. "Lead the way."

She stepped past me, once again overwhelming me with her aroma. Because the wound was covered, I was in control . . . but barely. If I hadn't taken precautions and drank so much blood while we'd waited at headquarters, I might not be so well off. There was no way to tell.

A shiver wracked my spine. I'd not been this tempted by a

person since the week after my transformation from sailor in the Royal Navy to the newest vampire of the Laurent clan.

"It's super close," Meredith whispered, gliding through the gallery with steps almost as light as my own. "I can feel it, it's like a thudding in my chest."

Suddenly, she stopped. Her slender-fingered hand dipped into her pocket, cobalt nails disappearing as her two-toned eyes shuttered closed for a moment.

Moonlight poured into the room from a small window above, bathing her in a silver glow. The rest of the room faded.

In this light, using her magic, she'd never looked more like a witch. Or smelled like one. If there was one scent more powerful than that of her blood, it was her magic. Sweet honey spiking the fresh forest and jasmine aroma that normally clung to her skin.

I inhaled, tempting bloodlust and dragging the pleasing scents deeper into my being. Then, I froze.

Something else punctuated the air. Something not of Meredith. Nor of me.

Iron and dry cotton, scents typical of one supernatural order.

There was another vampire in the New Haven Museum. Or there had been recently.

"Meredith, don't move," I commanded.

She stiffened and then whirled about, eyes wide open and blazing. "What?"

"Don't move. I—"

"You know you're not my boss, right?" She crossed her arms over her chest, lips twisting in displeasure.

The instinct to dominate her, to make her do as I wished, rushed over me, and I glared at her, willing her to listen. But before I could compel her, I blinked. I didn't do that with coven members. We were a team, colleagues. In fact, I rarely compelled at all anymore.

But again, Meredith made things difficult, and my body responded in ways that it did not when others challenged me.

Why?

The simple answer was that few people ever challenged me. Giselle, Luca, and Hans did. Gunner too, but in his teasing way. All were leaders of their magical orders. Shay sometimes tossed me a bit of sass—though it was hard to take the nephilim seriously. She was strong for her age, but not compared to a vampire like me.

If I ever saw Raphael and Serena, they too would challenge me, as was their right. In the Blood of Laurent, we were equals —all Giselle's children, first of her blood. But it had been so long since I'd spoken to either of my closest siblings, let alone seen them.

Meredith stepped closer, the motion ripping me back to the moment, and my gaze barreled into her, again the power within me seeking to control her.

"What did you just do?" she hissed, glowering at me.

Again, I cut off the instinct to dominate, and blinked, feeling completely disoriented. "Excuse me?"

"I felt weird. Did you use magic on me? Do vampires have magic?"

Vampires . . . Bloody hell.

I still hadn't told her what I scented.

"Meredith." I took care to keep my tone low so the other vampire, should they still be present, would not hear. "We might not be alone."

"What? Is there a guard?"

"A vampire."

Her spine straightened, and she closed the distance between us. "The one who broke into Hans's house?"

"I can't be certain, I did not smell that blood. But even if I did, it would smell different than the person would."

A slow exhale parted her lips. "Is it close? I still think the Ringmaster might have hired the vampire that broke into Hans's place. Could be the same."

"Not close," I replied, tucking the other information she gave away for later.

The vampire had probably come through here, but it was no longer in the room. If they were, their scent would be stronger, and if they moved even an inch or breathed too deeply, I'd hear them.

Plus, if they were a newblood, as Luca believed, they would not be able to keep themselves from Meredith for long. She smelled far too tempting.

"Then we should hurry and get the hell out of here," she said. "The bone is close, I can feel it."

"I'll keep watch. Find it."

I trailed Meredith through the exhibit, which suddenly appeared larger than before. All the while, my gaze darted from side to side. The other vampire's scent lingered, but did not grow stronger. Wherever the creature was, it wasn't in this room.

The witch led me to the far back wall and huffed. "I feel like the femur is back here, but everywhere. Like whoever took it rubbed it on the walls or something." Her nose wrinkled. "What if they did that and left? 'Cause where would you even hide a bone in here? It's all photos."

She was right. It wasn't like one could hide a femur behind these canvases. Could the bone's magic really be so strong as to leave a trace? I usually disregarded other societies' magics as weak, but did Skull and Bones truly have a relic of note?

I doubted it. Surely nothing like the Pearl of Hell, which would have emitted a powerful resonance for Meredith to follow. The witch had been able to sense it even without the full extent of her magic.

Whoever took the femur likely knew about magic. Which meant that though the thief might have been trying to throw supernaturals off, the item we sought was most likely still present.

"Grab ahold of the finger again," I urged her. "Try to narrow your focus to only that."

She didn't argue, or even glare at me for telling her what to do, which hinted she might feel a bit lost. Or perhaps even scared. After all, a vampire had threatened her and might still be in the area.

"I have your back," I whispered.

She pulled the token of a long-dead king's mistress from her pocket. Softly, the air around her pulsed in a way I was sure she didn't sense. And then, a soft gasp parted her lips. "Left."

She turned around another partition.

"There!" she gestured with her hand, the finger bone in its grip.

I followed her direction. "In a storage closet? Seems a bit simple."

"Maybe it was temporary," she shrugged, striding over and grabbing the handle.

It didn't budge.

She grunted. "Locked."

Obviously, I didn't have a key, but that didn't matter. I

joined her at the door, and wrapped my hand around the knob. "Step to the side. Sometimes, wood splinters."

Meredith complied, and as soon as she was out of the way, I ripped the door open. A *crack* sounded, making me cringe. If the other vampire was still present, I'd given away our location.

"There," the witch murmured.

I gazed into the closet, filled with cleaning materials, and shook my head. There, laying on a shelf as if it were nothing more than a bottle of cleaner, was the ivory femur bone of Madame Pompadour.

My partner darted into the closet, seizing the bone. "Got it! Let's move before—"

Somewhere deep in the museum, glass shattered.

I ripped Meredith out of the closet so she could not be trapped inside, should an adversary appear, and whirled around to take in the exhibit. The other vampire was, indeed, still in the building, though not in this room.

Not that such little distance made a difference. They had announced themselves, which meant they were now hunting us.

"Meredith, we must leave quickly. Get on my back."

She balked. "I can run!"

"Not fast enough." Not if she wanted to avoid the newblood I suspected was stalking her.

Mindful of the femur bone we were risking our skin for, I grabbed the witch and flung her onto my back.

"*Oof!*" she breathed, but snaked one arm around my shoulders.

Again, the scent of her blood flooded my nostrils, but somehow, perhaps because I knew danger was lurking, I shoved down my desire to control her, finding it a little easier than it had been before.

I twisted slightly, and a flash of white told me she clenched the bone in her other hand. "Keep a tight hold. I won't let up until we're far from the museum."

As soon as the words were out of my mouth, I raced out of the exhibit room, scanning the space as I went.

Should I risk it and use the front door?

We had not dealt with the cameras in that part of the museum, and destroying them would slow us down even more. But if we didn't, humans might see us leaving. Then again, they might anyway, I couldn't run as fast as usual with Meredith on my back. Certainly not at the speed that would help me avoid being detected by the cameras. A witch could not handle vampiric speed.

Another thought struck like a matching being lit.

The other vampire hadn't seemed at all concerned by the cameras. Why? Was their sire that idiotic? Or that influential?

Did the vampire who'd sent their child know they would be able to deal with the newblood being seen and their image potentially thrown up on news sites?

Vampires didn't answer to humans, but we did have a governing body: the Covenant, a group of supernaturals who liked to keep it quiet that magical beings existed. But if the vampire in the museum didn't disable the cameras, that revealed a lack of regard for those in charge.

Who were we dealing with here?

We were nearly to the rotunda, where I'd have to make a choice to exit the way we'd arrived or use the door, when the air shifted. Around my shoulders, Meredith's arm tightened and her breath thinned.

I'd slowed ever so slightly, preparing for an attack to come from one of the closest exhibit rooms, when suddenly, I caught a flash in the air above. Before I could deduce what it was, Meredith was torn from my back and flung down to the ground just as a powerful hand shoved me forward to the floor, sending me into an uncontrollable roll.

I swore as I slammed into the wall with such force a painting hanging above dislodged to land on top of me. The newblood bastard had jumped from the second floor.

"Denz!" Meredith screamed, sending my usually static heart into overdrive.

I leapt to my feet, whirling to face the witch. She'd dropped the bone and instead held the dagger Luca had given her. Though sharp, it wasn't enough to decapitate a vampire, but judging by the ferocity on her face, she was undeterred.

"What happened to you, Denz?" Meredith demanded, swiping the dagger at the man in a tight black t-shirt and sunglasses. "Who did this?"

The vampire hissed, a bad sign. He was on the verge of losing control.

I launched myself at him, but being a newblood, he was fast and danced out of my grip, spinning in a wide circle away from the witch.

"Meredith! Get back!" I commanded.

She didn't listen but came up next to me, her gaze trained on her former partner. "He's a vampire? But how?! Is the Ring-master one?!"

"It seems whoever sprung him from prison had connections."

I darted forward as Denz attempted to veer toward Mered-ith, fangs extended. My fist collided with his face, and his neck snapped to the side.

Had he been human, the blow would have been deadly. But Denz was no longer human. No longer mortal. Without a stake or fire, the only way to kill him would be to rip his head off.

"Denz! We can help! You don't have to follow the Ringmaster anymore!"

Meredith's cries were still echoing in the space as the newblood launched himself at me, his eyes so black, I could feel the thirst burning in his throat.

"She's right," I said, my tone even, in control. I needed this newblood to sense my dominance.

I took a step forward, and Denz reacted to the motion, going backward.

Good. He likely felt my power, and I was effectively creating space between him and the witch. Now I needed him to make eye contact with me so I could compel him to stop this nonsense and tell me the identity of his sire.

"The coven can hide you, teach you," I continued.

"The Ringmaster won't find you! We're searching for him, going to stop him!" Meredith yelled, drawing attention to herself in a way that made the skin on my nape tighten.

"Death to the Ringmaster!" Denz spat, his attention snapping to her despite the danger I posed to him. "And screw your coven! You left me to rot!"

"I-I'm sorry!" Meredith shouted, the remorse clear in her voice. "I didn't want to. I—"

Denz darted toward me, and I sidestepped a punch to the gut.

"I made her leave you," I said, shoving him backward a few feet. "But it was a mistake. Let me right it, I can teach—"

"I don't need your teachings," Denz cut me off. "My sire is all-powerful, he'll teach me. As soon as I bring him *her*!"

Fast as lightning, he surged around me, and before I could spin to follow, the newblood had Meredith by the neck.

She kicked her legs as he lifted her so only her toes brushed the ground. Strangled noises came from her throat as his grip tightened.

"I'm not supposed to, but I can't help it," Denz murmured, his tone entranced. "I just can't . . ." A look of enchantment flashed across his face before his fangs sank into Meredith's neck.

"No!" I flew across the room. Though her open veins posed danger to my composure, I couldn't stop myself from grabbing the vampire's skull and ripping it upward.

His eyes blazed into mine, blood dripping down his face. *Meredith's blood.*

My throat constricted. The thirst that so often accompanied her presence, the yearning to dominate and taste her, rammed into me like a two-thousand-pound bull. I staggered backward, but recovered almost as quickly.

I had to remain in control. Had to save her. If I didn't, this newblood would drain the life from her in minutes.

From the rough gasping of her breath, he'd already taken too much too quickly.

The revelation somehow centered me, erasing my need to drink— and just in time. In the instant my thirst had overcome me, Denz had fixated once again on Meredith.

Her skin looked pale, clammy, and her hand trembled as she tried to swat him away.

I shot my own hand out, grabbing Denz by the chin, forced his gaze to lock with mine, then I lashed out with my power of compulsion. "Release her."

He blinked, as if in acceptance of the command, and relief flooded me.

But it lasted for only a second before the vampire sank his fangs deeper into Meredith's neck.

All the air seemed to get sucked from the room. My compulsion hadn't worked. Why?

I grabbed his head and pried it from the witch's throat. Once his fangs were clear of her body, I plowed my fist into his stomach like a battering ram.

Blood sprayed from his mouth, sending my own thirst into overdrive, but the blow had done what I intended. Under the force of my attack, Denz released Meredith.

She fell to the floor like a rag doll, and though my instincts warred—to check on her or to drink from her—I fought them both down, instead lifting Denz over my head and throwing him across the room.

He crashed into the stairs, but rose immediately, chest heaving.

"Who's your sire?" I roared.

The newblood stared right at me, unworried about my powers of compulsion—because they didn't work on him. They should, but they didn't.

That alone told me that his sire was powerful. A royal vampire. Someone in the web of vampires who could claim the Blood of Laurent. My family.

"Who is it?" I hissed. "Tell me, or I'll tear your head off right now."

A bark of laughter exploded from Denz, and he wiped the streak of blood from his face. "Perhaps one day, you'll learn. But not today."

He spun and sprinted up the stairs, moving so fast that his visage blurred. I dashed to follow, but the moment glass shattered above, it was no use. He was gone. He had burst through one of the windows above and disappeared into the night.

"*Fuck!*" My hands flew up to grip the sides of my head.

This was beyond comprehension.

"Tobias," Meredith's voice rasped from where she'd fallen. "Help."

My breath hitched as another dilemma presented itself. The witch was weak, possibly in need of blood, but could I trust myself to get close to her? To not drink?

"Tobias . . ."

My heart thudded hard inside my chest. Slowly, I turned.

Pools of red were spreading beneath Meredith, calling to me, enhancing the burn in my throat. But another instinct was rising too, responding to the faint beating of her heart.

Too slow. Too weak.

Denz took too much from her. Meredith is dying.

That thought firmly lodged in my head and heart, I closed the distance between us.

The witch lay splayed out, and staring down at her, I knelt, lifted her into my arms, and examined the wound Denz had left.

It was gaping. Pink-stained skin, flayed open. Life-threatening. The newblood had taken no care at all when he'd bitten her.

My throat constricted as the way to save her, or to buy her time, presented itself.

Vampire blood had healing properties; it wouldn't replenish her own blood, but it could put Meredith in a state of stasis, close the wound, and minimize scarring.

But sharing my blood would also mean bonding us, to some degree, and after what Giselle said . . .

What if my maker was right and we were fated? Soulmates? I couldn't be that for a mortal woman—couldn't do that to them.

But I couldn't let this one die, either.

A soft gurgling noise bubbled up the witch's throat,

banishing my indecision. I'd give her enough to get her to the coven's tomb so the healers could finish the job. I couldn't risk more than that.

Gently, I shifted Meredith to one arm and brought my opposite wrist to my mouth. Tearing into my flesh was easy.

The tang of blood was still on my own lips when I brought my wrist to hers. "Drink," I said, loudly. At any moment she might slip away, and I worried she couldn't hear me. "Meredith, you must drink."

Slowly, her lips parted.

I pressed my skin to those deep pink lips, exhaling when they closed around the punctures my fangs had created.

A soft sigh left her, and heat exploded through me, making me tingle—an indication she'd taken a sip.

To mortals, vampire blood tasted like the nectar of the gods. It was yet another way we seduced them into trusting us.

"Just a little," I warned as she sucked the life-force from my veins. "Enough for you to survive the transport to S&S."

Another pull, another explosion of heat.

My toes curled, and the desire to pry her lips from my wrist and kiss her came over me.

What the bloody hell? No.

Meredith took another pull, and finally, a little color returned to her cheeks.

No more. It had to be enough. Any more blood, and we risked forming a bond I didn't want. One she should never be forced to form.

"That's enough." I pulled my wrist away, and a pitiful sucking sound filled the silence as her eyes, wild and full of need, latched on to me.

"More," she demanded.

Some strength had returned to her voice, and though I doubted she could walk on her own, I decided to take that as a sign she was ready.

I gathered the witch up in my arms and, damning the consequences, ran out the front door of the museum and sprinted for headquarters.

CHAPTER TWENTY-SIX

MEREDITH

"You shouldn't have moved her so soon," a voice whispered into my consciousness.

"It was that or let her die," another voice, one that warmed my insides, growled defiantly.

"You could have given her more blood. It would have helped. She wouldn't have been so jostled in transport."

A long pause passed.

"I did the best I could."

"I don't know what you did, but it wasn't that."

I shifted, and moaned. My throat hurt so bad, like someone had rubbed it with sandpaper, and no sound came out.

What had happened?

Slowly, I opened my eyes and blinked heavily. I was lying on a bed, in a room I'd never seen before. Plants hung from the ceiling, vines trailing to the floor. The walls were white, and the space airy. Clean. Earthy with the spot of green. A skylight was positioned above me, letting in a beam of sunlight.

Where the hell was I? No one was around, so where were the voices coming from?

Painfully, I pushed myself up and scanned the area. I lay in some sort of hospital room. One with two beds and . . .

I sucked in a breath, catching sight of the bagged blood hanging at my side, the needle in my arm.

Blood.

Denz.

My throat constricted, and a strange, high-pitched, horrible sound flew out of my lips. I hadn't even known I was capable of sounding so scared.

"Meredith? Are you okay?" One voice I'd heard came closer, and my gaze landed on Luca and Tobias rushing my way.

My breath came faster as the memories of the New Haven Museum rushed back.

Denz was there. He'd been a vampire.

But had he really?

Yes, surely, he had. He'd looked different. The Denz I'd known had a beer gut, but the person I'd seen in the museum did not, hinting at a dramatic change. My old partner had attacked me, but Tobias . . .

What had he done?

I watched Tobias approach with hesitation in his eyes, but something else was there too. Not dismissal or annoyance, like when he usually looked at me.

Heat.

That made no sense.

"Meredith," Luca cooed, as if I were a child, from where he stood at my bedside. "You might not be able to talk and that's okay. Your windpipe was damaged. Nod if you're alright. Do you need a painkiller?"

I opened my mouth, determined to speak, to get answers.

"I'm—" I swallowed, pushing past the pain clawing up my throat. "Fine. Where am I?"

"The headquarters' infirmary."

I blinked. I'd been to the healing area once, to ease my hangover from hell. The space didn't look the same.

"You're in a secluded section. A private room," Luca explained, seeming to read the confusion on my face.

He looked terrible. There were dark smudges beneath his eyes, and his usually warm olive skin had taken on a gray pallor. He hadn't looked so bad last time I saw him.

"Only people who are not well-off are permitted back here," he admitted quietly. "Tobias and I were checking up on you."

"What happened?" Again, the image of Denz flashed in my mind, his fangs glinting.

"You and Tobias were on your mission for Skull and Bones when you were attacked by a newblood vampire." He paused.

"Denz," I murmured. "Really, though?"

Luca exhaled. "Yes, really. We weren't sure what you'd remember. You lost a lot of blood."

I remembered the sharp spikes of fear, and the sensation of fangs piercing my neck, but not much beyond that. Still, it was enough to put two and two together. Denz had bitten me, drank my blood.

"How did I survive?"

"Tobias gave you blood to drink."

"What?! Ew."

"Vampire blood has healing capabilities." For the first time, Tobias spoke. "It's not a panacea, but it will keep you alive, even if you're an inch from death."

The way he said it made me think that was exactly where I'd been. And that he hadn't liked it at all.

Pfft, as if he'd care.

"So why do I still feel like hell?" I asked, twisting my neck to face Luca, and cringing at the loud crack of my bones.

"I couldn't give you much," Tobias said stiffly, and I turned back in time to see him look away.

He was lying.

"You could have given her more, though," Luca muttered.

"She's alive. She's here. Isn't that what matters?"

I wanted to press that, sure, I was alive, but I felt like butt. Somehow, I stopped myself. If one thing was obvious, it was that Tobias had saved my life. The vampire who'd threatened me before had now *saved* me.

More than that, though he seemed upset with Luca, toward me he was worried.

I had no idea why, but I wasn't going to look a gift horse in the mouth.

"Thank you," I whispered. "Thank you for saving me."

"I wish I could have done more," he replied, his green eyes straying to Luca pointedly.

"Did Denz die?" I asked, wanting to change the subject.

The air crackled with intensity; there was definitely a subtext here I didn't understand.

"He escaped," Tobias replied, sounding miffed about it.

"Tobias couldn't compel him. Otherwise, that would not have happened."

"Compelling means control, right?" I needed to be sure.

Tobias nodded.

So, all those vampire shows I'd spent hours binge-watching had not been for nothing.

"Are you good at that?"

"Good?"

"Like, better than Denz would be?"

Tobias's eyebrows rose, but understanding fluttered across his features a second later. "Not all vampires can compel. Only those who remain very close to our origins. Apparently, Denz is now among that group."

"Can he compel *you*?"

"No. Actually, had I been better prepared, I think I might have been able to do it to him after all." Tobias looked flustered.

"Then why didn't you?" I asked, unable to hide the exasperation in my tone.

"He *surprised* me. That element of surprise allowed him to get past me, to you. After that, only your life mattered."

His tone dipped at the end, softened, weakening my resolve to keep prying.

I'd been shocked to see Denz too. Shocked and guilty. I'd left my partner in an Egyptian prison, and look what he'd become. Had I pressed to get him out and succeeded, this never would have happened.

"Thank you," I whispered again, as a wave of exhaustion came over me.

As if he could sense how tired I was, Tobias took a step back. "I should let you rest. And I still need to return the femur to Skull and Bones."

"Come back here when you're done," Luca said.

"Of course." Tobias turned and walked toward the door. With each step he took, a strange urge to call him back overtook me. I wanted to touch him.

I shook my head. What was that about? I'd almost died, and now I was going all soft?

The moment we were alone, Luca poured a glass of water and handed it to me. "You did well."

"Doesn't seem like it."

"Injuries are not uncommon on missions. Why do you think we have this wing?"

"Spa days?"

He let out a soft chuckle. "It is soothing in its own way. But seriously, Meredith, you can't judge the outcome based on the number of bruises received in the process."

"Or fang marks in my neck." My fingers strayed upward, only to find gauze.

"Those will heal," Luca assured me. "Tobias's blood will ensure it."

I took a sip of the water. "How long was I out?"

"It's midday, the day after your mission. Not too long."

I exhaled. I hadn't been laid up in this bed for a week.

"Like I said, we're proud of you. Tobias reports you found the femur quickly and stood your ground when you saw Denz. That couldn't have been easy."

"I feel guilty." My teeth dug into my bottom lip. "Can we help him?"

"Perhaps. A lot depends on who his sire is. In vampire society, the person who made you holds great power over you, as much as the governing supernatural body in this world—the Covenant."

"That sucks."

The coven master's lips twitched. "It does. But we will try to find him, to learn what happened and see if we can help. He was dragged into this, as you were."

"He got the short end of the stick."

"Indeed."

We stayed silent for a few seconds before the coven master sighed and took a step back, away from the bed. "I'll send a healer in to check on you, but I'm sure what you need the most is rest."

That was a bit rich coming from him. The dark bags under Luca's eyes hung heavily.

"I could sleep. You should too," I said, trying not to overstep—and failing.

To his credit, Luca only gave me a soft smile. "Soon. Term begins in a few days, and you'll need to be in class. I must ensure your enrollment is in order, and I still have course papers to go over."

I blinked. "Course papers?"

"For my class."

"You teach? I didn't know."

"I'm an adjunct professor." He shrugged. "It's very part-time, but the more the coven can integrate into campus life, the better. People ask fewer questions. Now, as I said, you should rest."

He turned and went to the door, throwing me one last glance as he opened it. "Sleep well, Meredith. You deserve it."

CHAPTER TWENTY-SEVEN

MEREDITH

"You seem tense. Are you sure this is a good idea?" Benedict asked from where he perched on his luxury cat bed.

He sounded nervous for me to leave, which wasn't as surprising as it would have been a week ago. Since I'd returned from the infirmary, the cat had been very concerned about my health and safety.

"Yeah," I replied. "I'll be fine."

"Don't sound too convincing."

My lips tightened. The cat was right. He was anxious that Denz might be coming back, and while that fear lingered within me too, I couldn't dwell on it. I had other things to worry about today.

In no way was I certain that attending Yale was a good idea. The concept of me fitting into the Ivy Leagues was too alien.

Would I hate it? Would the other students hate me? Did the second one matter? Would I survive the classes? The pressure?

"Meredith?" Benedict prompted.

"I don't know," I said simply. "But Luca wants me to go to

classes. Not everyone in the coven is integrated with Yale, but as many people as possible are. It's a good cover for S&S, and personally, something I can't say no to."

Because honestly, who passed up an all-expenses-paid education from Yale? Hell, I'd barely earned my GED online, so Luca sneaking me in here was a miracle in itself. I had to take advantage of this opportunity. It was one of the best I'd ever been given.

I hefted my book-filled backpack—a gift from Shay—over my shoulders. My neck only twinged a little, telling the injury I'd sustained really was mostly healed.

From the outside, it appeared as though nothing had happened. Thanks to Tobias's blood, my skin was smooth, unblemished, and even. Having a neck scar would have sucked and only set me further apart from the students of Yale.

"Very well. See you tonight. Harper's making salmon for dinner, so don't be late. Best of luck." Benedict circled in his bed and lay back down, prepared to snooze for a few more hours.

As both had insanely early classes, my roommates were already gone. So I locked up the house and began the short walk to campus.

On the way, my nerves jumped and danced. No one in the coven had spotted Denz since my attack, but would he have left New Haven? Tobias had told Luca that my old partner wanted me—and not just as a snack. He'd been sent to take me alive.

Probably for my seeker skills.

My blood chilled. The word was out already, and I wasn't sure I felt prepared to protect myself from supernaturals. Not after what happened at the museum.

Focus on today, I scolded myself, turning onto campus and

joining the flow of fresh-faced students rushing to their classes.

In the last week, New Haven had transformed. More students than I ever could have imagined had flooded into town and walked the paths between brick and stone buildings. The leaves teetered on the edge of changing color, and the air had crisped, telling that fall truly was coming.

My pulse quickened a touch as I lifted one hand to grasp the strap of my backpack. Being here, about to attend classes with the brightest young minds in the world, felt so weird. Like I was living someone else's life.

But I wasn't. This and working for the coven—searching for the Pearl, and maybe other dark artifacts after—was my life now. There was no more thieving to make the rich richer. Just studies, trying to pry darkness from the hands of those who would use it for evil, and watching my back for enemies.

For Denz and the Ringmaster and the Ordo Aeternum and the mystery person or group who had the Pearl.

My chest tightened. I still couldn't believe the coven didn't have a lead on who possessed it, but I held faith they'd figure it out.

Eventually, the person who took the Pearl of Hell from me would use it, and when they did, we'd be ready for them.

I stopped walking and pulled out my phone, bringing up the campus map Harper had downloaded for me. The building my first class was located in should be around here somewhere.

Before I could even zoom in on the image, someone slammed into me from the side, sending my phone flying from my hands to the ground. A *crack* sounded as the screen shattered.

"Dammit," I swore.

"Watch where you're going, freak."

Forgetting my phone, my attention snapped toward the voice to find Bentley Sloan smirking at me.

"You're an asshole," I growled.

"Better than an abomination."

So, Skull and Bones had told him about Shadows and Secrets, then. He knew we weren't human but *other*.

"Not so sure about that," I shot back, taking a step and scooping up the phone.

As I suspected, the screen was trashed, but I could still make out the map. Kinda.

Ugh, I did not need this added stress today.

"So, what are you?" Bentley lowered his voice and sauntered closer. "A demon seems about right. Lucifer your daddy?"

"None of your business."

His face darkened. "You know, the brotherhood works with aberrations like you now, but we might not always. My family holds sway." His gaze drifted left and right. "And once I can convince them to obliterate monsters like you, not even your snitch of a protector will be able to save you. You need to watch your back, bitch."

Snitch? What the hell is he talking about?

The question vanished as Bentley's face grew impossibly smugger.

It didn't matter what he said. Bentley was an ass, and he clearly had no idea the powerful forces he was dealing with.

But he would soon.

I closed the distance between us, pressing my finger to his chest. "Listen here, rich boy. I don't care who your family is or what you think they can do. Screw with me, or Shadows and Secrets, and I'll turn you into a frog."

CHAPTER TWENTY-SEVEN

His face faltered. "You can't."

"You bet your ass I can," I lied, and his face paled.

God, this was too easy.

"As easy as this." I snapped my fingers in his face, and he jerked backward, the confidence he'd displayed seconds ago slipping from his face like rainwater.

I logged that terrified expression firmly in my memory and whirled around, leaving Bentley Sloan standing there like an idiot.

* * *

I filed out of my Intro to Biology class as though I was walking on a cloud. The class, while basic, had also been awesome. Eye-opening. Invigorating.

It had been years since I'd been in a traditional school, and though I'd been scared to go back to that kind of structure, I was surprised to find that I'd actually missed formal education. Learning had always been fun, but as I had no memories from my life before the crash that killed my parents, I hadn't been so sure how I felt about school. As it turned out, I liked that too.

Once in the corridor, I pulled out my phone, turning it on and frowning at the broken screen.

During the lecture, I'd been able to forget about Bentley, but the cracked glass staring up at me brought him back to mind. I'd have to ask the coven for a loan to fix it. Or maybe I could use my paycheck? When did I get paid for my mission?

I made a note of my questions in my phone and pulled up the campus map again, squinting through the cracks. My next class was in fifteen minutes and only a few buildings away.

Sweet.

I could take my time, maybe grab a coffee beforehand. It was a basic math course, one of the credits I needed to fulfill my general education requirements. If any subject would put me to sleep, it was probably math.

I went with the flow of students, exiting the building and hanging a hard right. It wasn't long before I was smiling and walking through a green space—'*Old Campus*,' as a sign I passed proclaimed.

This was exactly what I envisioned being a student at Yale would be like. Old buildings of red brick towering around me. The smell of coffee lingering in the air from a passerby's cup, and a statue of some dude, probably a founder or whatnot, sitting in a prominent position in the middle of the green.

Wanting to pause and soak in my first day, I stopped and leaned against the closest brick building, savoring the moment. Not counting my run in with President douchebag, the morning had begun intimidating and alien, but now it was turning out to be magical.

"Dad!" a girl of about twelve burst out from behind the statue and ran at a man I had not spotted before. "Dad! Look what I found!"

"What is it, Mer?"

Mer?

My spine straightened, and I focused on the man, his tall, slender frame, his round glasses, his red hair. His gait was slightly awkward, and his oversized sweater with elbow patches was endearingly old-fashioned.

I cocked my head, trying to place him. The man looked familiar but also strange.

Shifting my gaze, my attention went to the girl. Dark-haired and—

I sucked in a breath.

One blue eye, one green.

The girl . . . was me.

"How?" I pushed off the building and strode across the grass to the center of the green, all thoughts of my next class forgotten.

"The statue, Dad. You rub the foot for luck!"

Dad. That was my father!

My heart rate kicked up as his image clicked into place in my mind. Yes, that was what he'd looked like. How had I forgotten for all these years? How had he been so cloudy, so nondescript in my head, when here he was, so very alive?

"Did you do it, Mer Bear?"

The tween version of myself turned to him, eyes wide. "Duuuuh."

Dad barked out a laugh, and though I had no memories of the man, the sound resonated within me, warm, comforting, familiar. "Well, what for?"

"To get into Yale! And be a professor like you!"

Professor? My father was a professor here?

"Best to aim higher, for your mother's position."

I picked up my pace, not wanting to miss a word.

Did they see me?

Quickly, I glanced around. No one was watching me, so I waved.

The two figures didn't turn toward me.

So I wasn't here. That meant this probably wasn't real.

I recalled then that Luca had told me I'd probably retrieve lost memories of my life.

My hand flew to cover my heart. This was a memory from my past! For some reason, my father and I had come here. Did we live in New Haven? It didn't feel familiar.

"I'm going to teach archeology," the younger version of me said proudly. "Be like Indiana Jones."

"Hopefully not *totally* like him." Dad huffed. "He doesn't treat the women in his life well."

"Not that part," little me assured him, and in the present, my heart swelled at my father's thoughtfulness.

I was standing right next to them now, waiting for the next word, hoping to get a tiny tidbit of my past back. As I inhaled, I caught a whiff of cedar. Was that my dad's scent? It warmed me to the core, making me think it must be.

"We should get to my office, Mer Bear," Dad said. "We're meeting your mother for lunch."

"Can we go to the sandwich shop?"

"Of course. I—"

"Rooms! Major news, Rooms!"

I gasped as the scene I'd been watching dissolved. Where a second ago, there'd been a father and a little girl, nothing remained.

"No! *No!* Come back!" I spun on my heel, taking in the green in one wild circle.

A few people stopped at my shout, but most were too involved with their phones or conversation partners to notice. But even if every student at Yale had stopped to stare, I wouldn't have cared.

For the first time in years, I'd seen my father, remembered him. We'd been together. Happy. A family.

"N-n-no!" A choked sob wrenched out of me as I gazed upon the spot where he'd disappeared.

"Rooms?" A soft voice came from behind me. Shay's. "What's wrong? Did I scare you?"

"She saw something," Harper's voice rang out, confident and clear. "What was it, Meredith?"

"My father," I whispered, dragging my gaze to my room-mates. "A memory. I finally have a memory of my past."

"Oooh," Shay breathed. "Congratulations!" Then she cringed. "I interrupted it, didn't I?"

Slowly, I nodded, and she bit her lip.

"I'm so sorry, Mer. Had I known, I wouldn't have interrupted."

"You couldn't have," I said softly.

More than anything, I wanted to rewind the clock and continue watching my father and me. Observe the past and what was probably a mundane day to us. But to me, it was everything.

"It wasn't real," I murmured. "Just in my head—and out here, like a movie. I don't get it. If it's a memory, why did it look like that?"

The girls stayed silent for a moment, then Harper spoke up.

"I don't understand it either. Neither of us know much about memories resurfacing. I'm sure there's something about it in the Beinecke, though."

"The what?"

"It's a library," Harper said. "It has rare books. Even a supernatural section—though no one can find or see it but us, of course."

"I want to go to it," I said quickly. "Can we?"

Now that my memories might be surfacing, I had hope. If there was a chance I could speed this process up, get moments of my old life and my parents back, I'd search the whole damn library. I'd read every book, every word, if only for another moment like what I'd witnessed.

"You'll need an escort to get in, since you're not registered in the supernatural section yet." Harper cut a glance at Shay.

"We don't have clearance to get you in. Luca, Tobias, or Hans would, though."

"Let's go get them!"

"Actually . . ." Shay stepped forward. "We need to go to the coven headquarters anyway. Something huge might have just happened."

Frustration tinged with anger rose inside me. Right now, with my father's voice so fresh in my ears, nothing was more important to me than getting my memories back.

"I want to go to the library," I said firmly. "I'm going to find Luca and demand he take me."

Harper came closer. "We understand. And you will. But Shay is right, this is super important. And I don't think Luca will have time to take you to the library. Look."

She held out her phone, and I glowered at the pair of them.

"Meredith, this is important. Read it." Harper nodded downward.

My jaw clenched, but something in the wolf's eyes made me do as she said.

My gaze went to the screen, scanned the page. Then my eyebrows pulled together. "I don't get it. What does this have to do with anything?"

"We think everything," Harper said, her tone ominous.

CHAPTER TWENTY-EIGHT

TOBIAS

The backdoor of the blood bank swung open, and the hedge witch poked her head out, wild curls flying in the wind.

"It's you this time? Thought Lisha would stop by." The look on her face told me she didn't think it, she *wished* for Lisha to visit.

Lisha had always been charming, and it had earned her an admirer.

"Nice to see you too, Mona," I replied wryly. "I might be chopped liver, but I'm also the only vampire in town."

"But the coven wasn't scheduled to pick up for another week, right?" She ignored my jest and opened the door wider, inviting me in despite her obvious confusion.

"We had an incident," I gritted out.

Meredith had required a transfusion, but in truth, most of the blood the coven stored for vampires had gone down my own throat. It was the only way I could be around Meredith and suppress the urge to assert my dominance over her.

Mona arched a sandy blonde eyebrow. "I see. Well, lucky for you, I'm prepared well in advance. How many bags?"

"Fifty."

She scoffed. "That's *a lot* more than normal."

"We're about to embark on a dangerous series of missions."

Mona's lips pressed together, and she turned on her heel, knowing better than to pry. Coven members didn't answer outsiders' questions about what went on in Shadows and Secrets. "This way."

I trailed the witch down the corridor, and soon enough, a chill set in. After passing three doors, she stopped before a metal one.

The cold would have tipped anyone off that this room was where they stored the blood, but my senses detected even more nuances. Inches of metal provided a strong barrier, and yet I could smell the metallic tang of the bags' contents, sitting on the other side.

The moment she opened the door, I was nearly bowled over by several other aromas, some enticing, a few revolting—as it always was with human blood. Some people simply did not treat their bodies well, or their blood grew bitter as they held their demons and sins inside.

An urge to fall to my knees and repent for the world—a notion instilled in me by my devout biological mother—crept in. No matter how many years passed, that impulse remained. I pushed it aside, as I did whenever my past tried to take hold.

"Mind if I take a look at what you've reserved for us?" I asked the witch.

"If you didn't, I'd be worried something was wrong with you. Lisha usually spends an hour sniffing the bags before carrying them out. It's all over there." She pointed to the right, at a long, metal table weighed down with bagged blood.

My lips curled up. "She's pickier than I am, but there are some varieties I simply cannot stomach."

"Makes sense. Hey, I have paperwork to do, and I'd rather not go up front. My co-worker microwaved kimchee before she left, and it smells horrendous up there. You won't be bothered if I stay in here and put on the news, will you?"

My nose wrinkled at the thought of nuked kimchee. "Not at all."

"Sweet." Mona pulled a stool over to a table cluttered with paperwork, and turned on a small, ancient television. "If you have any questions, I'll be here."

I nodded and turned to the supplies the coven required.

As it was more common for my kind to drink the blood than for it to be used in our tomb's infirmary, the vampires of Shadows and Secrets took turns coming to the blood bank and picking up our stock. Mona had been our source for three years, and as such, usually picked donors well.

After a short ten minutes, it became clear that, once again, Mona had done a splendid job. Of those on the table, I only pulled out five bags to swap. They were too sour-smelling, which wouldn't matter if the blood was only needed to heal injuries, but no vampire would want to drink something so tangy.

"I'd like to replace these," I held up the bags and turned back to the witch.

"Sure thing. I took the liberty of setting aside some more just in case that happened. You can set those here." She tapped a spot next to her. "And the replacements are on the next table over." Mona pointed, unable to tear her gaze from the screen as she shook her head.

"What's going on?" I walked over to see for myself, the blood still in hand.

"Some crazy break-in. Apparently, there's this vault in Switzerland that hasn't been opened for decades, but someone broke into it." She turned to look at me, brown eyes wide. "I guess someone owns it, but they never come to check on it. They make the payments and that's it."

I tilted my head. "What was stolen?"

"One thing. A gemstone."

My heart gave a single, hard thump. "How do they know?"

"There's a ledger of the contents in another safe owned by the same person—which, if you ask me, is even weirder. Anyway, once the break-in was discovered, the bankers checked what was left against the ledger."

"Did it say what kind of stone?"

"Opal." She shrugged as icicles of dread climbed down my spine. "The newscaster claims there were diamonds in there the size of golf balls! Why wouldn't they take those? Makes no sense."

Not to Mona, it wouldn't, but to me, a single opal made all the sense in the world.

I swallowed thickly as I set down the bagged blood. This was huge. I needed to return to S&S's hall.

"These five are all yours. I'll find five more and load up." I kept my tone level, when all I wanted to do was bolt from the blood bank and call Luca.

Had he seen the news? Probably not, if he was at the office —which was where he said he'd be—awaiting the shipment of blood. It was always a team effort to get the bags into coven headquarters without regular people noticing.

I turned back to the table Mona had noted earlier, determined to get this over with.

"Need any help carrying stuff out?" she asked.

"I have it handled."

The witch, helpful though she was, would only slow me down, and if my suspicions were valid, time had become much more precious.

Not bothering to resort to human-appropriate speeds, I sprinted back and forth from the van to the blood bank's supply room. Mona watched me, her eyes widening each time I ran in for another armful.

On the seventh and final trip, she shook her head. "If only you guys could compete in the Olympics! That would be something to see."

"Humans would never win," I replied with a smile, though inside, my anxiety continued to swell. "Many thanks. We'll return on the regularly scheduled day next time."

Hopefully. As long as I could get myself under control.

"If you need more sooner, hit me up," Mona said, clearly not believing a thing I said.

Though she was a hedge witch, I believed she might have a special talent for teasing the truth from words.

"Good day." I zipped out the door and down the hallway.

Reaching the van, I took great care in securing the bags. I might be in a rush, but the blood was a safety net the coven required. Once I was satisfied everything was in place, I shut the door and hopped into the front seat.

I'd no sooner started the van when my phone rang. Sliding my hand into my jacket pocket, hope rose within me that it was Luca. That he would already have answers.

Regarding technology, the coven master was old-school, even more so than me, but he did have a cell phone—even if he kept it turned off and tucked away in his desk most of the time. Considering his position, it was not an ideal quirk to have, which everyone had told him at least a dozen times.

However, he always pressed back that he knew when we needed help and always answered, which was true too.

But one glance at the screen, and my hopes plummeted. It wasn't Luca, but my maker; I suspected she wasn't going to have good news.

"Giselle." I put her on speakerphone and placed the cell in a holder.

"Did you see the news? The theft?" she replied, her tone low.

Was she with the rest of the OA, hiding but desperate to get a message to me?

"I did." I began to drive. No matter what she said, I needed to get to headquarters fast. "Was it you?"

"No. I was hoping it was you."

I paused, my mouth going dry. "Unfortunately not. But it must be the Opal. That's what you're thinking too, right?"

"It is." She exhaled a lengthy breath. "The timing is too coincidental."

"I agree." My shoulder muscles tensed. "I don't suppose you know if the same symbol you told me was left in Cairo was found in the vault?"

"I don't. We're in Edinburgh, and no one will be there to check until they've figured out a plan. But the bank that was robbed has a reputation of never being penetrated, Tobias. It's the most secure place on Earth."

I didn't know the bank's name; either I'd missed it in the newscast, or they hadn't mentioned it.

"What's it called?" I asked, suspicion rising.

"Take a guess."

I swore. "*Le Bastion*."

"Correct."

Le Bastion had been a bank for thousands of years. Many

prominent supernaturals kept their riches there—and *only* there. It was guarded by magic as well as modern technology. Whoever took the gemstone had done their homework.

"Has Raphael contacted you about this?" I asked my sire. My brother held a vault in *Le Bastion*. This news would, rightfully, worry him.

The sound of footsteps on the other end of the phone told me that someone was walking by. When I could no longer hear them, Giselle spoke again. "I'm not sure. I do not wish to involve him, not with the Ordo Aeternum watching me so closely. Plus, I believe he's at *Castel Romono* and you know he has no phone in that blasted castle of his." She paused. "Actually, you should go see your brother, Tobias. Not only for this . . . I worry for him. Fear he's been alone far too long."

I turned the van onto a main road, nodding. "I will."

Eventually. Once this is settled.

"There's something else regarding our family I need to ask you, Giselle."

"If I can answer, I will."

Meaning if the vampire I asked about was ranked above her and she was responsible for his or her secrets, she would hold her tongue. But silence would still be information. There weren't many Laurents who demanded my maker's allegiance.

"I recently was involved with a newblood who resisted my compulsion—"

"Pardon?" Her pitch rose. "How? That would mean—"

"A Laurent of my rank or higher made him. I'm not asking you who made the vampire, only if you've heard of any kin in this world who recently expanded our bloodline?"

There, that was a safe question. Nothing that would implicate my maker.

"I-I haven't. I'm sorry to not be of help, Tobias."

An exhale parted my lips. "I'll figure it out."

I turned the van onto the coven's street and parked on the side of the road. At times like these, I wished we had a garage, but the hall S&S had been founded in was too antiquated.

"It looks like we both have mysteries to solve," I mused.

"It does," my maker agreed. "I'll let you know if I hear anything of the Blood in this world. And the stolen item."

"As will I." I turned off the van, feeling very near helpless. "But for now, I must go."

"*Adieu*, Tobias."

"Goodbye, Giselle."

We hung up, and I allowed only a moment of shock to rumble through me before dialing Hans. He said he'd come help me unload, making transport of the blood into headquarters fast and covert.

Once we had finished the task and were away from prying ears, the coven would have to discuss what these new developments meant.

CHAPTER TWENTY-NINE

MEREDITH

MY LEGS BURNED AS I SPRINTED BEHIND THE WOLF AND NEPHILIM, wishing I could talk and run at the same time. Shay and Harper had filled me in on the basics of what had them so worried, but I still had a million questions swirling in my head.

The Opal was probably a sacred stone, but what did it do? Did it have an ominous name like the Pearl of Hell? How did someone find it now, when it had been hidden for so long? How would the two stones react if they were together? Would a reaction even occur, or did all seven stones have to be in play for their combined effects to be sensed?

We rounded the final corner that would put us on the coven's street, and I abruptly slowed my pace. On the sidewalk, Tobias, Hans, Silas the fae, and Josiah the necromancer were running to and from a white van with . . .

"Uh, is that blood?"

"We keep it on hand for the vamps," Shay said, not breaking step, though she slowed as well. "And injuries."

Of course. I'd been the recipient of donated blood.

At the thought of my time in the infirmary, my neck twinged; a reminder that, though I felt better, I might not be 100% quite yet.

"But won't people see?"

"Hans probably cast an illusion spell over the area," Harper said. "He's good at those, so passerbys without magic won't see what's happening. The only downside is illusions are short-lived. But it helps that Tobias parked so close to the coven tomb."

"Right," I murmured, shocked an illusion could be so thorough.

"You guys need help?" Shay asked when we were closer.

"This is the last bag," the silver-haired Silas said, grabbing a blood pouch and shutting both doors to the back of the van. "But Luca called a meeting in the Shadow Room. I assume you heard the news?"

Shadow Room? Chills washed through me.

I didn't even know where it was in the tomb, and that only made it clearer I needed to spend more time there and better familiarize myself with the society I'd thrown my lot in with.

"We did," Harper replied. "I need details."

Our foursome darted down the sidewalk and into the alley that hid the entrance to the coven. Thankfully, Hans was already waiting at the door, so no one had to go through a magical ritual to enter.

"Stone, Harper . . . Shay." The wizard nodded at each of us in turn, his gaze lingering on the nephilim for a beat longer than normal. "You aren't missing classes, are you?"

"This is more important than a class, Hans." Shay rolled her eyes. "And it's the first day. We won't do anything interesting."

I agreed, though Harper didn't look so convinced. She'd

come to headquarters out of duty, but I suspected she'd be freaking out about missing her class later.

"Just asking. Come on."

We trailed Hans down the hall and through the atrium. Once we reached the other end of it, Silas split off.

"Have to take this to the freezer. Tobias is doing inventory. We'll be right there."

"Got it. We'll wait to start."

Hans continued on until he reached a door about halfway down a hall I hadn't explored. When he opened it, we found forty people sitting around tables arranged end to end to form a rectangle. As I scanned the room, Sara, the strawberry blonde necromancer I'd met at the Gryphon threw me a shy wave. I returned the gesture.

Opposite the door, Luca was leaning down the table to speak with Gunner. When he sat upright and caught sight of us, the mage's dark eyes widened, and he waved in our direction.

Given that there were only three empty seats around the coven master, and four of us, I assumed he wanted Hans, and began to follow Shay to a trio of empty chairs close to the door.

"Wait, Meredith." Hans turned, his blue eyes piercing me. "He'll want to talk to you."

"Why?"

"You're our seeker, and something we might want is lost. Come on."

'*Our seeker.*' My skin tingled.

It was still strange for me to belong somewhere *positive*. I'd basically been the Ringmaster's property, but here, I was a coven member, an equal. The coven's seeker.

With each passing day, it became more and more clear to

me that I would stay. These people were my friends. Maybe one day, I could call them family.

The memory of my father rose in my mind, making my heart clench. Until today, I'd almost totally forgotten how it felt to have a family. Now that I remembered, I didn't want to go on living without that feeling.

No more running. No more hiding.

A place to belong, I thought, passing coven members who spoke in anxious voices about what the stolen opal could mean.

"Here, Hans." Luca pulled out the chair to his right.

I could tell he wasn't feeling well again. His dark brown eyes looked dull, his skin clammy.

On the other side of the coven master, Gunner waved, still smiling despite the seriousness of the situation.

"Meredith, glad you could make it." Luca's dark brown eyes caught on me, settling there for a moment. The warmth the man embodied rushed over me. "Please sit next to Hans."

"Oh, thanks," I said, suddenly uncomfortable.

No one was watching me, as the news of the Opal was all-encompassing, but it still made me feel weird to be given a place of honor, so close to the coven master.

"We're waiting for Tobias and Silas, right?" Hans asked. "Not everyone in the coven?"

"Yes. The rest are either out of town or, like our healers, unavailable," Luca replied. "Two members returned from a mission with grave injuries. Others will catch them up later."

The next second, the door to the Shadow Room opened again, and the vampire and fae darted in. Silas took the first available seat, but Tobias swung around the formation of tables, toward us.

He looked so self-assured, so full of purpose. The vampire knew his place here.

At that very instant, his emerald gaze snapped to me, and I swear his eyes burned into mine so hot it took my breath away. Inside my boots, my toes curled.

What the hell?

There was no denying Tobias was attractive—scorching hot, even. I also couldn't deny I felt drawn to him, even though he tended to annoy the crap out of me most of the time. But that particular physical effect had never happened before.

I ripped my eyes from his, locking them on the scarred wood of the table.

Although I was no longer watching the vampire, I sensed when he walked by me, passed Hans and Luca, heard when he pulled his chair back and settled into it.

Then a pair of hands clapped, and Luca's voice boomed out, "It's time to begin."

I exhaled, ready to be distracted by something other than Tobias. Dragging my gaze from the table, I focused on the mage leaning forward with his elbows on the table.

Quiet fell, and others mimicked the coven master's posture. While the atmosphere had been tense before, now the pressure mounted to uncomfortable heights. We were about to get answers.

"Everyone here has heard of the bank heist in Switzerland?" Luca asked. "The stolen gem?"

All around the table, heads nodded.

"An opal." He scanned the room. "I'm assuming I'm not the only one who thinks this might be another sacred stone. Specifically, the Opal of Heaven."

A shiver ran down my spine. Yup, that was another ominous name.

"It almost certainly is," Tobias confirmed. "I have information that it wasn't any ordinary bank that was looted. It was *Le Bastion.*"

A few people looked confused, but many more sucked in a gasp. Whatever *Le Bastion* was, it was major.

"The most secure bank ever to exist has been broken into, and another sacred stone taken." Luca leaned back and let out a soft breath, the effort of sitting upright apparently too much for him. "The question is, does anyone have any idea who could have coordinated such a heist?"

"It's not Ordo Aeternum," Tobias said. "They were, of course, my first thought, but I have knowledge it can't be them."

Luca nodded. Whatever Tobias knew, he had already heard and agreed with. "Any other ideas?"

Again, silence shrouded the room.

Luca cut Tobias another glance, and the vampire inclined his head, as if giving permission for something.

"Apparently, this symbol was found in the Egyptian tomb in which Meredith found the Pearl of Hell." The mage waved a hand, and flames flew up creating a symbol.

It was an upside-down triangle, its ends extending past the tip and curling outward at the bottom where it intersected with a V. Inside the inverted triangle, an X had been drawn from the top two corners of the triangle, and its ends also strayed outside the confines of the three-pointed shape.

My eyebrows pinched together. I didn't recognize the intricate shape at all.

"That's the Sigil of Lucifer," Josiah, the necromancer, noted.

"It is. Does anyone know of an underground organization using this? One that perhaps might be interested in the seven *lapis caelesti*?" Luca spoke to everyone, but when his eyes landed on Hans, they stuck.

The wizard stiffened.

There was something in the exchange, something I didn't understand, but judging by how Hans swallowed and shifted in his seat, he was uncomfortable.

Luca sighed. "I'd hoped someone would have information, but I see now that whatever individual or group is responsible has hidden their presence well."

"We need to suss them out," Silas said, his strange silver eyes blazing.

"And determine if they really were responsible for the theft at *Le Bastion*," Tobias added. "If they were, they would have likely marked the area again. Claimed it."

"Precisely. We—" A sharp gasp cut through Luca's words, and the mage's hands flew to his throat.

I twisted in time to see the moment his veins darkened to black, to see the beads of sweat appear on his skin.

He stood, his brown eyes widening, his expression growing wild. Terrified.

Blood thrummed in my veins as my pulse began to race. What was happening?

Gunner rose from his seat. "What's happening, man?"

"Luca?" Tobias also leapt to his feet.

His attention raked over the mage and suddenly, he dipped to pull a blade from his boot. When he stood tall again, he drew the weapon across Luca's upper arm.

The mage's eyes shuttered closed, and his knees buckled. Quick as a flash, Gunner darted forward to catch him before he hit the floor.

A loud moan rang from Luca's lips, but his body looked limp, his face grayer than before.

"What's happening?" I whispered, my heart ticking irregularly in my chest, making my breath thin and weak.

Tobias's attention shifted to me, and goosebumps erupted along my arms. When our eyes locked, it was like the rest of the world faded away.

Or at least, it was like that for me. Tobias appeared able to break our connection easily.

He refocused on the dagger, swiping a bit of blood from the tip with a finger and touching it to his tongue.

He dropped the dagger. "No." Fear laced the vampire's voice.

"What is it?" Gunner asked. "He's shaking."

"Shade poison. His blood's full of it," Tobias replied.

"What?! How could he not realize?" Hans shouted. "Their poison is supposed to be beyond painful."

"Bet your ass he did know," Gunner said, crossing his arms over his barrel chest. "His skin reeks of herbs."

"Yes," Tobias agreed. "I've smelled them too. And heard him ask the healers for a draught while Stone was in the infirmary. I thought they might be to sleep, but now I believe Luca has been taking potions to heal. You two remember what he looked like before."

Both the wolf and the wizard nodded gravely.

An image of Luca on the couch, sweating and weak, popped into my mind. He'd looked horrible then, but gotten better for a while.

"Likely the elixirs were simply getting him through the day. Bloody proud mage." Tobias echoed my line of thinking as he focused on the coven master, trying to decode his choices. "But it seems they aren't working anymore."

He twisted, and a lock of dark brown hair fell into his eye, making my breath hitch in the weirdest way. "Gunner, get him to the infirmary. We'll be right behind."

The wolf didn't hesitate. He shifted Luca in his arms as if the mage weighed nothing. Once the coven master was secure, Gunner bolted from the room.

The rest of those in the Shadow Room began to crowd around us, questions lining their faces, but Tobias held up his hands.

"We only know that Luca has shade poisoning. Now we have to figure out what to do about it. Everyone, steer clear of the infirmary. I'll lead this. Hans?"

"With you. Meredith, you come too."

"I don't know anything about shades." Other than how they stank to high heaven and one had tried to bite my ear off.

Not that any of that would help the coven master.

My stomach plummeted. Luca was ill, and it was partly my fault. After all, the shade had been coming for *me*.

Hans's blue eyes pierced mine. "Maybe not, but I have a feeling we might need you anyway."

CHAPTER THIRTY

TOBIAS

By the time our trio reached the infirmary, the healers were already hard at work. Gunner stood off to the side, uncharacteristically silent as he watched.

Stepping over the threshold into the sterile room reeking of antiseptic and disease made me want to punch a wall. The memories of Meredith in here were too fresh, too raw. Too unwelcome for a creature like me, who could never live with developing strong feelings for a mortal.

Not again. Not after what happened last time.

"How is he?" Hans approached the mage, who lay still in a bed in the main room.

He was the only occupant, though two other coven members were under the healers' care. Their injuries were so dire, they required more privacy, as Meredith had needed. That the healers hadn't placed Luca in a private chamber meant they were either in denial or hopeful.

I wished for the latter, but wasn't holding my breath.

"Unconscious," the lead healer, Daphne, said, blue eyes flashing up at us. She rose, and her long blonde ponytail slithered over her shoulder. She jerked her head, tossing it back in annoyance. "Tobias, Gunner said you tasted shade poison?"

"It's flowing strong within him."

The healer nodded. "When he came in after the attack, we gave him a remedy for shade venom. He healed, or he appeared to, but this . . ." She gestured down to the mage, his chest fluttering softly as he strained for breath. "This is not normal. The poison seems to be strengthening over time."

"We believe the attack was targeted at someone else. To kill them." I refrained from cutting a glance to Meredith, though I felt the witch stiffen at my side.

"But we've dealt with shade poison before," the healer affirmed. "We know how to rid the body of such venom. How Luca is worsening makes no sense."

The room stilled. This was not good. Our healers were among the best in the world. Of course, magic had many mysteries, but it was rare the coven's healers did not know what to do.

Hans stepped forward. "Will more elixir fix him?"

Daphne's eyes darted to the coven master and then back to the wizard. "I'm not sure. He's declining rapidly, and we'd already given him quite a strong dose."

"The strongest possible?"

"Not yet. That's just as dangerous. As always, the poison is in the dose."

"He's already in danger," Gunner argued. "Give him the heaviest dose possible. Luca is strong, he can take it."

Daphne sighed. "Maybe, but there's no way to test that."

"And why not?" My tone was tight with frustration.

"I'm nearly out of ingredients. Luca has been drinking so much elixir . . . And I haven't had time to contact our supplier.

Lucimisia, the herb I need, is rare. Only grown in one spot in this realm."

This realm.

I swallowed. That indicated it was grown elsewhere.

"It's native to Isila?" I asked.

Perhaps I could procure some quickly. I might be working against the Laurent king, but he didn't know that. As long as the herb grew in another kingdom of Isila, I could enter and leave without my bloodline ever knowing.

Theoretically, anyway.

"If only," Daphne replied. "It's a plant native to Hell, and has been transplanted here but only in one place. The environment is quite specific, requiring volcanic gas and extreme heat."

"Plants can grow in *Hell*?" Meredith piped up. She'd been so silent, I'd almost forgotten she was there. "How does it grow? What about the lava? Isn't there lava there?"

"It's rare, but yes a few plants grow in Hell," Daphne answered, her tone softer. "As for the lava, I can't speak to that. Never been there, thank the Goddess."

"Can we get it?" I pressed, wanting to get the conversation back on track.

"I'll contact our supplier. Someone will have to go get the lucimisia, though, because I can't leave Luca. However, the field's location is well hidden, so it won't be easy."

"Sounds like a job for a seeker," Hans muttered. "And me."

For a moment, anger rose inside me, but I beat it down. I might not like the thought of Hans and Meredith together, but he was right. If Meredith could help, she had to go. And she needed backup. We couldn't allow the mission to take too much time and risk Luca's life.

"Let me call the supplier," Daphne said. "I'll be right back."

The healer murmured a word of instruction to her apprentice, who'd been listening to our exchange silently, and left the room with the younger witch.

The moment the four of us were alone, our gazes strayed to our coven master.

He must have been in an extraordinary amount of pain. Why hadn't he said anything?

Before anyone could go to Luca's bedside, or even utter a word, the door to the infirmary burst open.

"How is he?" Shay blurted, rushing inside along with Harper.

My lips compressed. "You shouldn't be here."

"Whatever, Tobias. You may be Luca's right hand, and others might be too scared to cross you, but you aren't in charge."

"Hey now," Gunner said, tone light to diffuse the nephilim's obvious anger. "What are Hans and I, chopped liver?"

Harper rolled her eyes. "You guys are all leaders, but we don't care. What's happening?" She looked to Meredith, who drew in a shaky breath.

I stepped in front of the witch, shielding her, though I wasn't sure why when there was no threat present. The motion did not go unnoticed by Harper. She arched a ginger eyebrow, but said nothing.

"Shade poisoning," I answered. "We need more of a certain herb, but it is not close by. The healers are calling now. We—"

Daphne stormed into the room. "We have a problem!"

Everyone whirled to face her, and I stiffened. Her face was hard, anxious, filled with fear.

"What's up, Daph?" Gunner prompted. "You alright?"

"Not at all. Luca won't be either." Her hands shook as she spoke. "Our supplier's crops were set to flame the other day."

"*What?*" Hans growled, his blue eyes darting to me as he worked through what this meant.

Whoever had sent the shade for Meredith, and injured Luca, knew they'd done harm. How, I wasn't sure, but it was the only thing that made sense. Now, they wanted to weaken our coven, deprive us of the only source of remedy we had.

Was there a traitor in the coven? Someone that had informed the mystery enemy of Luca's decline? Or had the attacker simply hedged their bets? My gaze locked with Hans's, and I suspected he was thinking along the same lines.

"It's gone. All of it." Tears filled Daphne's eyes, and silence fell over the group, spreading and creeping into the corners of the infirmary until it choked the room.

"Then it looks like we need to go with plan B," Hans broke the quiet. There was a strain to his voice, and I alone understood why.

I turned to the wizard. "You can get there?"

"There's a way." He lifted his chin as if daring me to ask. Daring me to out him.

I had too much dangerous knowledge as it was. There was no way I'd ask where an entrance to Hell was located.

And despite how we often butted heads, I wouldn't out the wizard either. I owed him.

"Whatcha guys talkin' about?" Gunner came closer, as did the ladies. All wore confused expressions, which was completely reasonable.

To them, Hans was merely a wizard, but that was not the truth. Once, the man had saved me. Once, he'd been a partner who opened his veins so that I might survive a mission. Once, he revealed a dangerous, dark secret he kept hidden from the world.

Hans wasn't just a wizard, and if we were to save our coven master, he was the best person in the coven to procure lucimisia.

"I have certain attributes that will allow me to journey to Hell," he said finally.

All around, eyes narrowed as the others considered what those attributes might be.

"But I can't go alone," he continued. "I have a general idea as to where this lucimisia herb is, but not a precise location. I'll need help with that. I hate to say this, but I need Meredith to go too."

My fists clenched as my blood began to boil. No. She wasn't going to Hell. I wouldn't allow it. I might be conflicted about the witch, but I knew one thing: if she left this world, I would inch closer to insanity.

"She can't go."

No sooner were the words out of my mouth than Meredith stepped forward.

"One, you're not the boss of me. Two, I don't want to go, but if it means saving Luca's life, I will." She sought Daphne's gaze. "And that is what it means, isn't it?"

"I'm afraid so," the healer replied.

"Then I'll go."

"No!" Shay's tone was strangled. "Mer! It's so dangerous."

"Obviously," Harper muttered. "It's *Hell*. And what makes you think you can get through, Hans?"

He shook his head, not about to divulge his secret. "I just know I can. I know a way. And I—"

"Then I'll go too," Shay cut him off, tears brimming in her clear blue eyes. "Mer is our roomie, our friend! You two can't go alone!"

"Don't be ridiculous!" Harper whirled on the nephilim. "You're part *angel*! The demons will sense you right away, and you'll endanger anyone you're with."

"But I—"

Meredith closed the distance between her and the nephilim. "Hans and I will go. Doesn't the coven have other stuff to focus on? Like researching that vault?"

My eyes widened. In all the commotion, the theft of the Opal of Heaven had been forgotten, but Meredith was right. We needed to get to the vault in *Le Bastion*, needed to learn who it belonged to and if they had information on the Opal. If they might have a hunch who took it.

"And we require the lucimisia quickly. Within the week, two at the most. Luca won't last longer than that," Daphne said before adding. "If you can get a lot, bunches with the roots attached that would be best. Then our supplier has a chance of regrowing and no one will have to do this again."

"That settles it, then," Hans said. "We'll leave tonight. Meredith will need a bundle of lucimisia to help her seek. Can you spare it, Daphne? Some invisibility potion too."

"I keep the latter on hand, but remember it has limits." The healer exhaled a worried breath. "I'll keep just enough lucimisia to make Luca another batch of elixir, which means you two really must hurry."

"What about the Pearl, though?" Harper pressed. "Meredith has to find that too."

"Yeah, but until signs of madness start popping up, I'm kinda useless," Meredith pointed out. "I can't search the whole globe. I need a place to start, a general vicinity at the very least. Luca was waiting for that before sending me."

"Plus, Luca's gotta be well to hide the Pearl when we get it," Gunner said. "We need the mage to access his magic safe, or whatever he calls it. He's the only one in the coven who can."

They were all right. Though Luca claimed one other person in the world could get into his safe, a protection should he perish, no one held the knowledge of who that person was. Now that Luca was so ill, this seemed a gross oversight. My chest tightened at all the uncertainty. I couldn't help but think that Luca would know exactly how to handle this.

"I'm going with Hans," Meredith reiterated.

We were at an impasse, and the best way to move forward was to let go of this desire to both be around Meredith and distance myself from her. I needed to stay busy, to have a quest of my own.

"I'll work on getting into *Le Bastion*," I said suddenly.

Gunner shook his head. "I won't be able to sit here and wait. Do you think you'd have need for a wolf, Hans?"

Conflict rippled across the wizard's face. He was thinking of denying the alphablood.

"He's an excellent fighter," I murmured. "Taking too many would be a folly, but you'll probably need help fighting off creatures of the underworld. Invisibility potion only lasts so long, Novak."

Hans glared daggers at me, but eventually let out a huff. "Gunner, you can come."

"Well, then, I'm coming with you, Tobias," Shay said.

I wanted to refuse her, wanted to say this was a job best suited to working alone, but after I'd forced Gunner on Hans, it would look hypocritical. Plus, the truth was I didn't know that working alone would be beneficial. No one had ever broken into *Le Bastion,* not until today. I might require nephilim magic.

"Very well," I said. "We'll leave tonight too."

CHAPTER THIRTY-ONE

HANS

The door slammed behind me, and my nose wrinkled. The air in my home was stale. Sour. The trash needed taking out.

When had I last been home? When I'd retrieved Meredith?

I shook my head. I'd been spending too much time at headquarters again. That would come as no surprise to anyone, least of all me.

I always preferred Shadows and Secrets' tomb, even sleeping on a stiff cot in the basement, to my own home. This put-together dwelling, so modern and beautiful it would make my father faint, was one place where I couldn't escape my past. Nor what I'd left behind.

Weak. I was so weak. I couldn't face coming home because it reminded me of a duty I'd long given up on fulfilling?

Briefly, I closed my eyes, and an image of the shack I'd grown up in appeared on the back of my eyelids, instantly adding to my torment.

"*Argh!*" My eyes flew open, and I marched into the kitchen, flinging open the fridge.

"Thank the Goddess." I reached for the beer that had appeared inside.

The fridge that provided whatever a person wanted had proven well worth the time Luca and I had put into charming it. Especially now, when all I wanted to do was drink myself into oblivion and forget.

Popping the cap, I turned and hurled the metal disc in the general direction of the trash, not even caring when it pinged off the edge and rolled across the floor to rattle to a stop under the dining table I'd only used twice.

I stomped into the living area and slumped onto the couch, my gaze straying to the drawer in the coffee table I kept locked, hidden, like so much of myself.

Look at me, it seemed to call. *It's been so long.*

My fingers itched to touch the contents of the drawer. Within seconds, I recognized refusing the call was futile.

"This won't go well," I muttered, and pulled the key from its secret compartment on the underside of the coffee table.

The metal was covered in dust, which I wiped on my pant leg before inserting the key into the drawer's locking mechanism. With a twist and a gentle tug, I revealed the larger compartment, inch by inch.

A book of photographs stared back at me, its red cover faded. The smell of my father's fresh-baked *cozonac*, a treat he made more often than our neighbors, had long since disappeared from the material binding the pictures. And yet, I swore I could smell the festive bread from my homeland, mixed with the scent of old, yellowed paper.

I inhaled, hoping to taste the sweet bread too. Failing, I frowned. That's the way it was with my past; the good parts were always an inch out of reach.

But the bad haunted me.

Now that I was going back to Romania, going home, there would be no avoiding my family. My mistakes. Where I came from or what I was.

So why try?

I opened the book and flipped to the middle, only to feel like I'd been punched in the gut.

Snow-capped mountains rose, a picturesque backdrop to an image of a little blonde girl. She smiled at the camera, her curls falling in perfect ringlets, her teeth straight and gleaming.

Her eyes, black as night.

My mouth went dry, and I swallowed another glug of beer, trying to force down the pain rising inside me.

It wouldn't be long after we stepped foot in my secluded village that Meredith and Gunner would learn my secret. My shame. There was no way I could hide it, not when the villagers knew. Tobias would no longer be the only one clued into the darkness inside of me. The very part of me that, ironically, was the key to healing Luca—a man I'd do anything for, including travel to the pits of the underworld.

Was I doing the right thing by allowing Gunner and Meredith to join me? Despite his fun-guy exterior, the wolf was hard as nails, a fighter to his core. And though I barely knew her, I suspected the witch was too. After all, she also had a rough past and had gotten herself out of many binds.

But this, my homeland and the realm we were about to enter, was more than 'rough.' It was the stuff of nightmares.

And I was connected to Hell in a way I could not deny, no matter how hard I tried.

I just hoped that when the seeker and the wolf learned of the darkness inside me, they wouldn't look at me differently.

ALSO BY ASHLEY MCLEO

The Winter Court (Crowns of Magic Universe)

A Kingdom of Frost and Malice

A Lord of Snow and Greed

A Hallow of Storm and Ruin

Coven of Shadows and Secrets (Crowns of Magic Universe)

Seeker of Secrets

Hunted by Darkness

History of Witches

Marked by Fate

Kingdoms of Sin

Bound by Destiny

Spellcasters Spy Academy Series (Magic of Arcana Universe)

A Legacy Witch: Year One

A Marked Witch: Internship

A Rebel Witch: Year Two

A Crucible Witch: Year Three

The Spellcasters Spy Academy Boxset

The Wonderland Court Series (Magic of Arcana Universe)

Alice the Dagger

Alice the Torch

Standalone Novels

The Alchemist of Silver Hollow (Magic of Arcana Universe)

Curse of the Fae Prince (The Spring Court: Crowns of Magic Universe)

The Bonegate Series - A Fanged Fae sister series

Hawk Witch

Assassin Witch

Traitor Witch

Illuminator Witch

The Royal Quest Series

Dragon Prince

Dragon Magic

Dragon Mate

Dragon Betrayal

Dragon Crown

Dragon War

ABOUT THE AUTHOR

Ashley lives in the lush and green Pacific Northwest with her husband, their dog, and the house ghost that sometimes makes appearances in her charming, old home.

When she's not writing urban fantasy and portal fantasy novels she enjoys traveling the world, reading, kicking butt at board games, and frequenting taquerias.

For all the latest releases and updates, subscribe to Ashley's newsletter, The Coven. You can also find her Facebook group, Ashley's Reader Coven.

www.ingramcontent.com/pod-product-compliance
Lightning Source LLC
Chambersburg PA
CBHW061049190726
48286CB00006B/1680